---- ★ ----

Through the tall window next to the door, I could see why Martha was upset. A light coming through a door at the far end of the room illuminated a sink and a pair of spindly legs lying sprawled on the floor.

"She hasn't moved a muscle since the first time I looked," Martha wailed.

Martha was right about the door being locked. I tried the window and it was locked, also as Martha had said. I didn't waste any more time looking for a conventional way in. I had broken the bottom window and was halfway inside the room when the ambulance, siren blaring, crunched to a stop behind my car. I finished climbing through the window and opened the door from the inside to admit the EMTs, who had been guided by Martha with her arms waving extravagantly enough to guide a 747 to dock.

---- ★ ----

Previously published Worldwide Mystery titles by
LINDA BERRY

DEATH AND THE EASTER BUNNY
DEATH AND THE HUBCAP
"THE THREE WISE WOMEN"
   in THE LAST NOEL (anthology)
DEATH AND THE ICEBOX

DEATH *and the* WALKING STICK

LINDA BERRY

W✪RLDWIDE®

TORONTO • NEW YORK • LONDON
AMSTERDAM • PARIS • SYDNEY • HAMBURG
STOCKHOLM • ATHENS • TOKYO • MILAN
MADRID • WARSAW • BUDAPEST • AUCKLAND

DEATH AND THE WALKING STICK

A Worldwide Mystery/December 2007

First published by Five Star.

ISBN-13: 978-0-373-26622-7
ISBN-10:   0-373-26622-7

Printed in U.S.A.

Acknowledgments

As always, I must thank my cousin, Johnny Shuman, who inspired the creation of Henry Huckabee. When Hen says something particularly pungent, Johnny probably said it first. Johnny tirelessly answers my questions about police work in south Georgia, even when I go over the same things again and again, and he never points out where I have messed up anyway. Bonnie McCune and Suzanne Young are loyal, honest, unflinching friends who do everything they can to help me weed out flaws in the writing. My sister, Dr. Jackie Swensson, the English teacher, shares her expertise in the matter of commas, dangling participles, and subordinate clauses. My husband, Jerry Berry, always provides what I need most—everything from computer expertise to encouragement. Thanks to them all, and to the other friends who've told me they like the places and people I've imagined and put in these books.

ONE

"SHE'S AN UNPLEASANT old turkey buzzard if I ever saw one," said Henry Huckabee.

"Now, Hen, she's just a poor old lady." Actually, I said "pore ol' lady," because I wanted to exaggerate my insincerity and get on Hen's nerves as much as possible.

Hen is Henry Huckabee, the Chief of Police of Ogeechee, Georgia, a town about sixty-five miles west of Savannah, with a population that's hovered around three thousand people for most of its hundred years. I am Trudy Roundtree, his cousin, the first (and so far only) female officer the OPD has ever had. "She" was Althea Boatright, five-foot-two, eyes of blue, ninety-seven pounds, and eighty-one years, as I was in a position to know since I had so recently taken charge of her driver's license. She reminded me more of a plucked chicken than a turkey buzzard, but I made allowances for Hen's heightened emotional state.

Whether she was plucked chicken, turkey buzzard, or poor old lady could be debated. What was not debatable was that Althea Boatright had been at the controls of her Lincoln Continental when it crushed the life out of Mr. Charles Sykes of Jesup, pressing him between her grillwork and the side wall of the post office, that beehive of late-morning activity in Ogeechee.

"It was the awfullest noise I ever heard," testified ear-witness Caroline Strickland, who had been discarding most of the contents of her post office box directly into the handy wastepaper basket near the big picture window that over-looked the parking lot. "The crash. Lord, I thought I was done for! Thought she was gone plow right through the wall and get me, too. Althea's horn blowing and the man's scream cut off like that, I'll hear it the rest of my life, I swear, and on top of it all that yappy dog."

Oh, yes. The dog. Althea admitted to some responsibility for the accident because her dog, known variously as "that yappy dog" (Caroline Strickland), "that overgrown rat" (Henry Huckabee), and "Precious" (Althea Boatright), had gotten tangled up in her feet and made her hit the foot-feed instead of the brake in the stress of the moment.

"She probably had the dog navigatin' for her," Hen fumed. "Had him up there on a pillow so he could see out."

"That's right." I fanned his flames. "Did you notice the pillow matched the one Miz Boatright sits on so she can see over the dashboard? You don't think it was actually Precious driving, do you?"

"Precious! Lord help me," Hen said. "You got statements from everybody?"

Yes, I had. Besides Caroline Strickland, there had been Cooter Wilbanks. "Never saw anybody in my life look so surprised, when he saw that car coming straight at him like that. He waved like he thought he could stop it that way, like it was a nervous cow or something, and even after he was hit, it looked like he was trying to reason with it, talk his way out."

And Tara Hilliard, earnestly, around her tears. "It was awful! It was awful! That poor man! I hope he was saved. He was just standing there, like he was waiting for somebody. I guess he was waiting for the Angel of Death and didn't know it. Oh, to be cut off like that, with no chance to say goodbye to your family or make peace with your enemies or anything!

I hope he was right with God. You never know when your time will come. Are you—"

"I'm a Methodist. Thank you, Tara. We'll get in touch with you if we need anything else."

And Holton Hooks, wobbling on his walker. "I heard he wasn't even from here. What was a man from Jesup doing at our post office, anyway? Shows what happens when you start ramblin' too far away from home."

"Open and shut," I summarized for Hen. "No extenuating circumstances, unless you want to count Precious."

"I don't want to count Precious as an extenuating circumstance or anything else in any way whatsoever," Hen summarized for me. Then he brightened. "Unless you think we could get that overgrown rat as an accessory—aiding and abetting, something like that."

What had him in such a bad mood was trying to decide what to charge Althea with. Everybody in town knew she was a menace, had been a menace for years, driving around with that dog. Since it was our clear duty to do what we could to protect the citizenry by getting Althea Boatright off the road, we didn't want to blow this heaven-sent opportunity. But coming down too hard on that angle might give somebody the idea they should sue the police department for failing to get her off the road sooner. A range of seductive possibilities beckoned. Vehicular homicide, with or without intent, was our favorite. Reckless disregard for the public safety was in the running. Since she was a good Methodist senior citizen, we had reluctantly scratched the possibility of getting her for driving under the influence, unless maybe it was the influence of her medication. Hen had deputed me to find out if she was on any kind of drugs that would qualify, in case we got so desperate we had to come down to that. I'd been trying to convince Hen that revoking her driver's license would be enough punishment. No need to try to send her to jail.

Hen's comment about Althea's unpleasantness notwith-standing, at the scene I had been struck—not in the same way Mr. Sykes had been struck, I'm happy to say—by her unchar-acteristic docility. She asked several times, "Is he dead? Is he really dead?" and once she was convinced of that, she seemed to lose all her starch. For once, she hadn't tried to bluster or explain it away. She agreed it was terrible. She agreed that she was at fault, even if only to the extent that she hadn't kept Precious under control. I guessed she'd been under heavy fire from her family to quit driving, and she realized this was the last straw for her as well as for poor Charles Sykes of Jesup. Whether it was mostly guilt or embarrassment it would have been hard to say, but it boded well for the future safety of the streets of Ogeechee.

Hen consulted his notes and looked up at me. "Littering?" he asked hopefully. "Assault with a deadly weapon?" At this point, his rantings were interrupted by the arrival of Officer Jerome Sharpe.

Jerome's a recent addition to the force, and he's worth his considerable weight in shelled pecans, a standard higher than gold around here. At six-foot-four and three hundred pounds, and ornamented with a gold earring and dark curly hair as long as Hen's regulations will allow, one of Jerome's best qual-ities is that the very sight of him scares the living mischief out of most people. People who might keep pushing because they think they can get away with something when they see me coming fade and dwindle in Jerome's presence. Trouble simply evaporates. Even Hen, at about six feet and about two hundred pounds, looks small next to Jerome. What chance do my five-foot-six-inches and (about) one hundred thirty pounds have?

I know Jerome's slow, deliberate movements are the result of an ingrained habit of trying not to cause accidental damage by bumping into things, but the general run of evildoers seems to see controlled menace. I know he prefers gentleness and quietness, but we hope the word never gets around. Comparing him to a freight train isn't too far off: he's almost as big, he usually moves slowly but purposefully, and his voice has a deep rumble that seems to assure you everything is moving along on the right track and on schedule.

He's a big hit with women of every age, and color, but professionally he's developing something of a sub-specialty in irrational women. One of his groupies, Elma Coleman, lives east of town, or, as Hen says, her body lives over there, but her mind stays somewhere out in the ozone. She's been one of Jerome's special women ever since the first time she called in to report that there were some snipers shooting at her from the roof of the Magnolia Blossom Motel, a new establishment just across the highway from her house, on what she probably thinks still ought to be a peach orchard.

Imagining everything from a drug deal gone bad to teenaged squirrel hunters run amok, we responded quickly. We don't get anything as interesting as snipers every day of the week. Not even every week.

When we got there, though, it didn't take us long to ascertain that there were no snipers on the roof of the Magnolia Blossom Motel and absolve the premises of any sinister goings on. The only odd thing we found was little old Mrs. Coleman, eighty-five if she's a day, nervously peering at us through her lacy front curtain.

We flashed our badges, and she opened the front door as far as the security chain would allow.

"There's nobody up there, ma'am," Jerome told her. "Maybe we scared 'em off."

"Well, of course you can't see them," she whispered, releasing the chain and grabbing his sleeve to hurry him inside where he'd be safe. I followed unassisted.

"Of course you can't see them," she repeated in a normal tone. "They're wearing that camouflage stuff that makes them invisible."

"Uh huh," Jerome rumbled, nodding wisely. I had to turn my unruly face away from Mrs. Coleman. "That makes a big difference in how we go about this," he continued, in a matter-of-fact tone that suggested utter control of the situation, now that he had all the facts. "Don't you worry, now, ma'am. I've had experience with this kind of thing, and I know just what to do."

Apparently he did know just what to do, besides laying on the "ma'am," which actually does seem to help in cases like this. Mrs. Coleman and I watched him stroll back to the motel and roust up the manager. They talked for a few minutes, then Jerome went back to his cruiser and rummaged around in the trunk. He disappeared from view, and the next thing we knew, Jerome appeared on the roof of the Magnolia Blossom Motel. From that distance, it was hard to tell exactly what he was doing, but he seemed to be walking back and forth across the roof, holding a spray can of some kind out in front of him. He spent a while walking and spraying, covering every corner and crevice. Finally, he turned to face Mrs. Coleman's house and gave a big thumbs up, along with his dazzling smile. Have I mentioned that dazzling smile?

He returned to the cruiser and opened the back door, at the same time going through a pantomime I couldn't interpret. Then he put the can of whatever it was in the car and reappeared at Mrs. Coleman's door, looking satisfied with himself, as well he should. When he announced that he'd taken care of the snipers, Mrs. Coleman and I both believed him.

"What were you doing up there?" Mrs. Coleman asked.

If he tried to tell us he'd used insect repellant, I wasn't sure even Mrs. Coleman would believe him, but he surprised and impressed me by being more subtle than that.

"Hit 'em with special sniper paint," he said. "Once they knew I could see 'em, they caved right in. I got 'em locked in the cruiser, ready for special delivery to the lock-up."

I remembered the can of spray paint he'd taken from some eighth graders who were using it for what Hen called "unsanctioned outdoor art."

"I didn't see them," Mrs. Coleman said, doubtfully but trustfully.

Jerome didn't miss a beat. "It's distance sensitive," he explained. "Only works up close, messes up the light waves. But don't you worry. I got 'em all right."

She was convinced. She rewarded him—us—with homemade chocolate chip pecan cookies, still warm from the oven.

Since then, Jerome has periodically gone over to clean the snipers off the Magnolia Blossom Motel and have some of Mrs. Coleman's cookies. I'm not sure which of them initiates the contact. Jerome may do it whenever he's having a slow day and needs a cookie fix. Since I used to be just about the only member of what Hen calls his "fringe patrol"—his code for people who are on or beyond the fringe of normal society—I'm happy to share that niche, to let Jerome infringe, so to speak.

"You think we can get jail time for Althea Boatright?" Hen asked him now.

"Old lady like that with no prior offenses? Nah," Jerome said. "Just get the town up in arms. It'll be enough to get her off the road. Even when she doesn't run into anybody, she's a nuisance. Don't sweat it. There's not a chance in a truckload she'll be able to pass the driver's test again."

"Public nuisance," Hen muttered, and made a note.

"She must keep the cruise control on that car set at five," Jerome continued. "Creates a dad-dogged parade any time she goes anywhere. Musta been going faster than usual when she mowed down that fella. Most of the time, even old Holton Hooks could outrun her."

"Now you mention it, we get her off the streets, we can probably hit Leland up for a fat donation next time we try to raise money to send kids to some camp besides the Rogers Correctional Institute," Hen said. "Having her hanging around over there can't be good for business."

Grinstead's Market is just across the street from the station house. Althea shops there because it's the family business. She was married to—and widowed by—Bert Grinstead before she was married to Rowland Boatright. Her son, Leland, is a Grinstead. When she and Rowland Boatright got together, she changed her name but not her interest in Grinstead's Market. Leland probably would appreciate it if Hen made it a little harder for Althea to drop in for unannounced inspections of how he runs the store.

"I've noticed that when Althea comes for groceries, there's a rush of people coming out of the store to move their cars away from hers," I contributed.

"Might be a good idea to check with Leland before you settle on the charges," Jerome said. "Might be you could get a bigger donation out of him if you lock her up instead of just gettin' her off the streets."

"You could play Leland against Homer, pretending you're going to let her off, and see which one will be more grateful to see her locked up," I suggested. Homer is the son of Althea's second husband, Rowland Boatright. Homer and his sister Susannah have been in one lawsuit or another against Althea over the Boatright estate ever since Rowland died.

"With or without Leland and Homer, the town will probably put up a statue in your honor if you get her off the streets," I said. "Or maybe in honor of Mr. Sykes, a martyr to the cause."

Jerome ambled off, brushing at the errant cookie crumbs

on his shirt which both Hen and I had been too polite to mention. We heard him rumbling at Dawn, the dispatcher.

"Kid's got a good head on his shoulders," Hen said, completely ignoring my comments. "Lucky for us he went into law enforcement instead of crime, or even football, like those cousins of his."

"Yep," I said, thinking about the fringe-dwellers I was now sharing with Jerome.

Hen sighed. "Okay, no jail time. But she is an unpleasant old turkey buzzard."

For once, I couldn't bring myself to argue with him.

TWO

WE HAD ANOTHER helping of the old turkey buzzard the next week when we went to the Hatfield House. Yvonne Hatfield has converted her old family home into a base for her business—mostly catering, but open on Sundays for dinner. She's filled the spacious front room with tables, and hung the large windows with lace curtains, knowing the old-fashioned charm of the place was as attractive to her clientele as her old-fashioned good cooking. The mismatched dining tables and chairs have their own friendly attraction. Diners come from miles in all directions for the family-style meals. No ordering, no need to keep track of who eats what, or how much. Yvonne and her helpers keep bringing out bowls of whatever they're serving that day until all the diners have eaten all they can hold. One price fits all. Take a seat wherever you can find one. As soon as you're settled, the food starts coming—sooner than that if you're joining somebody who got there first.

Hen's Sunday entourage consists of his wife, Teri; his daughter, Delcie; and his mama, my aunt Lulu. They're a nice-looking bunch. Seven-year-old Delcie is always beautiful, with her short, white-blonde hair and the startling blue Huckabee eyes. Teri's always neat and colorfully dressed. Aunt Lulu's not *always* anything. She changes her hair color and color-coordinated wardrobe periodically, whenever she or Pauline (of Pauline's Cut-n-Curl) gets bored. Her current hair color is something she and Pauline call Canadian Sunset. It's a pinkish gold, and apparently it required a wardrobe of orange, mauve, and lilac. If she thinks old age won't recognize her if she keeps changing her appearance, it seems to be working. She's in her early sixties, which apparently isn't nearly as old as it used to be. She's vivacious, attractive, interesting, and active, with a wide range of friends.

Sometimes I'm part of Hen's bunch—I am family, after all—but sometimes I'm not. Sometimes I'm part of my own bunch, which includes only me; sometimes I have my own sub-bunch which extends to Phil Pittman.

The Pittmans have been putting out the local newspaper, *The Ogeechee Beacon,* for generations, longer than anybody now alive can remember. Generally, the small-town newspaper business can be kept under control, and Phil can arrange his time, but not always. Lately, with his daddy's failing health and his sister Molly's recent marriage, more and more of the business has fallen on Phil.

That Sunday, things at *The Beacon* were under control and Phil was with me. We took two of the seats with the Huckabees. For the record, and he'd tell you this himself, Phil is not the all-purpose, universally acknowledged, chick magnet Jerome Sharpe is. Phil's sex appeal is targeted more toward those women who like freckled faces, a bashful manner, a quick sense of humor, and thick eyeglasses. Also for the record, I fall into that category. Phil falls into the category of men who like low-maintenance, brown-haired women with a lot of attitude and big mouths. It also helps that he's not put off by the fact that I carry a gun. And maybe he goes for the iceberg blue eyes that are part of the Roundtree heritage.

When I came back home to Ogeechee a few years ago to try to put myself back together after my husband died in a hunting accident, Phil and I picked up a low-key friendship from back when we both went to Ogeechee High School. We're still waiting to see where it will carry us. Neither of us is in any hurry. We enjoy each other's company, and we share enough of the same interests that we don't mind people thinking we're a couple (as long as it isn't "a cute couple"), and we're both contrary enough to enjoy knowing our occasional weekends out of town together give the more-than-usually conservative element in Ogeechee something to talk about.

Hen has trained his bunch to bee-line for the car as soon as the choir cuts off on the last amen so they can get to Hatfield House in time to get a head start on the Baptists, but that Sunday the Huckabees were seated at Hen's *second-choice* table, the one out in the middle of the room.

Homer and Melva Boatright sat alone at Hen's first-choice table—the one by the front window that seats six. Homer had already loaded his plate, and exuded a satisfied, anticipatory air. Melva, silvery hair carefully coiffed, wearing an expensive-looking dress, was choosing a slice of tomato from the platter in front of her.

"They left before the benediction, I swear," Hen muttered as Phil and I took the last two seats at the Huckabee table. "Homer'd do anything to get that table, up where he can keep a good eye on everybody, even if it is a table for six and only two of them."

"Behave yourself," Teri instructed him, sending a smile in the general direction of the Boatrights, in case they'd overheard Hen's not-very-muted grumbling. "You're just mad because you didn't get here first so you could sit where you can keep a good eye on everybody."

"That's my job," Hen said. "He just does it because he's nosy."

"Glad to know you're always on the job," Phil said, spreading his napkin in his lap. "Anything interesting on the blotter this week?"

Like Hen, Phil is always on the job.

"Stop fussing about where you're sitting, and pass Phil the ham," Aunt Lulu instructed. She's always on the job, too.

We began passing platters and bowls: butterbeans, zipper peas, squash, fried okra, ham, boiled new potatoes, pork chops, applesauce, cornbread, sliced tomatoes. Yvonne Hatfield, her generous body wrapped in a flowered coverall apron, bustled out from the back with a pitcher of tea in each hand, and swept through the room, pausing at every table to ask, "Y'all doin' okay? You drinkin' sweet or unsweet?" She poured as directed, scanned the tables, and moved on, calling toward the kitchen, "We need biscuits out here, Leon!"

Between bites of food and briefing *The Beacon,* Hen found time to taunt one of the late-arriving Baptists. "Brother Crowell must have been a little long-winded today. Don't he know he'll get in trouble if he keeps letting the Methodists beat y'all to dinner?"

"He's new. We'll get him trained," Gordon Albritton paused to answer. His wife stopped to speak to the Boat-rights, who seemed unaware of Hen's irritation—or perhaps were aware and found it added flavor to the meal.

"Reckon I'll have to remind him we do our own hirin' and firin', not like y'all, where you have to put up with whoever the bishop sends you on rotation," Gordon said. "He's not in too much trouble today, though, unless Yvonne's out of…what is it today?"

"Nah, you're not that late," Hen said, indicating the spread of food.

Gordie joined his wife, who'd moved on to a small side table.

Close behind the Albrittons came Susannah Boatright, who took one of the empty chairs at Homer and Melva's table. Except for her compact frame, a distinctive broad nose, and an aura of money, she bore no resemblance to her brother.

Susannah's hair was streaked-blonde and her dress was a pale green, plain except for an eye-catching pin at the throat.

Althea Boatright came in with Leland and Clarice Grinstead about that time. They might have made a family group with Homer, Melva, and Susannah, at their six-person table, seeing that Althea had been married to Homer and Susannah's father, but the newcomers sat as far from the Boatrights as possible, over by the dessert table. There'd been so much hard feeling over how Rowland Boatright left his property that even Yvonne Hatfield's cooking couldn't bring them all to the same table.

"Mama, your blue-eyed baby boy needs the butterbeans again," Hen said. How he can eat while he's talking non-stop is beyond my understanding.

"You're not a baby!" Delcie protested. Young as she is, she promises to be a linguistic nitpicker worthy of the Huckabee name.

"I used to be," Hen assured her.

"You sure did take a lot of peas, Delcie," Teri said. "You think you can eat all of that?"

"I heard there was some trouble out at Ebenezer Baptist," Phil said to Hen.

Hen's guffaw startled diners all over the room. "Where'd you hear about that?"

"I have my sources," Phil told him, giving me a wink and adjusting his glasses. I turned my attention to my pork chop.

"Tell us! Tell us!" Delcie begged, lifting a spoonful of peas and looking at her mother to make sure her virtue had not been overlooked.

Hen's method of keeping his adoring family from worrying about his line of work is to tell such entertaining stories about the state of crime in Ogeechee that they get the idea all the criminals are bumblers. The trouble at Ebenezer Baptist church was perfect for this purpose, since the degree of criminality was not threatening and didn't even involve the Ogeechee police.

"It has to do with drunkenness," Hen said. "I'm not sure it's appropriate to talk about it on Sunday in front of all these righteous churchgoers."

"I did hear it involved a churchgoer," Phil said.

This time, Hen stifled his guffaw in his napkin. "But not a righteous one. Best part about the whole thing is the sheriff's department had to deal with it."

"What happened?" Aunt Lulu asked.

Hen wiped his chin with one of Yvonne's heavy-duty paper napkins and settled back into story-teller mode. If there's anything Hen likes better than eating—and that's a big *if*—it's telling stories. He adopts a semi-rustic, semiliterate good-old-boy persona that is ideal for storytelling and for making people underestimate him. He may be the only small-town chief of police in the state with a bona fide law degree, but it's easy to forget that when he's being folksy.

"Seems like there was a fella looking to take shelter from the weather on Saturday night, and he took it inside the church."

"Sanctuary," Aunt Lulu said.

"There must be more to it," Teri said. She knows Hen.

Hen nodded. "Didn't take sanctuary in the sanctuary *per se*. Took sanctuary in the baptistry."

"Sounds pretty uncomfortable to me," Aunt Lulu said.

"Well, it's a good-sized dunk tank, so he mighta made out all right," Hen offered. "Since he's spent a good share of his adult life in a confined space, maybe he felt more secure that way. It's a wonder he could get down in there without hurting himself, though, because he'd imbibed way too much of the fruit of the vine."

"What does that mean?" Delcie asked.

"In plain English, he was so drunk he wasn't thinking or walking straight," Hen explained to his daughter.

She nodded.

"He crawled in there with his bottle and settled down and didn't wake up till somebody came and started running water in there so it would have time to warm up some for a baptism on Sunday morning. When that cold water hit him, he came to and let out a howl that scared the religion right out of the deacon who was in charge of filling up the baptistry. Upshot was, the trespasser got baptized and the deacon wound up causing such a ruckus that the family of skunks who'd been peacefully napping underneath the building got riled and made their presence known."

"They made a stink?" Delcie guessed.

"Yes, darlin' daughter, they just let fly with good old *eau de skunk*."

"Phew," Delcie said. She shivered elaborately and knocked over her glass of milk.

"Hen!" Teri admonished, mopping up the milk.

He paused momentarily to look aggrieved at the lack of logic that would blame him for Delcie's spill, but he went on with the story.

"The people who'd gotten themselves all dressed up for church and were looking forward to a baptism were mightily put out to arrive at the church house and find all the doors wide open and pie plates full of coffee grounds sitting all over the place. I hear a few of the more imaginative members of the congregation thought they'd been taken over by some obscure cult with a peculiar taste in incense."

"What were the coffee grounds for?" Phil asked.

"Some folks'll tell you they absorb the odor. Maybe they do, but they didn't do it quick enough for the Ebenezer people," Hen said.

"Are you makin' this up, Daddy?" Delcie looked at him with wide eyes, while her fork began methodically mashing peas and potatoes into a greenish whitish paste.

"No, ma'am, I am not," Hen said, making a face at the mess on Delcie's plate. She giggled. "In my line of work, I don't have to make up things like that. Hey, Jim L., Martha."

While Jim L. Tootle returned Hen's greetings and shook hands with Phil, his wife Martha bent and whispered to Aunt Lulu. Aunt Lulu brought her napkin up to her face but didn't quite cover a quick glance at Susannah Boatright.

"You're sure?" she whispered to Martha.

"That's it, all right. You'd think she'd have better sense, wouldn't you?" Then, as if the rest of us had only that moment materialized, Martha smiled like an actress who's just finished a star turn, and took her husband's arm. Martha's affection for the dramatic is illustrated by what must be an artificially white streak in her equally artificially black hair. I've never seen her wearing anything but black and white. Once, when she lit into Hen over his handling of an incident involving a pack of loitering teens, and irked him more than usually, he compared her to that woman in *101 Dalmatians,* but he didn't do it to her face. Now, whenever I see her, that's usually what comes to mind. Today, though, naturally I thought of skunk.

Hen watched Jim L. and Martha take seats with the Baptists, then turned to his mother. "What was that about?"

Aunt Lulu chewed her bite of tomato twenty-five times and daintily wiped her mouth before she answered. "Nothing."

"Mama, what did she mean 'that's it, all right'?"

"She was calling my attention to…all the jewelry." Without turning her head, Aunt Lulu made a gesture that included the room.

"I thought I heard that," Hen said. "Something about a brooch?"

"Honestly, Henry, I think you've been in police work so long you've forgotten how to behave yourself, eavesdropping and cross-examining your own mother."

"I've been in police work so long I recognize evasion when I hear it, Mama. What are you and Martha Tootle up to?"

"Well, just look around," Aunt Lulu said.

Naturally, we did, but, seeing nothing that would seem to justify Martha Tootle's dramatics, we came right back to Aunt Lulu.

"What's a brooch?" Delcie said.

"It's an old-fashioned word for a piece of jewelry like that pretty thing your mama's got pinned to her jacket," Hen said. He glanced at his own mama, who didn't give him a chance to resume his interrogation.

"I guess you think that's a clever way of calling me old-fashioned, but not so clever it got past me, young man," Aunt Lulu said. She turned to Delcie with the same enthusiasm a drowning sailor would show for a life preserver and launched into a grandmotherly tutorial. "Instead of its being an old-fashioned word for a piece of jewelry, I'd say it's a word for an old-fashioned piece of jewelry. See, your mama's is silvery and modern looking, so we'd probably call it a pin; this one I'm wearing, with the stones in it, is more like a brooch. It was my mother's."

Delcie was used to this kind of thing and knew how to play the game. She looked around the room.

"Miz Albritton's is a pin," she said.

Teri and Lulu looked in the direction of Mrs. Albritton and agreed that the small free-form gold object would probably be called a pin. Mrs. Albritton, looking up and seeing them looking at her, smiled uncertainly. Lulu, Hen, and Teri smiled back. Delcie's survey had already moved on.

"And Mr. Beasley's is a pin."

Yes, we agreed, the small American flag in Mr. Beasley's lapel was surely a pin.

Delcie scooped up applesauce and scanned the room. "And Miz Smith's is a brooch."

"Miz Smith's is a fortune," Hen said, eying the multicolored jeweled hummingbird on Mrs. Smith's sedate gray lapel.

"What's a fortune?" Delcie asked, spoon in mid-air, applesauce dripping onto her lap.

"Oh, goodness, Delcie! Pay attention!" Teri said. "Hen, stop it. Is everybody ready to go?"

"I haven't finished my applesauce," Delcie said. "Miz Thompson's is a…"

"And I haven't had dessert," Hen said, pushing his chair back. Yvonne Hatfield keeps the platters of food coming, but she operates on the theory that if you can't get up and walk a few steps to get your dessert, you don't need any. Hen headed for the sideboard and its array of pies and cobblers. Following him, I was almost tripped by Althea Boatright's walking stick as she pushed away from her table and swooped on Homer, Melva, and Susannah.

"Where'd you get that?" Althea demanded, holding on to a chair back and all but poking Susannah in the chest with the mischievous walking stick I had so narrowly dodged.

"What in the…!" Homer swiped the walking stick away from his sister. "Have you completely lost the rest of your mind? What are you doing?"

"Susannah, I asked you a question." For all the notice Althea paid Homer, he might not have been there. "Where'd you get that?"

"It's mine," Susannah said.

"She found it," Homer said.

"She stole it," Althea said, "and I want to know how she got her hands on it."

Even Yvonne Hatfield's cooking couldn't compete with this. Everybody else in the room was staring, their faces reflecting various degrees of confusion, interest, and amusement.

"You said you didn't have it," Melva chimed in. "How could anybody steal something from you if you didn't have it?"

"Whether I knew exactly where it was or not, Rowland's will left it to me, and you know it."

"Maybe it was with that bunch of stock certificates you claim you can't find either," Homer said.

"Come on, Mama." Leland Grinstead was at Althea's elbow. "I bet Precious is getting tired of waiting in the car."

"I'm not going anywhere without my brooch," Althea said, taking a swipe at Leland with the walking stick.

"You can have it over my dead body, you greedy old woman," Susannah said.

"Hen, do something!" Teri whispered.

"I am doing something. I'm having my dessert and enjoying the show." Hen smiled around a bite of pecan pie.

"I don't think that was an incitement to murder," I said. I'd meant to reassure Teri, but I earned a scowl from both Althea and her stepdaughter.

Homer Boatright frowned at Althea, then spread the frown to everybody else in the room. "I want you all to know that brooch belonged to our mother."

"You've read Rowland's will, so you know he left it to me," Althea said. "Your mama doesn't have any use for it, anyway. Give it here."

"Not on your life." Susannah brushed past Althea, who took a clumsy swipe at her with her walking stick.

"Anyway, she didn't steal it," Melva bleated. "Clarice gave it to her. Didn't you, Clarice?"

The front door slammed behind Susannah. Althea had

started after her, but, at Melva's words, she turned on her daughter-in-law so fast she nearly fell into Phil's lap.

"You?" Then back to Melva. "If she did, then she stole it! It wasn't hers to give." Back to her daughter-in-law. "Clar—"

But Leland and Clarice had broken out of whatever trance they were in.

"Come on, Mama. We'll talk about it in the car," Leland said. Althea might not have gone willingly, but Clarice was leaving, and it was clear to everybody that Althea had serious intentions of talking to Clarice.

The silence after the door closed behind them lasted only long enough for people to draw enough breath to speak. Then Melva Boatright's voice cut across the slowly rising murmur.

"They know how much it means to Susannah. And Homer," Melva said to the room, as though addressing a jury. She smoothed the front of her solid-colored, too-tight dress, which showed off her own uncontroversial jewelry and a gravy stain under her chin. "Their daddy never would have left it to Althea if he'd been thinking straight."

"We're not through with her," Homer said, strengthening the jury image when he added, "You all see how irrational she is. She's crazy as a bedbug. And you can just bet she's got some of the other things she said she couldn't find, some of the things Daddy left to us. If she doesn't know exactly where every coin and stock certificate is I'll…I'll…"

While Homer was trying to think of an oath potent enough, Hen weighed in. "No question about that pin…brooch…if y'all recognized it, but you might be wrong about the other property, Homer. I always heard your daddy had a secretive side. Maybe he sold it off without telling her about it, and then never got around to changing his will."

Homer snorted. "His will? He didn't have a will of his own after he married her. He was secretive, all right, I'll admit that, but he kept careful account of things. It's there, or it was. The Grinsteads have it. All of it."

"Maybe it's in one of the hiding places your daddy made," Melva suggested. "You could get a court order and take a look."

Homer sent her a withering look. "Think about it, Melva. Just on the off chance Daddy did leave anything hidden and the Grinsteads haven't already found it, do you think we'd ever see it if we told them where to look? Leland's so much like Althea he might not have had a daddy at all."

"Do you really think—?" Melva started but Homer didn't let her finish the thought.

"They've got it, don't you think they don't."

"And the house," Melva said to the room at large. "Don't forget the house."

"Yes, they have the Boatright house," Susannah said.

Finally, Homer seemed to realize what a spectacle they'd been. "We don't need to go into all this here," he said, frowning at Susannah and pulling Melva toward the door. "Nobody wants to hear us going on."

That wasn't true. We had been fascinated by the show and would have listened all afternoon, but the Boatrights left.

"Just one more bite, now, Delcie!" Teri said.

By this time, Delcie's peas and applesauce, with the assistance of some mashed potatoes, had come to resemble a section of the Okefenokee Swamp. "I don't like it when it's all mixed together," she said.

"And how did it get mixed together, Miss?" Teri asked.

Delcie made a face.

"You're not supposed to take it if you're not going to eat it," Teri persisted.

Delcie batted her eyes and looked at her daddy.

"You better pick the least mixed-up part and eat at least one more bite, like your mama said," Hen said, fixing her with a stare that had been known to make criminals quail. Delcie quailed.

Martha Tootle paused at our table on her way out to have another word with Aunt Lulu. "I told you, didn't I?"

"Yes, indeed you did," Aunt Lulu said.

"Oh! I almost forgot! I'm supposed to find a substitute for our bridge group," Martha said. "Can you play bridge at Ellen's on Tuesday?"

"I'll look at my calendar when I get home and call you. Seems like there was a library board meeting or something I was supposed to do. Who else is playing?"

"Ellen and Althea and me. Emmy's going out of town. Cancel whatever else you have going. This is bound to be more interesting. We'll have plenty to talk about."

"You think Althea would bring this up?"

"She won't have to," Martha said. "I will. Don't you worry about that. Call me." Martha delivered her exit line as she moved on toward the door. "I wonder whether Homer and Melva are so hard up she can't afford a new dress or if she just doesn't realize she's outgrown that one."

And Hen muttered just loud enough that I could barely hear, "If somebody had run over that old turkey buzzard instead of the other way around, it woulda been a public service."

"I don't suppose I can put any of this in the paper," Phil said.

"Not unless you want to get *The Beacon* messed up with that wrangle-happy family," Hen said.

"But I'm sure your readers would appreciate it," Aunt Lulu said. "Not that the paper isn't always interesting. I didn't mean that."

"I'll have to see what I can do with the skunk story, then," Phil said.

"It's a skunk story either way," Hen assured him.

THREE

WHEN I PICKED up the 911 call, at 11:47 on a Tuesday morning, I was only a few blocks from the Boatright-Grinstead house. I shot across Highway 280—which doubles as Court Street when it's in Ogeechee—and skidded to a stop on the graveled street beside the house, stopping behind a shiny new yellow Volkswagen. Martha Tootle? Yes. Jim L. spoils her something awful, but he must have drawn the line at a black Beetle.

Martha, her dark hair wild and its white streak blazing in the morning sun, leaned over the porch rail, her body at an awkward angle as though she didn't want to turn away from the window. Her wardrobe choice for the day, black and white stripes, combined with her erratic movements, gave the impression of a nervous zebra.

"Trudy! But I need an ambulance, not the police! I mean Althea does!"

"Why? What's the matter?"

"I don't know. She's just lying there. I tried the doors, even the one around back, by the kitchen, and I couldn't get in to see about her, so I called nine-one-one. I don't know why people have to lock their doors. We never used to. I'm surprised this old house even has locks. Do you lock your doors, Trudy?"

"I keep trying to remember to," I admitted, but she wasn't listening.

"I couldn't get in, but I wanted an ambulance, not the police. What are you—"

Rattled as Martha already was, I didn't see any point in confusing her further by trying to explain that my scanner picks up 911 calls, or that often there's a good reason for police to appear on the scene of an emergency. "Show me."

By now, I was on the porch with Martha. The Grinstead house is one of those old ones, with a wide porch that stretches across the front and partway down the right side. A door at the end of the side porch leads into a room that might originally have been intended for a home office for somebody genteel like a doctor or a lawyer. It had been converted to what modern realtors call a mother-in-law suite, but they left most of the beautiful old detailing, including intricately grooved paneling around the lower part of the wall. Althea's room.

Through the tall window next to the door, I could see why Martha was upset. A light coming through a door at the far end of the room illuminated a sink and a pair of spindly legs lying sprawled on the floor.

"She hasn't moved a muscle since the first time I looked," Martha wailed.

Martha was right about the door being locked. I tried the window and it was locked, also as Martha had said. I didn't waste any more time looking for a conventional way in. I had broken the bottom window and was halfway inside the room when the ambulance, siren blaring, crunched to a stop behind my car. I finished climbing through the window and opened the door from the inside to admit the EMTs, who had been guided by Martha with her arms waving extravagantly enough to guide a 747 to dock.

Martha started to follow Porter Smith and Liza Kirkland, the EMTs, calling, "Althea? Althea?" but I pulled her out of the way, toward the bed.

"Give them room, Martha. No point in calling for help and then not letting them help."

"But…"

"They'll know what to do for her." Standing there, I noticed a faint unpleasant smell, at odds with what looked like a clean, well kept room.

There was a sudden rush of racket from the bathroom, yapping, whining, and the mutter of voices, and then Porter, a veteran emergency technician, appeared at the door holding a flat basket, which he thrust in my direction. "Can you keep this vicious guard dog out of our way?" he asked, and turned back without waiting for an answer. That accounted for the unpleasant smell. It was the smell you can't get out of the carpet if you have a dog who doesn't know how to behave.

I passed the basket and its whining contents to Martha. She dug her fingers into the dog's long hair and buried her nose in the back of its neck. Precious squirmed and whined, doubtless unhappy that Martha wouldn't let her return to her mistress.

"Don't worry, Precious. Don't you worry, now." Martha was emitting the same sort of meaningless soothing sounds you make when a child takes a tumble.

I gestured toward the bathroom. "How'd you come to find her?"

"Oh." She turned her attention from Precious to me. "Well, we were playing bridge today, at Ellen Chandler's. Lulu was subbing for Emmy, so it was Ellen and Lulu and Althea and me. We usually play most of the day, but Althea said she wasn't feeling well, so we stopped after one rubber." Martha huffed a little. "She might not have been feeling well, but she was feeling good enough for her and Ellen to practically take the skin off me and Lulu. I lost thirty-seven cents."

"Is that bad?" I asked.

"It's a penny for each down trick," she said, as if that explained it. "Althea likes to get out of the house, and it isn't easy for her, now that she can't drive herself. She doesn't drive any more. You know."

"I know."

"So we've been taking turns picking her up for bridge, depending on where we're playing, and I picked her up today, so I brought her home."

Martha hadn't been paying much attention to me, even as she answered my questions. Now, some movement in the bathroom distracted her even more, and she craned around me to get a better look at what was happening in there. Her movement knocked loose a walking stick that had been leaning against a chair that stood out from the wall near the head of the bed. She bent down to put Precious and her basket on the floor and retrieved the stick, pushing the chair out of the way as she replaced the walking stick against it.

"Is that when she collapsed?" I asked, when Martha stood again.

She looked at me in confusion. "What?"

"Did Althea collapse when you brought her home?" I prompted.

"Oh, no. I mean, I don't think so. Not right then, anyway. Not while I was here. I helped her up to the door—she has a hard time managing Precious and the steps—but I didn't come inside."

I'd noticed a slowing of activity in the bathroom, which didn't augur well for Althea Boatright. "Precious goes to bridge with you?" I asked to keep Martha distracted.

"To bridge, to church suppers, and anywhere else Althea goes," Martha said. "It isn't so irritating now that she's so old and doesn't run around and get into everything, but when she was a puppy, now, that was something else!"

I asked again, "So you brought Althea—and Precious— home but didn't come in with her? You left?"

"Oh. Well, I didn't see any reason to go in." She said it as though I'd accused her of something. "She said she'd be all right, just needed to lie down, so since I was already out of the house and it was so early, I decided to go by the grocery store on my way home and get something so I could surprise Jim L. by fixing him a good supper, which he usually doesn't get on my bridge days, but while I was at the store, I got to thinking if Althea was sick enough not to want to play cards, she must be pretty sick." She drew a breath. "With Leland and Clarice both off at work, I knew she'd be here by herself, and I got to worrying that I'd been in too big a hurry to drop her off, so I came back by from the grocery store to see if she was all right. That's when I saw her through there and called nine-one-one. Jim L. makes fun of me for carrying a cell phone, but he'll have to admit it came in handy today. I don't know what I'd have done without it."

Precious slowly crawled over the side of her basket and wobbled toward the bathroom. Suddenly, Porter Smith loomed in the doorway, startling Precious into a full stop. Porter was shaking his head. Precious considered him for a moment, then resumed her approach. Porter scooped her up.

"We were too late," he said, apparently to Precious. "Nothing we can do for her now but get Carlisle over here."

Those words, which put Althea into the category of "unattended death" instead of "medical emergency," changed everything. We now had to treat Althea's room as a potential crime scene. That doesn't mean we had any suspicions about Althea's death. It's routine for the very good reason that in a case where a crime has been committed, if the scene hasn't been treated properly any possible evidence has been destroyed or contaminated. There's no way to recover from that.

While Porter called Carlisle Sapp, who runs one of the local funeral homes and also serves as coroner, I hustled Martha and Precious outside and called Hen.

I knew I'd have to admit to Hen that we'd been inside and hadn't been careful, but there were some things I could do to mitigate the damage. Explaining to Martha that I'd talk to her again and get her statement, I got the camera from my cruiser and began photographing the scene. I made a note that Martha and I had moved the chair.

For the next hour, under Hen's direction, we worked on the scene. As recording officer, it was my job to keep track of everything and everybody, and I did a thorough job to make up for my earlier lapse. I didn't even make fun of Hen, as I otherwise might have, for the meticulous attention he made us give to simple thoroughness. He wasn't doing it to punish me for my carelessness—my own conscience was doing that—but because he's a good policeman. In short, to use Hen's phrase, we were looking for "anything boogery," anything that might suggest that Althea's death was more—or less—than it seemed.

I stepped to the bathroom door to take a look. Althea Boatright had been an unpleasant force in life; in death she was just a small crumpled pile.

"We straightened her out, trying to see what we could do for her," Liza Kirkland was saying. I wrote that down.

Behind me, Porter said, "It looks like she slipped and hit her head on the side of the tub and just sank right there. Probably didn't even twitch."

It looked straightforward enough. "I wonder what made her slip," Hen said.

Porter and Liza looked around, then at each other, then back to Hen.

"Did one of you put the bath mat there on the tub?"

"No." In unison.

"Was there water on the floor?"

"If there was, it dried up before we got here." Porter indicated their uniforms, perfectly dry.

"Might have had a sudden massive coronary and that made her fall," Porter suggested. "Or, old people, sometimes a hipbone just snaps and they fall. That's probably what happened. Just her bad luck the tub was there."

"Could she have tripped over the dog?" I asked with an uncomfortable shiver. Had poetic justice, or a providence with a sense of humor, decreed that the same dog that caused Althea to kill Charles Sykes would be the end of her?

Porter emitted a snort that was probably a stifled laugh. "I know it's not funny, but I flashed on that old comedian who moved in slo-mo and just sort of toppled over. I remember once he tripped over a peanut, shuffling along like he always did. I guess she could've tripped over the dog. However it happened, it looks like Miz Boatright would've been able to catch herself though, doesn't it?" He shook his head at Althea's bad luck.

When I got back to Martha Tootle, she was sitting on the porch steps wailing into the back of the helpless dog's head.

"Oh! If I hadn't got to talking to the new preacher's wife at the grocery store, I'd have been back sooner. Oh! I'll never forgive myself!"

But you'll enjoy telling about it, I thought.

Porter spoke from the doorway. "Well, ma'am, if it makes you feel any better, I don't think a few minutes would have made any difference. Even if you'd been here, even if *we'd* been here, when she fell, we might not have been able to do anything for her."

Martha rebounded somewhat. "You mean it was sudden? Thank you for saying so. That's a mercy, anyway."

Leland arrived on the scene at that point. "What's going on?" he wanted to know, although he must have guessed it wasn't anything good, with all the uproar. "Clarice?"

"No, Leland, not Clarice. It's Althea," Martha said.

"Mama? I thought she was off playing bridge." Only then did he seem to take in the whole scene: the ambulance, the police cars, the hearse. "Oh, no."

"I'm afraid so." I stood, blocking the steps.

"What happened?"

He tried to push past me and Martha and Precious still on the steps, to get to the porch. I didn't budge.

"I'm sorry, Mr. Grinstead, but you can't go in right now."

"What do you mean I can't go in? That's my house, and it's my mama."

Hen appeared then, to my intense relief, blocking the door to Althea's room. "We'll be through in a few more minutes, Leland. I'm sorry about your mother."

"What are you doing? You're not a doctor." I'd moved off the steps, figuring Hen could do the blocking, and Leland was crowding Hen, trying to see past him. Hen crowded back, but gently, smoothly.

"We're making sure if there are ever any questions about how she died, we'll be able to answer them. You know Carlisle. He's being respectful. While they're finishing in there, maybe you can tell me if she'd been having dizzy spells or anything like that lately? Anything special about her health you were worrying about?"

Hen had calmed Leland somewhat by the time Carlisle and Porter were finished and brought Althea out on a stretcher. Hen, Martha, and I backed away to clear the way, but Leland seemed rooted. They paused while he lifted the drape over Althea's face. He reached for the railing as though he didn't trust his legs. Even his neatly pressed short-sleeved shirt and clip-on bow tie seemed to wilt. He looked up, bewildered.

"What happened?"

"We don't know for sure," Hen said. "It looks like she fell

and hit her head on the side of the tub. Carlisle will take her to the mortuary to wait for the van from Atlanta."

"Atlanta?"

"Since she died like she did, not in a hospital or with a doctor, there'll be an autopsy to find out what to put on the death certificate. The folks in Atlanta may be able to tell us more about what happened. There's no point in us trying to guess."

"Doesn't matter anyway, does it?" Leland asked. "It doesn't matter whether it was her heart or a dizzy spell or a stroke. Does it?" Then, more like himself, more like his mother, "Why didn't somebody call me? Just let me run across this when I come home for dinner!"

"Don't get worked up, now, Leland," Martha said. "I know it's a shock, but everybody was thinking of Althea." For once, she said the right thing, or close enough to the right thing to calm him down.

Martha went on speaking, softly, gently, reminding me of her crooning to Precious. Yes, something in Leland's reaction reminded me of Precious. The same stunned confusion. Both forlorn. I'm probably twenty years or more younger than Leland Grinstead, but I was orphaned so suddenly when I was so young, that I've had a long time to get used to it. Leland's daddy's been gone a long time, too, but he had his mother for more than half a century. He'd had a long time to get used to having her around, and now, suddenly, she was gone. Not even a lengthy illness to prepare him.

"It'll take a while for the carrier to get here from Atlanta," Carlisle said to Leland. "I know you haven't had a chance to take it in yet. You want to spend a little while with her before I take her off? Or ride over with me to wait?"

"Thanks, Carlisle," Leland said. "I'll take a minute here. I just can't believe it. I can't take it in."

The rest of us moved away from the hearse, then, while Althea's son said goodbye.

Leland's resemblance to Althea—so strong that it was hard to see any traces of his daddy—was especially strong at this moment. The small frame, always angular and spare, now seemed shrunken; the face, always thin and pinched, was now colorless. Althea's blue eyes were closed, but Leland's were clouded. He looked as old as she did. This was the first time I'd seen any show of affection or attachment to Althea. Although it shouldn't have, it took me by surprise to realize that not everybody thought of her as an unpleasant old turkey buzzard. It was a reminder of how lucky I am. Cranky, mouthy, opinionated as I am, I know there are people who love me.

After a few minutes, Leland called, "Okay, Carlisle."

Carlisle turned to Leland. "You want them to send her back to me when they're through, or you want to do business with somebody else? Shouldn't be more than a day or two." In mortuary circles, that may pass for tact.

"Uh. Yes, we'll want you to take care of things," Leland said.

"Well, come on over whenever you feel like it, and you can pick out the casket, and we'll go over the arrangements."

Leland nodded.

Carlisle went on his sedate way with Althea.

Martha offered Precious to Leland, who waved her away.

I took the dog and put her down inside the door to Althea's room. She tottered the short distance to the bed and disappeared under the drape of the bedspread, wending her way through the legs of the chair, as if following a familiar path.

Behind me, I heard Martha.

"Where is Clarice, Leland? You want me to call her? You want me to stay till she gets home?"

"No, you go on. I'll be fine by myself. I need a little while to get used to things. I'll call Clarice. She's probably out showing a house or something."

I was still standing on the porch beside Leland when Martha let out a shriek, which I thought out of place and out of scale, in the circumstances. Then I saw her staring into the back of her car.

"I forgot all about my groceries! Look at the ice cream! It's melted all over my new car! Jim L.'ll have a fit. What a mess! And I don't know about this chicken. Trudy, do you think I ought to throw out the chicken?"

FOUR

ONE OF HEN'S favorite lectures is on the subject of how the job of the police is to serve as well as protect. In practice, that means we do a lot of police work that doesn't look like fighting crime. Giving talks about the dangers of drugs at high school assemblies, doing welfare checks on people whose neighbors haven't seen them in a while, and rousting snipers for somebody like Elma Coleman all come under this heading. So, I suppose, does going to talk to a group of women who are suspicious about the death of one of their friends.

That accounts for my joining Aunt Lulu and her bridge-playing friends a week or so after Martha Tootle found Althea Boatright lying dead on her bathroom floor.

Althea Boatright had made the trip to Atlanta, and, accompanied by an autopsy report that said she had died from a depressed skull fracture, had come back to Ogeechee and the Sapp Funeral Home, where friends and family paid last respects before services at the Ogeechee United Methodist Church, where the choir sang, and Leland and Clarice Grinstead, and their son Jordan, were consoled by the pastor's words and a vast number of floral tributes (even if many of the flowers did come from people who do business with Grinstead's Market).

Althea's earthly pilgrimage came to an end when she was laid to rest at the side of Bert Grinstead at the Ogeechee City Cemetery. I don't know if Leland considered trying to bury her next to Rowland Boatright or not. Probably not, since he'd have wanted his mama and daddy to lie next to each other, but it might have been tempting for him to pretend to think Althea should rest there, to annoy the Boatrights and for any leverage it might have given him in ongoing Grinstead-Boatright litigation. Leland's resemblance to Althea was more than skin deep. He would fight for everything he thought he could get— if not for himself and Clarice, then for his son, Jordan.

Aunt Lulu, Ellen Chandler, Martha Tootle, and I were gathered in Aunt Lulu's family room. I'd expected Aunt Lulu to be put out that Hen hadn't come to talk with them, but she might have been satisfied that he was willing to send me. Possibly, she thought I'd be more receptive to their point of view, or, if I couldn't manage to be receptive, at least I'd be more polite.

I must be more susceptible than I realized to girl talk, because I found myself thinking this group might have assembled because they set each other off so well. There was Martha Tootle and her dramatic black and white. Today's ensemble starred a black T-shirt with a magnificent white magnolia blossom across the front, paired with white linen-looking pants. It was much more attractive than the zebra get-up.

There was Aunt Lulu and her Canadian Sunset palette, interpreted today in mauve silk, set off with a string of orange, mauve, and lilac beads, with earrings to match.

And there was Ellen Chandler, whose style, in spite of her odometer up in the low seventies, was very trendy, very teeny-bopper, thanks to her twin granddaughters, Lucinda and Cinda Lou, who are in the fashion business. The twins treat Ellen like a mobile billboard to advertise their imaginative wares, with themes that range through the plant and animal kingdom with stopovers in geometry. Ellen's a good-sized woman, and she makes a fairly impressive display. The fact that she goes along with this shows her good nature, as well. Today, an elaborate manicure featured long, cherry-red fingernails with a different flower painted on each one, courtesy of Lucinda. The manicure matched the coordinated T-shirt and earrings—hand-painted flowers on the shirt, the same flowers, in wood, dangling from her ears—provided by Cinda Lou, who runs a boutique in Gatlinburg.

Martha Tootle and Aunt Lulu, stylish though they are, pale in comparison to Ellen. The contribution of the absent one, Althea, to the group's diversity might have been to be comparatively colorless and unimaginative, like a parody of a little old lady. Camouflage for her strong personality.

I held up the low-maintenance end of the feminine spectrum. It struck me, too, that I was by far the youngest woman in the gathering, with Aunt Lulu's sixtyish coming in second, with Martha close behind her. Ellen was surely at least ten years older, and there must have been another ten years between her and Althea.

"Ice cream on yours, Trudy?" Aunt Lulu spoke from the kitchen, through the pass-through into the family room.

"Real ice cream?" In her occasional nods toward weight control, Aunt Lulu sometimes makes the mistake of buying low-fat, low-sugar, low-taste products. I'd rather have nothing.

"I knew you were coming," she answered, which meant it was the real thing. It also meant she wanted to butter me up. She'd have made Hen eat dietetic. When I realized she'd brought out her good china and hand-embroidered napkins to go with it, and put a generous dollop of ice cream on top of a generous serving of her famous blueberry crumble, I began to worry. First, it worried me that Aunt Lulu would think elegance mattered enough to me that I could be swayed by it. Second, it underscored the importance of the meeting. What had Hen let me in for?

I tried to hide my fears under polite conversation about the dry weather we'd been having and what it would mean for the orchards. Finally, when Aunt Lulu had bustled around to the family room side of the pass-through and finished doling out the dessert and the coffee or tea of our choice, I couldn't stand it any longer. I broke.

"Hen tells me y'all have some concerns about the way Althea died."

That was a judiciously edited version of what Hen had told me, which had been more like, "Martha Tootle has a bee in her bonnet about Althea Boatright, and I want you to go over there and swat it dead. She probably feels guilty about running off to the grocery store and leaving the old lady alone to die."

At my words, Aunt Lulu and Ellen turned to Martha, but I wasn't fooled into thinking that meant they didn't have the same bee in their bonnets. Aunt Lulu doesn't abuse her position as mother of the Chief of Police. She must have had some reason to bother Hen—and, under his trickle-down system of delegating unpleasant chores, me—about it.

"It was her walking stick, Trudy," Martha said. "You were there. You saw it."

"Yes." I remembered the walking stick that Martha had knocked to the floor.

"Well, then." Martha seemed to think she'd made a point.

"Well, then, what?"

"Well, then, how did she walk to the bathroom?"

"Carefully?" I suggested. "It wasn't very far."

"But she never took a step without the stick. She had a deathly fear of falling."

I didn't want to emphasize the aptness of Martha's phrasing, so I merely said, "I see your point. It was unusual for her to walk anywhere without the stick."

"Not unusual. Unheard of." Martha's magnolia blossom heaved.

"That's right, Trudy," Aunt Lulu confirmed. Ellen stopped with a spoonful of crumble halfway to her mouth and nodded her agreement.

"So, there's obviously something suspicious about her death," Martha said.

My duty was clear, and I started swatting, putting all the sincerity and matter-of-fact authority I could muster into it. "No, there is not obviously something suspicious about her death. The forensic pathologist who performed the autopsy didn't find anything suspicious about Althea's death. You all said she hadn't been feeling well." They all nodded. "Then, why do you have trouble believing she fell accidentally?"

I thought maybe they'd back off if I started throwing around words like "forensic pathologist" and "autopsy," but I underestimated them.

"Because of the walking stick," Martha insisted.

"Why don't you tell me what you think happened." I took a spoonful of ice cream and closed my eyes to savor it. And to listen, of course.

"We think somebody came in and killed her and dragged her body to the bathroom to make it look like she slipped," Ellen said.

"Or maybe whoever it was took her in there and threw her down against the tub to kill her." Of course Martha Tootle would take the more dramatic view. "Could your forensic pathologist tell if that's what happened?"

"A forensic pathologist can tell if a body has been moved after death." I saw no harm in admitting that much.

"Even if it was just a few seconds after death—before the blood starts pooling?" This was Aunt Lulu. I'd forgotten that she'd been reading up on forensics, taking an unwelcome interest in police work. I'd have to be careful.

"Maybe she'd been drugged or poisoned and the killer wanted it to look like an accident so nobody would investigate," Martha said. "And you're playing right into his hands."

"Or her hands," Aunt Lulu supplied, beating me to it. My feminism isn't always militant, but I don't think it's unreasonable to hold out for equal treatment in society and language.

I tried again. "The police pathologist in Atlanta who performed the autopsy found no unexpected drugs in her system. We know what medicines she was on. Nothing else turned up. That means she had not been poisoned." I didn't feel it was necessary to explain that the OPD had a head start on Althea Boatright's medications because of the now-unnecessary investigation of the vehicular homicide.

"What about expected drugs?" Aunt Lulu asked. "She took a lot of medication. Maybe she had too much or not enough of whatever she'd been taking."

"If that's what happened, it would be difficult to prove, especially difficult to prove it wasn't accidental. Contrary to what your reading might suggest, we in law enforcement have to have evidence that will stand up in a court of law, not hunches. Listen, now. I understand that you're all upset about her death. And, Miz Tootle, I understand the point about the walking stick, even though I think it would be hard to prove she never ever took a step without it. But you have to understand that without some weighty evidence—real evidence, now, not just a feeling—to suggest foul play, there is nothing to warrant a police investigation of the death of Miz Boatright, if that's where all this is headed. And the forensic pathologist found no such evidence. None whatever."

"But he—it was a he, wasn't it?—he didn't know about the walking stick."

"The walking stick doesn't prove anything," I argued. "If y'all weren't being so obstinate, you'd be able to suggest three or four reasons for Althea to be in the bathroom without her walking stick."

"That's not all." This was Ellen.

In spite of the way she dresses and a marital history that includes so many husbands there's no way for most people to know which lineage she's actually tracing when she mentions a relative, she has a down-to-earth approach to life that makes a lot of sense. I was interested in whatever she might offer. "What else do you have?"

"We might not have thought any more about it, but my niece Debra works at the Veterinary Clinic and she told me that even before Althea's funeral, Clarice had Precious put to sleep. Debra thought it was mean, is why she mentioned it."

I'm afraid my exasperation showed, and my silver spoon clinked against Aunt Lulu's good china. "Please don't tell me you're saying Clarice killed Althea, and had to kill Precious because Precious was a witness."

"Now, Trudy," Aunt Lulu said.

"Well, what then? Precious managed to kill Althea and Clarice was exacting vengeance? Actually, when you think about it, maybe Althea did trip over Precious…and…"

I trailed off gracefully, in the hope that they'd like that idea and give up on a police investigation. Silly me.

"When Ellen told me about Precious, I asked Clarice why she did it, and she said Precious was grieving so much over not being able to find Althea that it was the only merciful thing to do," Martha said. "That may be true, as far as it goes, but Althea was always talking about how Clarice didn't like her—Althea, I mean—and especially how she didn't like her living with them. Althea didn't like it much, either, especially since she was more cooped up than she used to be."

She glanced at me when she said that last part, and then graciously added, "I don't mean it was your fault she couldn't get out, Trudy, just because you're the one who took her license."

"I'm glad you realize that," I said.

"I heard about the big whoop-de-do at the Hatfield House over that brooch," Ellen said, studying a fingernail as though trying to identify the particular species of daisy. It was an unconvincing attempt to appear casual. "Maybe Althea lit into Clarice about it later and Clarice killed her in self-defense."

"I've been wondering about that," Martha said. "Why would Clarice give the brooch to Susannah? She was bound to know it would cause trouble with Althea."

"Clarice and Susannah are cousins on the Walters side," Aunt Lulu said, "and maybe Clarice felt Althea was in the wrong. Trudy, Althea told us Clarice had been messing with her things. That's probably when she took the brooch. Maybe she was in there looking for something else and Althea surprised her by coming home early."

"We are way, way off the subject here," I said. "Somebody is going to have to explain to me how Clarice Grinstead's putting a pathetic dog out of its misery—or even giving away a piece of old jewelry—makes her guilty of killing her mother-in-law. I must have missed something." I applied myself to dessert again.

"The thing with Precious just shows how she felt about Althea," Martha said. "It's transference or something psychological. Althea was always talking about how mean Clarice was—and not just about keeping Precious out of the rest of the house and off the carpet, either."

"I told Althea from the beginning she'd be sorry if she gave that house to Leland and Clarice while she was still alive," Ellen said, flicking a petunia for emphasis. "Not that I don't think Clarice did the right thing about Precious. Even if Precious had been a sweet-tempered little dog, which she wasn't, she was so old she couldn't walk or control her bladder. I wouldn't have put up with it as long as Clarice did. You ask me, she should have done it even sooner, so they could have buried Precious in the same box with Althea."

"Ellen!" Martha tried to act scandalized, but I could tell she loved the barbarity of the idea.

Ellen was unperturbed. "I'll go even further. Whoever did Althea in—if somebody did—whoever it was might have done her a favor, like Clarice did Precious. And, Martha, I don't want to hear any more of this 'if I'd gotten back sooner I might have saved her.' If you'd gotten to her sooner they might have had to plug her into machines and life support and artificial breathing and I don't know what all. I hope I get hit by a logging truck when it's my time, might even decide to run out in front of one, if I can still run. I'd rather be roadkill than finish up in some smelly warehouse for old people where somebody has to wipe my drool and change my diapers. Don't look at me like that."

I'm sure all of us had been looking at her "like that." We all looked somewhere else.

"You know I'm right. One way or another, we're all circling the drain, and Althea had been circling longer than most. I'd like to have some say in how I go." Ellen simpered here, and waved her entire garden of fingernails, in a much-belated attempt to lighten things up. "I'd like people to remember me at the height of my powers. Like Cleopatra."

"We were talking about Precious," Aunt Lulu said.

"Same thing, except we aren't so humane with people," Ellen insisted. Another idea lit her face with mischief. "If you'd got back sooner, Martha, maybe they'd have killed you, too."

"Ooh!" I could tell the horrible prospect, now safely avoided, thrilled Martha.

"Let me see if I know where we stand," I suggested. "Miz

Tootle, you say since Miz Boatright's walking stick wasn't found beside her, it means somebody killed her. Miz Chandler, you say even if that's true, it was an act of mercy. Aunt Lulu, where are you on this?"

I could tell she didn't like the direct question. "Well, Trudy, if it's suspicious, isn't it up to the police to investigate?"

"Yes, ma'am, it is. But to justify an investigation," I tutored, "it has to be suspicious to the police. That means there must be evidence of a crime. We don't have that here. There is no reason to investigate the death of a sick old woman. You'd have to give me more than your opinion that she never took a step without her walking stick and the fact—I'll take your granddaughter's word on this, Miz Chandler—the fact that her daughter-in-law had her dog put to sleep. Even if I thought those things were significant, there is also the fact that she was locked in. Miz Tootle, you were there. You know perfectly well the house was locked and those locks have to be locked with a key. If somebody killed her, how did that somebody get out?"

Martha shrugged. "That's a no-brainer, Trudy. It was somebody with a key."

"Are we back to Clarice Grinstead? I thought she was your friend."

"She is, but so was Althea my friend, and if Clarice committed murder, she ought to pay. Isn't that why we have police? And you have to admit, Clarice could have locked the door behind her. Or Leland."

"Or Jordan," Ellen said, pronouncing it Jer-den, like the old-line Jordans do to distinguish themselves from the nouveau Jordans, which showed she knew who she was dealing with. You've really got to be in the know in Ogeechee to look at J-o-r-d-a-n and know how to pronounce it.

"Maybe Leland and Clarice were impatient to inherit

Althea's money," Ellen continued, fiddling with the iris dangling from her earlobe. The other earlobe had what looked like a peach blossom, and the mismatch distracted me so that I almost missed her next comment. "I don't know whether Althea still had part ownership of the grocery store or not, but my ex-daughter-in-law's first husband could look it up. Maybe she was tight with her money and Leland wanted to put more into the store. They've got to do something if they don't want to lose all their business to that new Food Lion."

"You think Leland would kill his mother for money to put into the store? What kind of minds do y'all have?"

"It's human nature, Trudy," Martha said, shaking her head at my innocence.

"Maybe they didn't do it just for the store," Ellen said. "Maybe it was for Jordan."

"Well, Miz Chandler, why don't you find out more about that, as long as y'all are making up a list of suspects and their motives?" Yes, I know I sounded a little cranky.

"Absolutely," Ellen agreed. "And what will the police be investigating?"

"Maybe another helping of blueberry crumble?"

I can't say I enjoyed the break while Aunt Lulu went to fetch me some more dessert. She forbade us to say anything while she was out of the room, and I was afraid I wasn't the only one trying to use the hiatus to reorganize my thoughts.

My fears were justified when Aunt Lulu returned and said, "It's not just the Grinsteads who have keys. The Boatrights, Homer and Susannah, grew up in that house. Maybe they still have keys."

"That's right, Lulu," Ellen said. "I'm sure sorry I wasn't at Hatfield House for dinner that Sunday. Sounds like Althea was on such a tear it might have made a saint want to kill her. It's no secret how Homer and Susannah feel about their daddy giving Althea everything. And Melva! Well, she's always wanted more than Homer could give her. And my daughter's husband, the one who's a contractor like Homer, says Homer's business hasn't been doing so well. Maybe it's more than being sentimental about some of that property that has the Boatrights worked up."

"Why would Homer Boatright think he'd benefit from Althea's death?" I asked.

Aunt Lulu took that one. "Well, Leland's probably not as tough as Althea was, in a business sense. The Boatrights might think it would be easier to get him to settle."

In spite of all the evidence that it wasn't working, I tried sarcasm again. "So, to sum up, we have as murder suspects in the death from natural or accidental causes, the son, daughter-in-law, grandson, stepson, stepdaughter, and step-daughter-in-law of the deceased? Is that everybody?"

Martha shook her head. "No, it isn't. Elfreda Wilcox used to clean for her, until Althea accused her of stealing and fired her. Elfreda might have had a key."

"That's motive all right, but I can't see Althea giving Elfreda a key," Ellen responded. "More likely, she'd have watched every move Elfreda made while she was there."

"Then how could Elfreda have stolen anything?" Aunt Lulu asked.

They were having such a lively exchange that I hoped they'd forgotten me. I kept my eyes on my dessert.

"That's a good question, Lulu," Martha said. "It was so unfair of Althea! None of Althea's friends used Elfreda after that either, and Elfreda needed the work. She has that no-good granddaughter to support."

"That's not true," Aunt Lulu said. "I still use her."

"And so do I," I said, forgetting I was trying to be invisible.

Martha was not deterred. "Well, I know Elfreda lost work

because of Althea. And I also know I saw Althea wearing the bracelet she accused Elfreda of stealing, after she accused Elfreda, but she never apologized. Talk about motive!"

"And it wouldn't have made any difference if she did apologize," Aunt Lulu put in. "The damage was done as far as Elfreda was concerned. It's like our preacher said about gossip. It's easy to spread, like a handful of seed you scatter out in a field, but you'll never be able to collect it all again. Some people couldn't believe Elfreda wasn't guilty of something."

"Or maybe they felt so ashamed of themselves that they couldn't face her," I suggested.

Aunt Lulu nodded. It was probably my imagination, but I thought Ellen and Martha both looked a little shamefaced.

Since I had the floor, I continued. "Let me caution the three of you against sharing this theory of yours with anybody else. *Anybody* else. Like the seed in the field Aunt Lulu was talking about, it might be hard to neutralize everything you say. Just think about the damage it might do to all these people—these suspects you've been talking about—if somebody got the idea you were accusing them of murder. If nothing else, you might find yourselves in court."

"Well, maybe it wasn't one of them," Martha conceded. "Maybe somebody else broke in."

"Then how did they break out?"

That stopped them long enough for me to say, "Well, thanks for the dessert, Aunt Lulu. It's been real nice talking to y'all, but if there isn't anything else, I'd better get on with serving and protecting." I put down my plate and stood and smoothed my uniform.

Of course there was something else.

"We have—Ellen has—one more suspect for you," Martha said, all but emitting sparks, she was so excited.

"It's about that man she ran over," Ellen said.

"He's dead," I said. "He didn't do it."

"But what about somebody taking revenge?" Martha said.

"Come on, now! Everybody knows *that* was an accident."

"You said you'd have to have a reason to investigate," Ellen said. "And maybe you didn't have a reason to investigate that, but what if he wasn't a stranger like everybody thought? What if Althea knew him and had a reason to want him out of the way?"

"Oh, my goodness." I sighed and sat back down.

"It's true," Ellen said. "Or it might be true. At least it's true that she knew him."

"How do you know that?"

"My son Darwin's wife Florine works at a nursing home in Jesup, and he said she told him there's a woman there who was talking about the accident when it was in the paper over there. Darwin says Florine says this woman says they were all in high school together. Did you know Althea came from Jesup?"

"It was before my time," I said, testily I'm sure. This was fourth-degree hearsay, or worse. "But even if—"

"If you'd known she knew him, you wouldn't have been so quick to call it an accident, would you?" Ellen asked.

"Maybe not, but she was still an old—"

"Especially since she didn't tell you she knew him?" It was Aunt Lulu on the attack. The others have to be careful never to criticize the police department, but she can get away with it. Up to a point. "Nobody's saying there's any way the police in Ogeechee could have known or should have known. But now that you do know, don't you think there might be more to it? And that it might lead to something about Althea's death?"

"Possibly."

"So you'll investigate?"

"I'll see what Hen has to say. He's the boss, you know."

I made my escape. Safely out in the fresh air, I began to enjoy the prospects of the day. Usually if we have a murder there's no mystery about it because it has happened in front of witnesses at a juke joint. I could hardly wait to see Hen's face when I told him we had a murder case—a murder mystery, no less!—complete with an extensive roster of suspects.

FIVE

BEING THE WELL-DISCIPLINED, loyal, upright, clean, moral officer that I am, of course I hurried right back to the station house to fill His Highness in on developments. It didn't hurt that I was interested in seeing how Hen would handle a case in which his dear mama had such a lively interest. It was bound to shed light on his character. Besides, in spite of all the odds against it, the meeting with Aunt Lulu and her friends had raised at least one question that I, the aforementioned well-disciplined, etc., police officer, thought needed an answer.

My report, however, had to wait. Hen was leaning against the doorframe leading to his tiny, cluttered office, and he was holding forth on the subject of the Redneck Olympics, an annual event in nearby Dublin. It must have been a slow day, crime-wise, in Ogeechee. Either that, or his accumulated paperwork was driving him to distraction. Maybe both. Jerome Sharpe was filling the doorway that led to the file-and-computer room across from Hen's office. Relaxed, arms crossed, he leaned against the frame, listening. He wore an expression of patient forbearance.

"Dwight's brother's daughter came in first in the armpit serenade category," Hen said, to catch me up. Dwight Wilkes started working for the OPD after he retired from being a guard at the state prison. He lasted at the OPD for a few years and then retired again. I have a sneaking suspicion that Hen's personality and policies didn't offer Dwight enough scope for his not-so-latent sadistic tendencies.

"Dwight says little Debra Lou brought tears to everybody's eyes with her rendition of 'Dixie.' A real crowd-pleaser, Dwight says," Hen said.

"Just how little is Debra Lou?" Jerome asked.

"She's about seventeen now," Hen said, "and that question shows why you're such a good officer, son. You don't take anything for granted."

I didn't want to admit I'd taken for granted that little Debra Lou resembled little Shirley Temple, so I kept quiet.

"According to Dwight, the runner-up did 'Georgia on My Mind,' but he ran into trouble with some of those long notes," Hen continued. "Dwight thinks it was his material that cost him. You just can't lose with 'Dixie.' "

"I wish I was in de land ob cotton," Jerome said without expression.

"Uh huh," Hen acknowledged.

"So it was 'Dixie' and not Little Debra Lou that was the crowd-pleaser?" I asked.

"Dwight didn't describe her costume," Hen said.

"This whole thing sounds like something a bunch of seventh-grade boys would dream up," I said. "It's coming back to me why I've never made the effort to get over to Dublin and see it for myself. That and the fireworks display at the school and everything else going on right here in Ogeechee."

"Maybe those seventh graders grew up but their sense of humor didn't," Jerome said. "Ol' times dere am not forgotten."

Hen nodded. "Ain't it the truth. Little Debra Lou and what we might as well call her rendition prove that."

"Don't get the idea I'm not enjoying this," I said, "because I really *really* am, but before we sink any lower, do y'all want to hear about my meeting with your mother and her friends?"

"Even Jerome would probably rather hear about the Redneck Olympics than what went on at a meeting of genteel senior citizens with overactive imaginations," Hen said. "That right, Jerome?"

"Yassuh, boss," Jerome said, in case we hadn't already picked up on his mood, which we had.

"Aunt Lulu won't like it when I tell her you called her a senior citizen," I said.

"Don't tell her, then. And while you're at it, you might as well not tell Martha Tootle I said she has the attention span of a squirrel," Hen instructed.

"Yassuh, boss," I said. Solidarity.

Hen ignored me, as he had ignored Jerome. "We've got some people here in Ogeechee that could give those Dubliners a run for their money in the Dumpster dive, and I'm thinking I'll see about entering Teri's daddy in the bug zapper spitball. I've seen that man shoot a stream of tobacco juice with enough accuracy to put out a match at thirty paces."

"Man must not have much to do, he's got time to develop a talent like that," Jerome said.

"How does it work?" I asked, glancing at Jerome. "Would he have to spit bugs into the zapper? Would even a redneck do that?"

"Sure, you get him drunk enough," Jerome said.

It suited me for this topic to rattle on a little longer. It would give me another few minutes to think how to present my unanswered question so as to get authorization to investigate.

"I reckon I'll have to ask Dwight how that bug zapper thing works," Hen said. "Might be if Teri's daddy won't do it, Delcie would. I bet I could make a real competitor out of that girl, with the gap she's got in her front teeth."

"That gap'll be closed up by next summer," Jerome pointed out. "Tough luck, Chief." He looked at me. "That poor child won't grow up having any idea how to behave herself with him as a daddy, in spite of everything her mama and grandma can do. Maybe you'll have to take that category yourself, Chief," he added for good measure.

"I'll find out how it works," Hen said, his rumbling laugh joining Jerome's. Boys, honestly!

That brought an end to the Redneck Olympics report. Jerome backed out of the doorway he'd been blocking, no doubt heading for the computer and paperwork.

"How's Miz Coleman doing?" I asked.

"I don't know for sure," Jerome said. "Looks like I did such a good job getting those camo men off the motel, they've taken to wandering around in the woods and down by the old Durrence Pond. I told her they were probably hunters, and she shouldn't worry about it. She's thinking it over."

"You shoulda left 'em up on the roof where you could find 'em," Hen said, turning toward his office. "You don't watch out, you'll lose your cookie supplier."

I followed Hen into his office, taking advantage of my knowledge that he'd rather do almost anything than paperwork.

"You satisfy those women, get 'em off my back?" he asked.

"I did my best, but, knowing who I was up against, I wouldn't swear to it."

"You told them that even if we believed there was foul play involved in Althea Boatright's death, which we do not, we'd need something to go on?"

"I did explain that to them. I think I went over it twice, using different words."

"Good. Is that your whole report?"

"Nassuh, boss," I said, trying to imitate Jerome again.

Hen sighed. "What's the problem?"

"If you're not in a big hurry to get back to that mess on your desk, I think you should listen to the suspect list they developed."

"If it's a list of people who didn't like Althea Boatright, I don't have the time."

"Sure you do." I ran through the list.

"Lordy, lordy! Dublin can have their redneck games, but we could give 'em a run for their money when it comes to the Small Town Gossip Olympics."

"You get no argument from me, but—"

"We've got the freestyle aspersion casting."

"Hen—"

"And there's jumping to conclusions, spreading rumors, uh huh, and the running innuendo, the all-out gossip-spreading speed trials, hint-dropping, the flying leap of logic, the death-defying—"

All I could do was wait until he ran down. He had to, eventually. Even Hen's vocabulary and imagination are not infinite. When he stopped, I told him the one thing that I thought ought to be looked into.

If Precious was such a crippled old dog—and remembering her awkward movements at the Grinstead house the day Althea Boatright died, I could testify on that point myself— how could she have jumped down and gotten tangled up with Althea's feet as Althea claimed she had, and made her run down Charles Sykes? Was it really an accident, or had Althea murdered the man and gotten away with it since we didn't even suspect any connection between them at the time and, therefore, had no reason to suspect an intent? I put it to Hen that the honor of the OPD was at stake here, not only to look into that possible crime, but to find out if the death of Charles Sykes had anything to do with the death of Althea Boatright. If she had gotten away with committing murder, that might have led somebody to want to kill her.

"Oh, hang!" Hen swore. But he agreed that we ought to see what we could find out about a connection between Althea Boatright and Charles Sykes.

I had an idea how to go about it, an idea that started with

Ellen Chandler and led through her son Darwin's wife Florine to a nursing home in Jesup.

"You get on it, then," Hen said. "Whether you turn up anything or not, just doin' it is bound to pacify, mollify, gratify, and possibly even appease my mama and her cronies."

Pacify? Mollify? Gratify? Appease? Fat chance. But I got on it.

SIX

A CALL TO ELLEN Chandler put me in touch with Florine, at work at the Azalea Acres Nursing Home in Jesup. Florine assured me that I could come whenever it suited me because Irene Dasher, the woman who said she'd been in high school with Althea Jordan Grinstead Boatright and Charlie Sykes, wouldn't be going anywhere. I was so jazzed at how easy that had been that I whipped through a stack of paperwork before I left for the day.

Even if Leland Grinstead was being considered (in some circles) as a murder suspect in his mother's death, since Grinstead's Market is just across the street from the OPD, it's where I usually get my groceries, so I stopped by on my way home to see if they still had a sale on chicken breasts that I could have for supper. I thought I'd bake them in mushroom soup the way Grandma used to. If I fixed several at once, I wouldn't have to cook again for a while.

I had detoured on the way to the meat counter, and was making the requisite fuss over DeeAnn Crenshaw's new baby, when I noticed Martha Tootle hemming and hawing and jiggling her cart while she studied the labels on cereal boxes at the far end of the cramped aisle.

When DeeAnn moved off and I resumed my quest for chicken, I realized Martha had been stalking me instead of a nutritious breakfast fortified with all the essential vitamins and minerals. "Trudy," Martha said in a loud whisper.

"My goodness, Miz Tootle, what's happened to your voice? You were all right this morning."

"Nothing," she whispered. "I have something to tell you."

"Okay."

"Not here. Meet me in the parking lot."

"What is it?"

"Shh! I'll wait for you outside."

I took my time choosing a package of chicken from the nearly identical possibilities and was equally careful to get exactly the can of mushroom soup I wanted. Nevertheless, Martha Tootle hadn't given up. When I got outside, she was pacing back and forth beside her car, fiddling with a walking stick.

"What's up?" I whispered out of the corner of my mouth.

"Are you all right, Trudy?" Apparently my version of cloak-and-dagger theatrics wasn't up to her dramatic standard.

"Never mind. What do you have to tell me, and why couldn't you talk in the store?"

"I didn't think you'd want anybody overhearing."

"Overhearing what? What is it?"

"I have some of that hard evidence you were carrying on about this morning." She waved the walking stick in my face. "I got this from Althea's just now."

"From Althea's?"

She brushed my question aside with a gesture that reminded me of Jerome and his cookie crumbs. "Well, from the Grinsteads', if you want to be technical about it."

"You're talking to the police, remember. If you're talking about breaking and entering, I may need to take you in."

"Of course not! After you left, Lulu and Ellen and I talked some more, and we decided I should go talk to Clarice."

"And ask her whether she killed her mother-in-law?" I guessed. It shouldn't have surprised me that no matter what agreement I thought we'd reached, the meeting hadn't adjourned simply because I left.

"Trudy, I'm never sure when you're joking!"

"I think I was joking," I said.

She frowned as she processed that, but quickly recovered. "You told us there weren't any unexpected drugs in Althea's body, so we thought I could maybe get Clarice to let me have Althea's medicine and we could see if somebody had tampered with any of it."

"Subject to who you mean by that last 'we,' that isn't such a bad idea," I said. "You did mean the police, didn't you?"

"Well, we've all known enough sick people that we, my friends and I, probably know more than you'd think. We'd be able to tell if the right pills were in the right bottles, or maybe if somebody had emptied out capsules and put something, maybe a double dose or a half dose, something that would have been serious, but not a different drug. You see what I mean?"

"Yes, I do." I was having a hard time balancing between amusement, annoyance, and concern for the busybodies. "Did you get her to give you the medicine?"

She looked pleased with herself. "I didn't just come out and ask for it, not right off the bat. I took over some brownies, and we talked about their loss—you know—and I'd made up a story about Jim L. having some of the same problems Althea did and wanting to know what Althea was taking for it."

"And Clarice just gave it to you?"

Martha grew more vivacious. "She told me to take whatever I wanted to. She was cleaning out—I mean really cleaning out—Althea's room, getting ready to put in some new carpet and turn it into a sort of a den, like she's been wanting to ever since she moved into that house, and she was pitching out practically everything of Althea's. Clothes, letters, shabby underwear. I swear, Trudy, it was pitiful to see it. Made me sadder than the funeral, even, to see the pitiful things she left behind. I'm going to go right home and clean out some things before I die and somebody else goes through all my drawers."

"That sounds like a good idea. I think I'll go get started on it right now." I was trying not to be rude to a citizen and trying not to worry about my groceries.

"And that's not all," Martha persisted. "We decided that while I was at it I should see what I could find out about where Clarice and Leland were when Althea died. You know, check on their alibis."

"Hen is going to love this," I told her. "That's sarcasm, in case you have any doubt."

"I recognized it, thank you very much. But you have to admit it would help if we could eliminate people from our list of suspects."

"If we had a case, yes. But we don't." I wasn't about to admit to any uncertainty on that point, but I couldn't resist asking, "Could you eliminate them?"

"Not really. Leland was at the store, like he is most of the time, but nobody pays much attention to where he actually is every single minute, and with Clarice in real estate, she could have slipped home between appointments. I guess we could check with the people she said she was showing a house to about exact times."

"Or you could give me the name—or, better yet, give it to Hen—so the police could check it out. After all, you've meddled with evidence—"

"Not if there's no crime being investigated!"

"—and alerted a possible suspect—"

She adopted a haughty air. "We didn't feel that we should bother the police at this time."

"On behalf of the entire Ogeechee Police Department, I thank you," I said.

"There's that sarcasm again, isn't it, Trudy? Anyway, you got me distracted. What I wanted to show you was this." She brandished the walking stick playfully. "I'd swear in court, on a stack of Bibles, that this isn't—wasn't—Althea's walking stick."

"It probably won't come to that. Even a court of law thinks one Bible is enough. And I don't think you want to perjure yourself, or put your eternal soul in jeopardy, just to make a point."

"It's the truth, Trudy." She adopted an injured air which didn't impress me.

"Really? So what?"

"So if this isn't hers, then her killer took hers by mistake and left this."

"I'm interested, in spite of myself," I said. "How can you be so sure this wasn't Althea's? It looks to me like every other walking stick from that display down at the pharmacy. Was hers monogrammed or something like that?"

"Something like that," Martha said, looking frankly pleased with herself. She began twirling the cane. With her black slacks and jacket and white shirt, she made a fair imitation of a tuxedo-clad, song-and-dance man.

"Martha, I've just bought some chicken, and you know how fast it spoils."

"Oh. All right. I'll get to the point, but you are taking all the fun out of it. See, Trudy, the day Althea died—was murdered—when I took her home, I put her cane in the backseat for her. When I got to her house and reached for it, I grabbed it near the bottom. It was all rough. When I mentioned it, she said it had been chewed up by that ugly white mongrel dog that comes from that bunch of white trash Wilkses that lives back in the woods behind her house. I swear somebody'd be doing the town a favor to go in there with a bulldozer and clean them out."

"You may be right about that. And?"

"Oh, yes, what am I driving at. Well, Althea said that dog attacked her one day when she was out back burning some trash and she had to fight him off."

"I know about that," I said. "She called the police about it, and told Hen if he didn't do something about that dog she'd be going to the town council about the quality of protection citizens were getting from the police and maybe suggest they look for a better police chief. Althea wasn't one of Hen's favorite people."

"She could be hard to deal with," Martha admitted.

"So all this is about the dog running loose?"

"No, it most definitely is not! It's about the dog chewing the cane." Martha grabbed my hand and thrust it against the end of the walking stick. "Look here. Feel this. This cane is perfectly smooth." Martha ran her fingers up and down the length of the cane to demonstrate. "It isn't the same one. According to Clarice, Althea had only one walking stick, and this one was in her room, but it isn't the one she had with her at bridge that morning. All we have to do is look for whoever has Althea's cane."

"That's interesting, Miz Tootle, and I'm not being sarcastic this time. If there is a killer and it is somebody who uses a walking stick, it certainly narrows things down for us."

Martha smiled in triumph. "It has to be somebody who uses a walking stick, Trudy. If the killer doesn't use a walking stick, there never would have been a mix-up."

"I don't want to worry you, but if someone killed Althea and made off with the wrong walking stick, whoever it is has probably realized it by now. And that means the killer—we might as well use the word—will notice anybody who seems especially interested in walking sticks and Althea's medicine."

"We'll have to be discreet then, won't we?"

"Discreet is a good idea, if it isn't already too late, considering you asked Miz Grinstead for Miz Boatright's cane and medicine and checked her and Leland's alibis. I think it's time for you and Aunt Lulu and Ellen Chandler to turn this over to professionals. Let's go over to the station house right now. We'll lock this in the evidence room, just in case. And you need to talk to Hen."

"Well, no, uh…"

"You don't want to confess that you've had so much fun playing with the walking stick there's no hope of getting the killer's fingerprints, if any, off of it?"

The cane fell with a clatter to the asphalt of the parking lot. Martha's eyes grew wide, and she clasped a hand to her bosom in the classic stricken heroine pose.

"You don't have to fake a heart attack," I said. "Even without fingerprints, the cane might be useful evidence."

"You really think so?"

"I don't know what to think, to tell the truth, but I might as well tell you, I did convince Hen to let me do a little investigating."

"Really?" She brightened. "Well, then, there's the medicine, too. Maybe there'll be something wrong with that."

"We'll lock that up, too. But don't expect too much. It doesn't make sense that somebody who had tried to kill her by messing with her medication would risk being found out by going there and knocking her against the sink or the tub or whatever it was she hit. That's what they call overkill."

"Maybe whoever it was got impatient?" She was totally irrepressible.

"You're right. It's too early for us to eliminate any possibilities. The exchange of this walking stick for Althea's does suggest that somebody left the wrong stick by mistake. But there could be some other perfectly reasonable explanation for that. And it is possible that there was something wrong with her medicine. We'll get the police lab to take a look."

"But Ellen's—"

"Listen to me. Either y'all think there was something fishy about the way Althea died, or you don't. If you do think so, then you all—all of you—have to quit messing around with the evidence. It's for the police to investigate, not Ellen Chandler's network of experts, no matter how good they are. And there's another thing y'all haven't thought about."

Martha pouted skeptically, so I explained. "If you're right, and somebody did kill her, it's practically got to be somebody you know."

"Oh! Trudy! You don't think I'm in danger?"

I shrugged with what I hoped looked like nonchalance. "Maybe. But what I meant was that your investigating would alert the killer that we're investigating."

"Oh my!" Martha said, turning pale. "Whoever it is might find out I have the walking stick. Oh! Leland and Clarice both know, and I thought he looked upset when he saw me taking it! What am I going to do?"

"You might have to stop shopping at Grinstead's," I suggested. "Leland might corner you in canned goods and finish you off with some pears in heavy syrup."

"You ought not make fun," Martha said. "I'm not even going to try to figure out when you're joking any more. My life may be in danger." She directed an incongruously bright smile over my shoulder. "Oh, hello, Homer."

I turned to see Homer Boatright headed in our direction from the far corner of the parking lot.

"Afternoon, ladies," he said without offering a smile to go with the words. As usual, his small frame was neatly dressed in slacks and a knit golf shirt. With his fringe of gray hair and the rimless glasses he always wore, he always had the serious mien of someone on important business.

"Goodness, Homer, you're limping. What happened?"

"Stepped in a hole at a construction site and messed up my ankle," he said with a frown. "Shoulda just gone ahead and broke it. I think it would heal faster."

"Don't you have a walking stick?" Martha asked next. I guess that's her idea of being discreet.

"Left it at home," he said. "Don't like using one."

"Why didn't you park in the handicap place and save all the walking?"

"Don't have one of those permits," he said. "Wouldn't want to get a ticket." He looked at me when he said that, so maybe he was joking. "Anyway, I don't like parking close to anybody else. People just as soon bang their junker car doors into your car as not. Do it on purpose, I think. Can't stand anybody having something better than what they have."

"Well, it might be worth the risk," Martha said. "Especially if you don't have a walking stick to help you."

"You offering me yours?"

"Uh. No. This isn't mine. It belongs to a friend."

Homer snorted and went on his way. We watched as he hitched his way on into the store.

"Must hurt pretty bad," Martha said.

I agreed with her, but I wasn't worried about Homer Boatright. I was thinking that if Homer had Althea's cane and had realized it, it would account for why he wasn't using it. And it would mean he'd recognize the one Martha had.

"Come on. Let's go turn in this evidence."

"Can I wait till Ellen and Lulu can go with me?"

"No. And I don't think you ought to follow Homer in there and check out his alibi, either."

"Sarcasm again?"

"No, that's the honest truth. I think you need to go straight from here across to the station house, for the benefit of anybody—like Leland or Homer—who might be watching you and that walking stick."

"You're right, Trudy." She used the tail of her shirt to pick up the walking stick.

"You didn't take anything else you ought to tell me about, did you?"

The walking stick clattered to the asphalt again. "Clumsy!" Martha scolded herself, and reached down again with her shirttail. "What did you say, Trudy?"

"I asked if you took anything else that might be evidence— anything besides the walking stick and the medicine?"

"Oh! No. We didn't talk about anything else that might be evidence."

That wasn't a direct answer to my question, but I put it down to Martha Tootle's innate sense of drama.

"I'll bring this stuff right over," Martha said. "You go ahead." She was reaching for her cell phone as I turned away.

I went on ahead and delivered the news to Hen. The good news, from one perspective, was that Martha had something that might pass for hard evidence of murder. The bad news was that she'd unquestionably ruined any fingerprints it might have carried.

And there was more to the bad news. If Althea Boatright's death had been murder, there was no longer anything approximating a crime scene to investigate. Was Clarice Grinstead's energetic cleaning-out prompted by nothing more than the natural desire to take care of the things left behind after a death—strengthened by her well-known dislike of Althea— or was she deliberately destroying evidence of murder?

SEVEN

THE NEXT MORNING, Ellen Chandler, Aunt Lulu, and I tooled down to Jesup in Aunt Lulu's Cadillac and found the Azalea Acres Nursing Home. It was a dreary, uninviting place that didn't come close to living up to its charming name, even allowing that it wasn't the time of year for azaleas to be showing off. The white frame building and sparse grounds—maybe acres, but surely not more than a couple—needed more care than they were getting in the July heat. My impression was that the inmates—pardon me, the clients, the patients—either were in no condition to notice or were powerless to complain and that the people who worked there had more than enough to do.

It is usually not a good idea to take civilians along on a police inquiry, but these particular civilians and this particular inquiry seemed to call for it. Hen and I had talked it over. The idea that we'd be putting them in danger was too far-fetched to consider, and it was possible they'd be useful. Ellen Chandler, after all, had been the link that got us there, and Aunt Lulu…well, what can I say? When she was widowed, she was left with enough income to free her from having to take a paying job, and she spends her considerable energy on various community causes, of which this investigation was unquestionably one. I counted myself lucky to have escaped without Martha Tootle, as well. It was my good luck that Jim L. had wanted her to go with him to Savannah for something or other.

Ellen's daughter-in-law, Florine, was holding down the reception desk. She was built along the same generous lines as Ellen, and I wondered if Darwin had consciously looked for a woman like his mother. Conscious or unconscious, it spoke well for the mother-son relationship.

"Glad to meet y'all." Florine's warm smile, as she acknowledged introductions and greeted us, was also like Ellen's. "Miz Dasher's down that way on the left. Her name's on the wall next to the door. I'd walk down with you, but I have to stay here and get the phone."

We turned to go, but Florine took up again. "I better warn you, though. She's losing her hearing, so it's hard to have a conversation with her. She knows she can't hear very well, so she talks constantly to keep from having to admit she isn't following what other people are saying. It's so irritating most people just leave her alone, which makes her even worse when she does have company."

"But she'll be able to talk to us?" I asked.

"Oh, yeah. She's able to talk."

"I meant have a sensible conversation," I said.

"I knew what you meant," Florine said, stifling a smile. "I just couldn't help myself. Uh huh, her mind is just fine. It might not sound like it, because she'll answer what she thinks you said, and it might not be what you really did say, but you have to blame her hearing, not her mind. She's pretty good at pretending not to hear anything she doesn't want to hear, too, but my husband does that and he isn't even going deaf." Florine and Ellen laughed together over this apparently endearing trait of Darwin's. "Miz Dasher's here so she can get medical attention in a hurry if she needs it, but she's still pretty sharp. Excuse me."

Florine turned away as the phone buzzed, and we started away down the hall.

"One thing that helps." It was Florine again, calling after us, one hand covering the mouthpiece of the telephone. "Miz Dasher does read lips pretty well. She does better if you look right at her when you talk."

"I know how that works," Ellen said as they moved on down the hall. "My second husband was really good at that trick. When he didn't want to know what you were saying, he'd look away. Maybe that's where Darwin gets it."

We made it to Irene Dasher's door with only two stops to explain to worried residents that the presence of an armed and uniformed police officer did not mean that a crime wave was in progress. One woman expressed her disappointment by snorting at me and clacking her walker angrily as she turned away.

The door beside the "Irene Dasher" nameplate was ajar. My knock pushed it open.

"Miz Dasher?" But instead of the frail old woman we'd expected to see, we were met by a man whose appearance called to mind old-fashioned descriptors like "dapper" and "spruced up." Shiny leather loafers, neat slacks, silky-looking sports shirt, fluffy snow-white hair—it all added up to a man who'd been what they'd have called a ladies' man in his day— which wasn't today or even yesterday. It wasn't so long ago he'd forgotten, though.

"Come in, ladies, come right in. I'm Buck Carlton, Irene's brother. Her younger brother," he added. His teeth may have been false, but his smile was genuine, energized, I guessed, by the appearance of a female audience.

He closed the door behind us, gallantly extending his hand to each of us in turn, guiding us into the room and toward chairs. I noted that he managed to pat Aunt Lulu's hand, and Ellen Chandler's, and mine, in the process. An equal-opportunity flirt, generously including a woman decades too young for him who was in uniform, to boot.

Even without his explanatory introduction, it was obvious that the dapper, flirtatious man and the woman in the recliner were kin—same hair, same deep-set dark eyes, same prominent chin. But there the resemblance ended. The narrow upper lip that made Irene Dasher resemble a rabbit had a different effect on Buck because he'd embellished it with a snowy white moustache. Irene Dasher might once have been stylish like her brother. If so, it looked like she'd given up. Her blue and gray plaid flannel housecoat gaped open to reveal a pink T-shirt on which white letters spelled out "GRITS—Girls Raised in the South." A voluminous blue cotton skirt billowed down to partially cover the orthopedic socks and moccasins on her feet.

"You're Althea Jordan's friends Florine told me about," Irene said. "I don't remember her married names right now. It'll come to me, but I'll always think of her as a Jordan, anyway. Law, it sent me back to see her name in the paper like that. We were in school together, you know, back a hundred years ago. I'm older than I look. Buck's my baby brother, still a young buck." She broke off to laugh after what was plainly a family joke.

"She's not really that old," Buck explained, no doubt worried that even the baby brother of a hundred-and-something-year-old would seem too old for us to take seriously, romantically speaking. "Florine said you wanted to ask some questions about Althea. Why are the police interested in her? What did she do?"

Ah, yes. Those were good questions, all right. Fortunately, Hen and I had given some thought to a good answer.

"We don't know that she did anything, Mr. Carlton. The reason we're interested is that there were some odd circumstances about the way she died. When we found out she had some old friends down here, we thought talking to you might help us clear up some things."

"She hasn't lived here for years," he said. Then, louder, facing his sister, "We haven't seen Althea in years, have we, Irene?"

On the drive down, I had done what I could to remind Ellen Chandler and Aunt Lulu that they were along on police business at the sufferance of the police, and that we were trying to accomplish certain things. "We're basically fishing for whatever we can learn about the connection between Miz Boatright and Mr. Sykes, so since we don't know what we're looking for, we might as well let the conversation go where it will," I had advised from the plushy backseat on the drive down. That was excellent, if unnecessary, advice, since, as it turned out, we wouldn't have been able to do anything else. Once started, Irene Dasher produced a torrent of words, all delivered in a soft, uninflected stream, as though, knowing herself to be hard of hearing, she was determined not to be too loud.

"I'm glad for your company. Not many people come by to see me any more. Of course, the ones that are dead have a good excuse." She paused here to insert a smile. "Not too many of my friends left. Thank the Lord, I have Buck. He's the best brother anybody could ask for. See those flowers there? He brings me flowers every time he comes, knows how much I miss my garden. You could come in here any day you want to and you'd find real live flowers, not those tacky plastic things some people have in their rooms, getting dustier and dustier all the time, and they think nobody can tell, even this time of year when nearly everything's burned up. Those old-fashioned petunias sure smell good, don't they? Not like the new kinds that are all show. Beats me how anybody can enjoy plastic flowers. Don't smell good or anything."

When she paused to draw breath, her brother confided to us, "She sure does miss that garden of hers." Then, turning to face his sister, "They came to talk about Althea, Irene, not gardens."

I began, "Althea—" but that's as far as I got.

Irene Dasher nodded knowingly and veered sharply away from plastic flowers and back to the fascinating topic of an old friend's death. "Althea, now, yes, that's why you came. Florine told me y'all were in the same bridge club or something like that. Never had time for cards myself, seems like such a waste of time when you could be outside in the yard, but I'm not saying anything against people who do play cards, not like I'm some religious fanatic or anything, I just never learned to enjoy it, that's all."

"And they didn't come to talk about cards." Her brother smiled around at us when he said it.

"No, Buck, I know it's not far. Ogeechee, didn't you say? Can't be more than forty, fifty miles. It was far enough Althea never bothered coming back here, though, once she moved over there. Always did think she was too good for Jesup. No offense, now, but I don't see that Ogeechee's any better, and I never have understood that business about only speaking good of the dead, never did see how somebody who wasn't worth spit when they were alive all of a sudden turns into blue chip stock once they're dead. Doesn't make any sense at all. Does it to you? No, not that I'm saying anything against Althea. We were friends."

She waved a quieting hand in Buck's direction when she saw he was about to speak. He smiled a conspiratorial smile at us, as though to make sure we weren't blaming him for her rambling.

"Haven't seen Althea since God was in kneepants, but we were friends when we were girls. Pretty thing, then. Her, I mean, but I was, too, not that you could tell, looking at me now. And lively! I bet she was full of vinegar till the day she died."

We'd have agreed with Irene Dasher if she'd given us the chance, but she didn't need our encouragement to keep her going.

"She was a friend of Buck's, too. He even went out with

her for a while—didn't you, Buck?—but she didn't like him as much as he liked her." She cut Buck a teasing sidelong glance. "Buck never did get over her is what I think. That's why he's a lifelong bachelor."

"Too many roses in the garden for me to find just one to pluck." Buck's response seemed automatic. I was not particularly charmed by what I assumed he considered a charming comment, the old lech.

Flapping her robe to regain attention, Irene Dasher was off again. "Run of luck? I don't know why you say that. It might have been luckier for her if she'd stayed with Buck, but I don't know."

Pluck? Luck? Buck? Who knew what she thought she'd heard?

"He's always had a roving eye, and I don't think Althea was the woman to put up with that. Had a good opinion of herself, Althea did. She'd have laid him out with a rolling pin, he tried running around on her. Maybe he'd've been different by now."

Buck briefly parted the flowing stream of Irene's words with another flash of that conspiratorial smile, but her words flowed smoothly around it.

"I think Florine said you told her there was some kind of scandal about Althea?" Ellen looked directly into Irene's face and spoke slowly, carefully stretching her mouth around the word "scandal."

"You want to know about that?" Irene tossed a knowing look in her brother's direction, waved a hand to indicate she was not inviting him to speak, and leaned toward her female audience. "If she'd stayed with Buck, she might not've got mixed up with Charlie Sykes in the first place. Law, that did turn out to be a scandal, all right! Althea told me Charlie just wouldn't leave her alone, thought she was the cat's pajamas. Well, Buck did, too, but Charlie had it even worse than Buck did."

A scandal involving Althea and Charlie Sykes? Was it really going to be this easy to find what we wanted?

"I had to break it off. She got too possessive," Buck managed to say. "You women always think you have to have exclusive rights to a man."

"Now, Buck, the way I remember it, she always said she dumped you," Irene said.

"A gentleman never—" Buck began, then flashed a smile instead of finishing the sentence.

"Althea always made out like she didn't care about Charlie particularly, but from what I could tell, she didn't mind him having a crush on her. Looked to me like she was as interested in him as he was in her. She started spending all her time with him, more time than they should have, as it turned out, and not all of it right out in plain sight, either."

Irene Dasher interrupted her narrative to assume a look loaded with significance before she continued. "The first thing we knew, Althea was in trouble. You know what I mean. Girls these days don't even call it trouble. They either have the baby and dare you to act like you don't believe it's a virgin birth, or they go somewhere and have it taken care of and never give it a second thought, but it was different back then. The only surprise was the Jordans didn't send her off to Europe, except that wouldn't have been a good time to be visiting Europe, with the war and all, or to visit an aunt somewhere, and pretend it never happened, but that wouldn't have been Althea's way. She claimed Charlie had attacked her, so her daddy sicced the police on him. That wasn't long after y'all stopped seeing each other, was it, Buck? Maybe she'd been doing some running around herself all the time she was going with you, plucking roses." She chortled at her own wit.

"Hmm?" Buck said. Unlike the rest of us, he apparently

didn't see any point in listening to everything his sister said. Of course, he'd probably heard it all at least once before.

Irene spoke more slowly and loudly for Buck's benefit, which I found so amusing I decided to turn and look out the window. "I said that business with Charlie came just after y'all broke up. She got over you pretty quick, whoever it was did the breaking up."

"A gentleman never—" Buck began again, then apparently remembered he'd already used that line. He looked directly at his sister and enunciated, "He got her on the rebound."

Having gotten the needle in, Irene nodded with satisfaction and resumed her monologue. "Rebound or whatever, Charlie said it wasn't him, for all the good that did, and, longer story shorter, he left town about the same time Althea did. We all took it for granted she'd be back after her trouble was over, but she never did come back. Charlie's the one we never figured to see again, and he's the one came back."

"I know it was all a long time ago," Ellen said, "but do you think she really was…in trouble? I've heard of girls saying that to try to get a fellow to marry them."

"I never—" Buck began, but Irene drowned him out.

"I never saw a baby, if that's what you're driving at, but that doesn't mean anything. Never saw her again, either. Next thing anybody knew she'd got married to somebody else entirely and was living over in Ogeechee."

She leaned forward again. "Everybody said Charlie ruined Althea, but even if she was my friend, I thought she was already ruined, spoiled and high-handed, and the way it looked to me, Althea and her daddy ruined Charlie, running him out of town like that. I wrote to him a time or two out in Texas where he went when he left here. Surprised everybody when he came back flashing money around like it was going out of style. Never did say where he got all that money, did he, Buck?"

"Not that I recall." The abruptness of his answer gave me the distinct impression he was pouting.

"Yes, maybe it was oil, but I don't remember, if I ever knew. They're more tolerant about people like Charlie out west on the frontier."

"What do you mean?" Aunt Lulu asked. I was glad the older women were with me. They were naturally sympathetic, not to say inquisitive and gossipy, and knew how to carry on this conversation. I wasn't having to do anything at all.

"No, I wouldn't say he was mean, but he did have a reputation for cutting the buck. If you ask me, cattle rustling would have been right up his alley, or maybe smuggling illegal aliens like you hear so much about these days, but that wasn't these days. It was a while back." Another glance at her baby brother. "Then he came back for that reunion, I remember, must have been thirty or forty years after we graduated, thirty or forty years ago by now."

Buck turned to his sister. "Are you trying to confuse these lovely ladies, Irene? You didn't graduate from high school eighty years ago!" Back to us. "Irene and Althea and Charlie were the class of thirty-nine. She's talking about two different reunions he came back for. The last one was just a few years back. Don't you remember, Irene? It was the year two thousand, and we all joked about making it into a new century."

"Two thousand? I do remember now." Irene was back in the game and carrying the ball. "Lord, how time goes by! Must have been that other one when Charlie came back so he could show off how well he'd done for himself. Seemed to be looking for Althea, too, wanted to show off for her especially." That much had been aimed at her brother. Now she turned to us. "Mostly, the ones that come to the reunions are the ones who've stayed here, so it's the same old faces, getting older and older. Or they've gone off and come back when they get old enough to retire, so it was a big hullabaloo when Charlie showed up. You're right, Buck, that one was a while back. Charlie wanted to know about Althea and when she married and who she married, and about the baby and all, like he hadn't been able to get over her even after all that time. I'm not a man, so maybe I've got a blind spot about what they go for, but she didn't look to me like the kind of a vamp that would have men drooling over her years later. You knew her, did she strike you like that?"

"I never thought about it," Aunt Lulu said while I was shaking my head. "But no."

"Maybe he was wondering if he had a child he'd never known," Ellen Chandler suggested.

"A man would have to start wondering in his old age if some of his wild oats had sprouted," Buck offered. "A man can't know for sure, like a woman can." He settled back in his chair, then, as though awaiting our applause for this bit of wisdom.

"That's right, you never know, but there must have been something about her even if her eyes were too close together," Irene said. "He should have stayed away from here."

I choked back a comment about bees flitting from flower to flower and asked instead, "Did he stay here in Jesup, once he came back?"

Irene cackled. "Stay? He sure did, not that first time he came back, but in two thousand. Settled down out on the family farm. Had to nudge his brother out of the way to do that, I heard, but that's another story. We'd see him every once in a while. Not that he lived here all that long. He died, got killed by a car. It was in the paper. Did you know that?"

"Yes, ma'am, we did. As a matter of fact, it happened in Ogeechee, and Althea was driving the car that killed him."

For the moment, neither of them had a thing to say. Buck recovered first and said with an air of satisfaction, "Looks like he found her, then, or she found him. And had a score to settle."

I took advantage of the moment.

"That's the main reason we're here, to see if we can find some connection between his death and hers."

"Well, I'll be!" Buck exclaimed.

His sister looked delighted. "You don't mean to tell me! Charlie Sykes lived all that time somewhere else, and when he came back to settle old business with Althea, she settled him! Can you beat that?"

"But what—" Buck Carlton's speech was cut off by a sharp rap on the door, which immediately opened to reveal a uniformed aide. "Dinner time," she said.

"Oh, no!" Irene Dasher wailed.

We had accomplished even more than I had hoped. Buck Carlton and Irene Dasher had established a definite link, with possibilities, between Althea and Charlie Sykes. It would be up to me to find a link between their deaths. "We'd better be going on home, Miz Dasher, or we'll be late for our own dinner," I said. "Thank you for letting us come talk to you."

"Listen to you," Ellen Chandler whispered, rising to her feet.

"You don't have to go already. This food'll be as good later as now. Buck, make them stay," Irene said pitifully. But futilely.

"It's everybody's dinner time, Irene," Buck said. "I'll walk them out." From beside his chair, he picked up a handsome walking stick that had a sleek silver horse's head for a handle.

"I hate for y'all to rush off like that. Seems like you just got here," Irene said.

"I'll be right back," Buck said.

We moved toward the door, Irene's rising voice following us. "That a new walking stick, Buck? Lord, you got so much money you can spend it on fancy walking sticks? You always were a peacock! Got more walking sticks than most women have shoes. He always was a peacock!"

The door swung shut on these last spiteful words.

Buck was philosophical. "It always makes her cranky when visitors leave. She loves company."

"You can tell she does," Aunt Lulu said.

"You have a collection of walking sticks?" I asked.

He beamed and lifted the stick he was carrying. "Yes, been collecting them for years. This one, now, is Italian. It's finished to look like mahogany, but it's beechwood."

"It's beautiful," Ellen said. "Do you have any plain old utilitarian ones, or are they all as fancy as that one?"

He frowned. "I don't really need one to help me walk. I just carry them to show them off."

We passed the receptionist's desk. Florine, on the phone, waved and smiled.

"I'll catch up," Ellen said. "Let me talk to Florine a minute."

"Your sister seems to be okay, as far as her mind goes," Aunt Lulu said, when we reached the front door and had to step aside for an aide and an old man in a wheelchair.

"Making a drug bust?" the old man cackled. "Always knew he was up to no good."

"Hello, Mack." Our escort didn't seem to be offended. He smiled at Mack and the aide, obviously wanting as many people as possible to notice him with women, before he answered Aunt Lulu's question. "Yes, Irene's still pretty sharp. Most of the time, anyway. She's no more forgetful than anybody else. She might be better off if she was more forgetful. Then she wouldn't know what she's missing. Like a police investigation into two old friends." He gave me a pointed look.

"Well," Aunt Lulu said.

"We'll let you know how it comes out," I promised.

"I'll see you to your car."

"There's no need to do that," Lulu said.

I stifled the impulse to remind him that we'd gotten there all by ourselves.

"Oh, but it is my pleasure," he said again, and followed us into the parking lot.

"We hadn't had anything to do with Althea in I don't know how long," Buck said. In spite of what he had said, I noticed he leaned on the fancy walking stick when he walked. "You said you had some questions about her death, but you didn't ask any."

"Okay, then," I said. "Here's one. Where were you the day she died?"

He smiled. "I know what you're doing. I read murder mysteries. I tell you and you pounce and say 'Aha!' and ask me how I knew when she died."

"We've read some of the same books," Aunt Lulu told him. "Try a better question, Trudy."

"Sure. Where were you on Tuesday, two weeks ago?"

"Let me ask one," Buck Carlton said. "What was wrong with the way she died? Why are you investigating? Florine told us she slipped and hit her head."

With him flaunting his fancy walking stick, I didn't want to tell him our walking stick-exchange theory. "It was quite a coincidence, her dying so soon after she ran over Charlie Sykes, that's all. So we just thought we'd satisfy our curiosity."

"And our reward was that we got to meet you and your sister," Aunt Lulu said.

He seemed to look at her with new interest. She did look nice. She'd been to the Cut-n-Curl the day before for a tune-up and was wearing a purple and pink striped shirt with a pink pantsuit.

"I'm surprised that a romantic man like you just turned his back on his high school sweetheart," she continued. I appreciated her coming to my rescue, but I swear she batted her eyes at him.

We'd reached the car by then. "Go ahead and let the windows down, Trudy, and let some of the heat out," Aunt Lulu said, still flirting with Buck Carlton.

"Yes, ma'am." I took her keys and did as I was told.

"Sure a nice car," he said.

"Yes, it is," Aunt Lulu said.

Ellen caught up with us then, and Buck Carlton insisted on helping each one of us into the car.

"I hope we'll be seeing more of you," he said, holding Aunt Lulu's door open and peering inside the car.

She started the car. "Thank you," she said, without specifying what for. After a long moment, he closed the door, and patted it tenderly, but he didn't move away. His hand trailed on the fender as Aunt Lulu put the car into motion. As we left the nursing home behind, I could see him still standing in the parking lot, gazing after us.

When he was out of sight, Aunt Lulu spoke. "Buck's just about as bad as Irene, isn't he?"

"But harder to get away from," Ellen said. "I think he's taken with you," she added.

"I thought it was the car he liked," Aunt Lulu said.

I settled back, thinking about old friendships and walking sticks, leaving it to Aunt Lulu and Ellen Chandler to work out whether to go home by way of Highway 301, through Glennville and Ludowici, or to take the back way, Highway 169.

As we pulled out of the parking lot, Aunt Lulu turned to me. "I'm wondering—if Althea was in trouble way back, what happened to the baby?"

"Good question," I admitted. "Maybe it was just gossip spread around by jealous school friends. Maybe she wasn't pregnant."

"Or," Aunt Lulu said. "What if she had that baby, and what if—*if,* mind you—and I wouldn't say this if Martha were with us because I know what an irresponsible gossip she is—what if that baby turned out to be Leland Grinstead?"

Ellen answered. "It's an interesting idea, but even if that were true, I don't see why that would give Leland—or anybody else—a reason to kill Althea."

"Unless the fact that he wasn't Bert's son is important," Aunt Lulu suggested.

"Whoa!" I said.

We traveled a few miles in thoughtful silence before Ellen asked, "What about Buck and his walking sticks? If he has a whole collection of them, he wouldn't be so used to one in particular that he'd notice if he had a different one. Do you think he could have had it in for Althea all this time?"

"Maybe we need to get to know Mr. Carlton better," Aunt Lulu said. "There was obviously a side to Althea we never saw."

"You watch out, now, Aunt Lulu. I appreciate your flirting in the line of duty, but even if Buck Carlton isn't an actual killer, he definitely sees himself as a lady killer. He's the kind who'd invite you over to look at his collection of walking sticks and let one thing lead to another."

"He's way too old for me," Aunt Lulu said. "If I was looking for romance, I wouldn't look at a man more than twenty years older than I am, a whole generation older. I'd probably go—what do they call it? tadpoling?—looking for a younger man, a tadpole, and see if he wouldn't grow up into my Prince Charming."

"Aunt Lulu, not even counting that you seem to have confused frogs and Prince Charming, you surprise me! Does Hen know you're on the prowl?"

"I'm his mother, Trudy. What do you think? And I am not on the prowl. I'm around sixty, which used to sound old, but it's looking younger all the time, isn't it, Ellen?"

"How would I know?" Ellen asked as Aunt Lulu moved

into the passing lane to get around a tractor. "I haven't been sixty for years."

Ellen seemed to hold her breath while Aunt Lulu pulled back into her own lane abruptly to avoid the car she hadn't seen coming from around a curve, then she added, "Two of my favorite husbands were younger than I was, if that's what you mean. It's a scientific fact that men reach their sexual peak at about age seventeen or eighteen and women peak later, so it just makes sense."

In addition to what we'd learned about Althea Jordan Grinstead Boatright's relationship with Charlie Sykes, I was seeing a new side of these two women, and I don't mean the back of Ellen Chandler's red, white, and blue, star-spangled T-shirt and shooting-star earrings.

"Matter of fact, I was thinking one of us ought to get a look at Buck Carlton's walking-stick collection," Aunt Lulu said.

"Was that why you were flirting so shamelessly?" I asked. "So he'd invite you into his lair?"

"Was I flirting?" Aunt Lulu batted her eyes. "It must have been unconscious."

"Somebody needs to talk to him again and check his alibi," Ellen said.

"I tried. He avoided the question of where he was the day Althea died, didn't he, Aunt Lulu?"

"Yes, he did," Aunt Lulu said, putting on a burst of speed.

"Aha!" Ellen said.

EIGHT

"I'M FINISHED WITH that little bit of ironing now." Elfreda Wilcox's voice was soft and low as it sifted through the screen door, but it startled me.

My hundred-year-old house is one of the few in town, I'd guess, that doesn't have air conditioning, so, hot as it was on the porch, I knew it wasn't much cooler in the house. At least the front porch is sheltered by big magnolia trees and there's a chance of catching a breeze. I'd been sitting out there on the swing as I tried to plot out a way to approach the subject of Althea Boatright with a woman who had good reason to despise her. I didn't suspect Elfreda of theft, let alone murder, but I reasoned that she probably had a perspective on Althea that nobody else had, and no reason at all to cut her any slack. Lacking a better plan, the Ogeechee Police Department was following up on the list of murder suspects Althea's friends had come up with.

There's a sense in which I had inherited Elfreda's services along with the big old house when my grandmother died. It suits me fine. Housekeeping doesn't interest me, and if I didn't have somebody come in regularly there's no telling how long it might be between the times I'd scrub a toilet or vacuum behind the couch. Ironing? I send my uniforms out, and I'd wear everything else straight out of the dryer if it was left up to me to iron. Elfreda doesn't charge what she's worth, so it's a small luxury to have her touch up my washables.

"Was there anything else you want me to do before I go?"

"Not today, but next week if you can give me some extra time, I think I want to get after that mess out in the garage."

"Oh, oh." Elfreda shook her head. She sank dramatically into the rocker next to the swing as though the very idea had knocked her for a loop. "Not enough that you swelter in this ol' house without even a swamp cooler, you want to get a heatstroke out there? You getting ready for a wedding or something?"

"I am not getting ready for a wedding. If I were, and if I were having any part of it here, there'd be better places to start fixing up than the garage."

We both laughed over that. My plans to fix things up has gotten to be a joke.

"I've started worrying about that being a fire hazard out there. I should have cleaned it out before the weather got so hot, but now that I've thought about it, I want to get it done. If you don't want to help me, do you know somebody who would?"

Elfreda began rocking slowly and fanning herself with her hand, not quite hiding what looked like a smile of satisfaction at getting a defensive rise out of me on the subject of my love life. "I don't think of anybody right off, but I could ask around. See if I can find somebody wants to risk a heatstroke."

"Well, let's get your money so you can go on home where it's cool," I said. We went back to the kitchen. I pulled a quart jar out of the cabinet and fished out a wad of bills. I counted off some of the bills and handed them to Elfreda. "You got time for a glass of tea? That'll cool you off a little." At her nod, I reached for glasses.

"If Latilda's not working somewhere steady these days, maybe she'd like to earn a little something." This was the approach I'd worked out in the heat of the front porch. Latilda is the woman Martha Tootle called Elfreda's no-good granddaughter.

Elfreda shook her head as she slid the bills into the pocket of the slacks that, along with tennis shoes and a T-shirt, are her invariable working uniform. With her wiry frame, smooth brown skin, and short curly hair, she looks younger than the mid-fifties, which I know to be her age. "That girl don't do nothin' steady, much less work. Lord knows, I don't see how she got so worthless. Thinks she'll always have some man to take care of her, I reckon."

"I'm disappointed in you. Are you telling me you couldn't teach her any better than that?"

Elfreda smiled. "Well, I tell you something you'll learn for yourself, you live long enough—life doesn't necessarily work out the way you have in mind. I know, and you know, that any woman with the sense God gave a butterbean will learn how to take care of herself and not depend on somebody else to do it, much less a man, but I'm not the only one in the family, and I'm not the one she decided to take after. Don't get me started on her mother!"

I pointed at the sugar bowl in the middle of the table and the bowl of little blue and pink packets that some people prefer, as I handed Elfreda a glass, and we sat in press-back chairs at the round oak table that's been in that kitchen since before I was born.

"It sounds like Latilda has a boyfriend, and one you don't hold in high esteem."

"Huh! You got that right, Miss po-lice detective. She's been going around with Deloy DeLoach. I don't know what she calls him, boyfriend, sugar—" here Elfreda paused and twisted her mouth in a smile at the range of possibilities "—but I call him a no-account, and I hold him in no esteem. Not like that boyfriend of yours, now. He's a nice man from what I hear."

"Uh huh." Moving right along. "Deloy DeLoach. Hmm. Oh, yes. He's Digger DeLoach's grandson, isn't he?"

"No, ma'am, Deloy's Digger's son. Digger's not as old as he looks. Hard work has kept me young, but hard work on top of worrying about Deloy has aged Digger." Elfreda put her elbows on the table, both hands on her cool glass of tea. "I don't do much worrying myself, don't see any point in it. I figure people reap what they sow and either learn from it or they don't. Latilda now, she's got grits for brains just like her mother, thinkin' that no-account'll take care of her. Take care of her right into the lock-up, that's what he'll do. A woman needs her own job. That newspaperman, now, he wouldn't expect you to give up policin', would he?"

"We haven't discussed it." Why couldn't Latilda understand it was her granddaughter I wanted to gossip about, not myself? I pointed the conversation back in the right direction. "Maybe Deloy'll straighten out under the influence of a good woman."

"Huh!" Elfreda's expression made clear her contempt for that idea. "Maybe he would, but a good woman ain't what he's got. They're a pair, those two, two biscuits out of the same batch. Even if she is my own granddaughter, I have to say it."

Apparently Elfreda's assessment of Latilda agreed with Martha Tootle's.

"What kind of work does Deloy do?"

"Huh! Sometimes Digger puts Deloy to work helping him, but you couldn't call that steady work. Well, now, to be exact, the work is steady, but Deloy's not. He might show up once in a while so he can get Digger to give him some money—Digger always was too good to him, and Deloy trades on that something awful—but work? Huh!"

"How can he afford a fine girlfriend like Latilda if he doesn't have any money?" I was getting even with Elfreda for her crack about a wedding.

"Huh!" This time the snort was accompanied by a glance heavenward, as though only God could answer that one.

"Sometimes I wonder that myself, then I think I'm probably better off not knowing."

"Elfreda, do you worry that Deloy might get Latilda into trouble? No, I don't mean *that* kind of trouble," I added quickly, thinking of the old story about Althea Boatright and Charles Sykes. "I mean with the law."

"Tell the truth, that pair could be Bonnie and Clyde and it wouldn't surprise me. She's just as likely to think up mischief as he is. Huh!"

Elfreda's "huh" was eloquent, capable of expressing a surprising range of nuance.

"Do you happen to know if Deloy ever helped Digger with work over at Althea Boatright's place?" It wasn't subtle, but it did get the conversation around to Althea.

Elfreda's face closed down at the mention of Althea's name. "Funny you should ask about that," she said. "Digger said Miz Boatright got it in her head critters and varmints was getting under the house—the house backs on that brambly woods that goes down to the lake, you know—and she wanted him to put some traps under there. Now, you ask me, crawling around under somebody's house is exactly what Deloy DeLoach is cut out for, and Digger must agree with me, 'cause he made Deloy do that job for him. Caught something, too, but it got away." She grinned. "I was hoping they'd catch a skunk, but it must have been something else, 'cause Digger didn't say anything about the smell and he knows how much I'd have enjoyed knowing about that. Must have been something big, though, to get out of that trap of Digger's. Too bad whatever it was didn't come up through the floorboards before Digger and Deloy ran it off and get Miz Boatright."

"Sounds like a horror movie," I said.

"Maybe that would have served her right. I didn't do much grieving when I heard she died," Elfreda said with stiff lips.

She shifted her position in the chair so suddenly that the chair leg squawked against the linoleum. "There's one good church lady might be wishing she was back enjoying this cool Georgia July with you and me instead of trying to cool off where she is now."

"She did you wrong, there's no question about that."

"She surely did. It was funny how many people found out they didn't need my help around the house any more after she told her lies. People don't think they can trust you in their house, they not gone let you clean for 'em, no matter how good a worker you are. She made things hard for me, real hard, and she didn't have any reason to do that. I know right from wrong, and even if I didn't, what made her think I'd want her old jewelry? Far as I know, I never even saw it. She used to keep a tray on her dresser with rings and things in it, but I never saw a pin fancy enough to call a brooch. Why'd she think I took it?"

"There is just no telling about that, Elfreda. She probably mislaid it, and it was easier to blame you than herself." I'd hoped to learn something by approaching the subject of Althea with Elfreda, but now I was sorry I'd upset her. "Just her own greediness, maybe, because that's the kind of thing she might have done."

"Huh! Don't know when she thought I could do any plundering or any stealing. It was all I could do to get the work done, she was underfoot so much, not like you, who's got the sense to stay out of the way and let me do what you're paying me to do. If she ever let me out of her sight, I don't remember it."

"You didn't have a key so you could come in and clean while she was gone? No, of course not," I added hastily, at the look of amazement on Elfreda's face.

"The kind of people who keep their houses locked up aren't real quick to give out keys," Elfreda explained the obvious.

"You, a police, you ought to know that about people. Anyway, most of the time, people like to be home while I'm there, so they can tell me what they want done."

"I heard that brooch turned up later. Did she try to make it up to you? Apologize?"

"Huh!" Elfreda's scorn for this notion was even more pronounced than over the idea that Deloy DeLoach might have an honest job somewhere and be good for her granddaughter. "Susannah Boatright, now, she tried to help out after that, letting me come to work for her. I took the work, too, but then I wondered if doing that didn't make it look worse, like maybe she got me to take the brooch and was paying me off that way."

"What a hateful thought!"

"Yeah, but people can be hateful. I don't know working for Susannah Boatright did me much good. Latilda told me I ought to sue Miz Boatright for defamation of character or some such. That's the way she and that Deloy think."

"You could have made a case for her owing you something."

"Now you sound like Latilda. She told me she figured I'd bought and paid for that thing, it ought to be mine. See how the girl thinks? I told her good luck explaining to Miz Althea Boatright!"

"Now you've told me something good about Latilda," I said. "It sounds like she's loyal to you." Then, hoping it would seem like the thought had just occurred to me, "You don't think she and Deloy would have tried to steal that brooch, really steal it, do you?"

"Like I said before, I wouldn't put anything past those two, let 'em get high enough on something to where they can't think straight, but then what would they do with it? Latilda's a mess, but she ain't so messed up she'd bring that thing to me, and if she couldn't do that, why would she steal it?"

"I have no idea," I admitted.

"I'd ask Latilda about helping you clean out that garage, but even if she wasn't too lazy, she'd probably be too smart to court a heatstroke. Might be you'd be better off talking to Digger about it, though. Maybe Digger and Deloy." She smiled.

"That's a good idea. I'll talk to Digger. If I hire him and he makes Deloy help, maybe I'll get Latilda for nothing," I suggested.

"That's the right idea. She's good for nothing, all right," Elfreda said, laughing, draining the last of the tea from her glass. "I better get on. Thank you for the tea." She stood and stuck her hands into her hip pockets. "I'll see you next week, unless you got some jewelry you're worried about."

"I wish I had jewelry worth worrying about," I rejoined.

"You want some nice jewelry, you drop a hint to that Pittman boy," she sniggered.

I followed her to the back door, laughing with her, and walked beside her car as she drove on around my circular driveway to get back to the street. Then I resumed my place in the swing on the front porch, trying to catch a breeze, and wondering.

Had no-good Latilda and no-good Deloy broken into Althea's house in search of the notorious brooch and killed her accidentally in the commission of the theft? Felony murder. I hoped not, for Elfreda's sake.

NINE

My HOUSE SITS on about twelve acres, and although most of it is in pine woods, and pretty much takes care of itself, the acre or so of yard needs constant work. My interest in yard work is greater than my interest in housework, but, even so, it rises only to the puttering and enjoying level, not the heavy maintenance level. I manage to keep the grass under control, with the help of my trusty riding mower, but when anything out of the ordinary arises, I call for help.

Digger DeLoach was the general-purpose yard-and-handyman Grandma had called on, so in the same way I'd had the good luck to have Elfreda, I had Digger. I wouldn't keep using either one of them if they didn't give satisfaction, and I don't doubt they'd fire me if I wasn't an acceptable employer, so it's worked out well.

I kept watch for Digger to appear for his regular stint at the place next door, and when I saw him taking a break from raking up the ever-present pine straw and branches that fall from the tall, brittle-limbed trees, I invited him over for a glass of tea and a discussion about the work I wanted done. I didn't tell him I also wanted to pump him about his son and Latilda Wilcox.

I'd just settled myself on the kitchen steps, with a cat in my lap, when Digger, a small wrinkled man in stained wrinkled overalls, rattled up astride his mower and stopped beside me. He wiped his hands and forehead with a bandanna, and reached for the tea, which he drained.

"Be right back," I said, discomfiting the cat as I reached for his glass and stood to go inside for more tea. When I returned, Digger had dismounted and was casting a professionally judgmental eye over my property.

"I know the yard's way overdue for its spring cleaning," I said, to forestall a sales pitch. "I have a whole list of things that need doing. I want to get the trash out of the garage, then get the yard behind it cleaned out, back to the trees, and some of the underbrush cleared out and hauled off. It's getting pretty wild back there beyond the grass. And rake up the old pine straw around the azaleas and put down some new. Can you give me that much time?"

"Well, now, that sounds like pretty serious work, maybe too much to handle this time of year. It's a busy time for everybody's yard, you know. Looks like your situation has been developing for a while. What's your hurry?"

At least he didn't ask if I was cleaning up for a wedding. "It's just started getting on my nerves," I said. It wasn't an explanation, but it was all I had.

"Well, if you're set on it and aren't in such a hurry you got to have it done right now, I can do it. You didn't think I'd get it all done today?" He rubbed the back of his wrist against his chin as he waited for me to answer.

I stroked the cat, which had deigned to give me a second chance. "Oh, goodness no. If you could just make a start and keep after it till it's done, that's all I care. It will be a lot off my mind to know I've got somebody reliable working on it."

"Well, then, we can do business," he said dusting his hand against his pants before offering it to shake on the deal. "I'll take a look around, get an idea of the situation, make me a plan of work, and see how far I get today. Won't be too far, though. Got to finish up at Griffins' and see to another job later on today."

"Okay."

"And I'll have to coordinate the schedule with my COO. My son Deloy tells me that stands for Chief of Operations, but I say it means Chief Ornery Officer. I'll have to line him up to help with the heavy work. I can take care of most of it by myself, rather work by myself, anyway, but I'm not able to do it all like I used to, with arthritis come on me like it has, and settling in this knee I messed up that time I fell off the roof of Miz Boatright's smokehouse and landed on that cement birdbath she had."

His bringing up Althea was a gift. I pretended to be interested in the cat's paws as I asked, "Are you still taking care of the yard over there at the Boatrights'? I mean Grinsteads', of course. I still think of it as Althea Boatright's place."

"Uh huh. It'll always be the Boatright house, far as I'm concerned. It may be just Grinsteads living there now that Miz Boatright's gone, but Rowland Boatright built it. If it is the Grinstead house now, it's only been for what, two weeks now, since Miz Boatright died? That is, if she left it to them, and it's been probated and all."

"My understanding is that she gave the house to them a long time ago," I said, remembering the session with Aunt Lulu and her friends.

He appeared to think that over. "Maybe she did, but she was a Boatright, and she was still living there, and she's the one I mostly did business with over there, so it's Boatright as far as I'm concerned."

"I can't argue with your logic," I said, scratching behind the cat's ears. Then I suggested, "It's bound to be different without her there."

"Uh huh, they need me even worse than they used to. Without her there to be in charge, they need an experienced professional like me who knows what needs to be tended to. Everybody has different ideas how they want things done, but it's my job to give satisfaction, whatever it takes, and it took some doin' where she, Miz Althea Boatright, was concerned. Yes, ma'am. I keep telling Deloy you can't build a business without customer satisfaction, but she was one to put that to the test." He grinned. "Only reason I kept on with her was so I could give Deloy a boot camp in customer satisfaction."

"I'm sure you kept her satisfied."

"Um hmm." He shot me a sly glance. "Much as any man could, I reckon. The big difference over there without her is that now I can just do what I come to do and get on. She was a good one for thinking up extra things for me to do once I got there, messin' up my schedule. Which I did not appreciate, with other customers to consider and all."

"What kind of extra things? Do you have some talents I haven't been taking advantage of?"

He put on a modest look and waved a deprecating hand. "Oh, just yard things, handyman things. I don't do electricity or plumbing, like that. Deloy's been egging me on to print up kind of a menu of the kinds of work I do with the rates and all. That's what he's good at, thinking up things for other people to do while he runs around with that gal of his. But sure's I printed something up, the next person would think of something that wasn't on the list, and I wouldn't know which category to put it in and we'd waste a lot of time talking about it" (as though wasting time talking was abhorrent to him!) "and I'd wind up doing it anyway. Besides, I don't go for the idea of writing down my rates so everybody knows what I'm charging everybody else."

The sly look on his face, replacing the modest one, led me to ask, "You have some kind of a sliding scale based on what you think the traffic will bear?"

"No, not exactly. The scale slides. You got that right, but what makes it slide is how much it's worth to me to put up with people. I don't think it would necessarily be good for my business if people found out I have what you might call a surcharge for some people, an aggravation tax." He grinned. "Deloy might call it my BAT—Business Aggravation Tax. You can see why I don't necessarily want everybody knowing that. No sense stirring up trouble."

"You mean I'm going to have to check with my friends to find out what you charge them, so I'll know how I stand with you?"

Now sly gave way to horrified. "Oh, no, don't you do that, now. It would just cause me trouble when they find out what I charge you. Anybody can't get along with you better get their head examined and go in for a personality adjustment."

I had to laugh. "I can tell you're the customer relations expert in the business, in addition to being prompt and reliable. What's your son's contribution?"

"Ideas, that's Deloy's strong point. It's the follow-through where he's weak. I try to go along with him, encourage him to take an interest in things, unless it's something I think would run the business plumb down into the ground."

"At least it sounds like he's taking an interest, if he's coming up with all those ideas."

Digger went back to rubbing his chin, a gesture I realized stimulated his garrulous bone. "I do take all those ideas as a good sign, even when I don't go along with them. But I don't know that it means anything. He's probably just puttin' on so I'll get off his back about getting a job somewhere else."

He cracked a grin, displaying gappy teeth. "I'd take it as a better sign if he was good for something besides foolin' around with women and hatchin' ideas. I'm trying to get him interested in the idea of a family business dynasty. I'd be the CEO, the Chief Executive Officer, and I'm bringing him up through the ranks so he'll be able to take it over."

"That's an excellent idea. He'll know the business from top to bottom."

"No, ma'am, not top to bottom. Bottom to top, that's the way I'll go about it. Sooner or later he's got to find out how much work there is to this here exterior horticultural maintenance business, and I reckon it might as well be sooner." His grin grew wider and he launched into a tale that must have been well polished from use. "We got our fleet of trucks ordered. Got 'em on hold right now while we work out the details on the logo for the doors. One of Deloy's bright ideas is how we need us a catchy name and a logo so people can remember us easy."

"I don't think you need to spend a lot of money on fancy trucks and advertising," I said. "If you're so busy you're having trouble fitting me in, it looks like you have plenty of business."

"You definitely do have a point there, I won't deny that, but another point is that I want to encourage the boy when I can afford it, and a catchy name wouldn't cost anything."

He rubbed at his chin again, waiting for me to respond. Hoping my rates, however favorable, didn't run by the hour, I cooperated.

"You have a catchy name in mind?"

Digger stood tall and proud as befit the founder of an exterior horticultural maintenance business. "Just about decided on DeLoach Integrated Garden Services. Now, I know that sounds pretty highfalutin, but you cain't count on finding ordinary, run-of-the-mill words to make up your catchy name, and DeLoach Integrated Garden Services makes DIGS. That's good enough even for Deloy, and he says it'll look real good on the trucks."

Something about the look on Digger's face made me ask. "You're not pulling my leg, are you?"

"Oh, no," he said with obvious delight. "I wouldn't do

that. Deloy does help me out when I need him. If I stay after him enough."

I joined in his laughter over this lurch toward common sense.

"And I do want me a slogan," Digger went on. "I'd been thinking about Three D, for Digger and Deloy DeLoach, that's three D's, you see, Deloy says 3-D went out in the fifties, not that he was around back then, and I need something that sounds more cutting-edge. He gets ideas a mile a minute, that Deloy."

"A slogan to go with your catchy name," I said exaggerating my admiration. "I hope we get my work done before you have all that. I won't be able to afford you once you get your empire set up."

"Well, now, a slogan don't cost any more than a catchy name." He chortled again.

I was beginning to see why it might take several days for DIGS or Three D to get my work done. "Since we're talking about your business name, I'll ask you something I've wondered about. If you don't mind telling me, how'd you come to be called Digger?"

"Matter of fact, it's my name, my real name. Or almost. My mama was a Driggers, and you know how kids don't always get things right, so it got turned into Digger. Now I haven't read into psychology much, but there just might be something to how your name makes a difference how you turn out. Like a boy named Percy, now, or Sue, like that Johnny Cash song, he's either got to be a sissy or real tough. I think maybe them calling me Digger made me think that's what I was, a digger, and it could be that's what turned me to yard work."

"You could be on to something. Gertrude always sounded prim and proper to me, much too old-fashioned for such a modern woman as myself, so I turned it into Trudy. I think it sounds more approachable."

The cat, apparently bored with our conversation, slithered

off my lap with only a slight dig into my thighs, and disappeared under the house. My cue.

"Got a whole herd of cats under there," I said. "I heard Althea Boatright thought she had something under her house."

"Uh huh. Something or somebody, she said, maybe a skunk or wild cats. These old houses, sitting up off the ground like they are, they're just asking for trouble. I know they used to put 'em up off the ground like that to get a little ventilation underneath and keep the water from running in if you get a big rain. Probably comes in handy if the plumbing springs a leak, too, but a lot of those houses are so old they probably didn't have any indoor plumbing. Yours wild?"

"What?"

"The cats you have under there. They wild? You want me to get rid of them for you?"

"Oh. No, I mean they're on the wild side, but not when it comes to finding their own food. I don't want to get rid of them. Was it cats? Under the Boatright house?"

"Beats me. I told Miz Althea if it was cats, the cats would run off other pesty things and wouldn't hurt anything so she ought to leave 'em alone, but she wanted me to put a trap out. She was as bad as Deloy for holding on to an idea, once it takes hold. Like one of them leg-hold traps, if you think about it. Enough to make you gnaw your own leg off just to get away. With the underneath of her house open like it is, all kinds of little things can get between those bricks, I told her. No way to keep 'em out. She told me it wasn't little things. I took a look, and it did seem like I could see around the opening into the crawl space where something had been comin' and goin' under there, something big enough to flatten out the dirt, too, not little pitty-patty cat tracks."

"That would worry me, too, thinking something that big was under my house. What did you do about it?"

"Had to put a trap out. Only way to satisfy her."

"Did it work?"

"Did it satisfy Miz elegant Althea Boatright? Didn't much ever satisfy her." He snorted, then apparently remembered that she was dead and gone. He added contrite to his gamut of facial expressions. "No, not exactly."

"You didn't catch anything?"

"Well, yes, we did. We caught us somethin'."

I was getting a little weary of his suspense building, but, short of crawling under the house with the cats, I saw no way out of asking, "Really? What was it? A raccoon?"

Digger was back to rubbing his chin again. "Nuh uh, not a 'coon. Whatever it was was big enough to get loose from the trap, and I'm not talking about one of those easy-on-the-varmints traps. Humane trap? There ain't no such thing. Anytime you trap something, it ain't humane. What they mean is it doesn't kill 'em or chop off a paw or something or make 'em bleed on your stuff. Have a heart, my hind leg! Never saw why you'd want to trap something if you didn't mean it any harm. I brought over the biggest trap I had, steel, with a snap on it that's supposed to break a leg."

"I haven't seen your trap, and I'm not asking to, so I'm assuming it wasn't the kind that would violate any of the laws, rules, and ordinances of our fair city." Yes, I know I sounded like Hen. I can do it when I want to.

Digger saw my point but was not at all contrite, and I got another dose of his smile. "Yessum, you're right. You can take my word for it on the trap. I wouldn't use anything against the law, no, ma'am. It caught something, too."

"What was it?"

"It wasn't an animal, far as I could tell, not a wild animal, 'less you count young'uns, and they can be pretty da—darned wild. 'Course I didn't tell her. It'd just give her something else to have a fit about, but there was a scrap caught in the trap, after whatever—or whoever—it was broke loose, and it wasn't animal fur, either."

"You mean…?"

"Some kind of cloth. I wouldn't be telling you this if I didn't figure you wouldn't hold it against me, and I didn't tell her because I didn't want to give her the satisfaction, send her off hollering bloody murder, but I think it was kids under there. House sitting up off the ground like that, it's an invitation to young'uns. Probably had a clubhouse or something under there. I'da liked to been there when that rascal explained to his mama how he hurt himself like that."

"Children?" The expression on my face must have worried him. "Those traps are against the law for a reason!"

"Now, don't you worry. Even if I did catch me a young'un, that little old trap wouldn't have hurt 'im too much. Maybe a bruise or a sprain, and maybe it would be a good lesson at the price. Messin' around under people's houses is illegal, too, likely to get him in worse trouble than that. It's trespassing, far as I know. And children, there's no telling what they might have done. They could have set the place on fire. All things considered, I'd rather have cats. Even skunks. But I didn't say it was children."

"You're right. You didn't."

Digger looked relieved. "Don't worry about it. There was a scrap of something, but not any blood or bones. Or anything dead. So whatever it was, I guess the trap scared 'em off. She didn't complain about it any more."

"Was that just recently?" I asked.

"Not too far back. Couple of weeks, maybe three. You really want to know, Deloy might remember. He purely hated doin' that."

Digger mistook my thoughtfulness for disapproval.

"Don't hold it against me, now," he said, rubbing his chin again. "I was just doin' what Miz Althea wanted done. I hadn't done it, she'da got somebody else to do it."

"You're right. I don't hold it against you. And neither does the police department. But I'd sure like to know what—or who—was under there. No chance you still have that scrap, is there?"

He looked so surprised, I backtracked. "Of course not. Do you remember anything about it? The color? What kind of material it was?"

He was shaking his head in evident amazement at the stupidity of my question when we were interrupted by the arrival in the driveway of a battered and noisy Dodge Ram pickup truck.

The driver revved the motor and yelled, "You about ready to go?"

Digger's mobile face now registered wrath, and he stalked to the driver's window, yelling in return. "Not yet. You've got me in the middle of a business meeting. How many times I told you not to make so much Go—gol-durned noise? You gone be my Chief of Operations, you got to learn some manners, act respectable."

In spite of the complete absence of logo, slogan, or catchy name, I concluded this was Digger's truck, part of the mythical fleet belonging to his future family dynasty, driven by his son, Deloy, who now revved the engine again. The woman in the passenger's seat looked from father to son, smiling broadly, enjoying the ruckus. With her wild dark hair and generous mouth, she looked like a woman who would enjoy almost any variety of ruckus.

"Turn off the da—dratted truck," Digger shouted.

The woman reached lazily forward, and the noise of the truck died out.

"You pick up that stuff in Vidalia I sent you for?" Digger asked at a much lower decibel level.

Deloy jerked his head in a gesture toward the bed of the truck. Digger took a look and nodded in satisfaction. "Looks like you did that right," he admitted.

"I made him," the woman said. "Gone make something out of this boy yet."

Deloy scowled.

I strolled over to the truck. A closer look inside showed a handsome, well-built couple. Both were wearing cut-off shorts, sleeveless T-shirts, and thong sandals. Maybe I imagined the smell of alcohol; the smell of cigarette smoke was a certainty. If ever a pair looked carefree and made for trouble, this was that pair.

"She's been asking about what we trapped at the Boatright place," Digger told them.

They'd been mostly ignoring me till then, but now I had their attention. I didn't want it. Remembering earlier speculation that Latilda and Deloy might have been behind whatever happened at Althea's, I was annoyed with Digger for being so blunt.

"Nothing we could skin or eat," Deloy said, blowing a stream of smoke in my direction.

Latilda, Elfreda's wayward granddaughter, wriggled in delight.

"But whatever it was, it quit bothering her?" I felt like I had to ask something else, if only to show I wasn't intimidated by Digger's Chief Offensive Officer.

Deloy shrugged.

Latilda was missing, or ignoring, the tension in the air.

"It's a big ol' house," she exclaimed, clapping her hands in delight. "You could plumb get lost under there with the spiders and—" She cut her eyes mischievously in Deloy's direction. "He goes crazy when he's caught in a tight place like that."

Deloy released me from his glare and turned it on Latilda. "I don't like dirty, dark places is all."

"No, you like dirty, bright-lights places, don't you? And bright-lights girls like this here Latilda?" Digger flung an accusing finger in the direction of Latilda. "You think all you got to do in life is drive around and rev up your motor and everything you want'll just come crawlin'."

"He don't like crawlin' things, either," Latilda said with a giggle.

Either Deloy wasn't as dangerous as he looked, or she thought she had his number. She obviously wasn't any more afraid of him than she was of Digger. At any rate, it didn't sound like Deloy had been voluntarily crawling around under Althea's house. Latilda, on the other hand, might have been capable of that, or anything else. Maybe she was the one to be afraid of.

"I've got to get to work," I said. "Just let me know when you're going to be working here."

As I headed toward the house, I could hear Digger telling Deloy and Latilda how they could help him finish up next door at the Griffin place.

TEN

"WHAT'S THE MATTER with you, Trudy?" Aunt Lulu's voice held concern as well as annoyance. I was annoyed with myself, to tell the truth. Usually, I think I track pretty well, but I hadn't been very quick on the uptake in my conversation with her because it hadn't made sense to me. We were talking on the phone, and I suppressed the unworthy idea that she'd called because she thought it would be easier than facing me. The result, from my point of view, was I couldn't tell whether her pull rope had come untied (as Hen might have said), whether she was pulling my leg, or something else entirely.

"I'm sorry, Aunt Lulu, but I swear it sounds like you want Phil and me to double date with you and Buck Carlton."

"You shouldn't swear, Trudy. And I wouldn't have put it like that."

"But that is basically it?"

"Well, yes."

With that much cleared up, odd as it was, I snapped back to normal. I think. "Didn't you say he's too old for you?"

"Well, yes. I did and he is. But you've got to admit his old connection with Althea makes him a suspect. And if we go over there, we can get a look at his collection of walking sticks and see if one of them is hers."

"Ah. I'm glad to hear it isn't just romance you have in mind."

"Give me some credit, please. Will you consider it?"

"What? Consider him a murder suspect or consider going on a double date with you?"

"Either one. Both. Think of it as a social outing with investigative overtones. I don't know why you're so surprised that I'm seeing him again. After all, you and Ellen as much as suggested it." Here we went again, out into the surreal.

"I don't remember doing any such thing."

She ignored my quibble. "Well, you must have said something like it, so when he called and asked if I'd like to come have dinner with him and see his walking sticks, it sounded like a good idea. I thought you might want to come, too, that's all."

"A first date and you're inviting extra people? What did he say to that?"

"He hasn't had a chance yet. I thought I ought to ask you first."

"Thank you. Very considerate."

"Well, with you and Ellen acting like you thought Mr. Carlton might be some kind of a sexual predator, I thought you might be worried about my going alone. But I don't want you to worry about it. If you and Phil don't want to go, I'll be all right. My mother always said a girl could protect herself from unwanted advances with a hatpin."

"I've never seen you wear a hat, and I don't believe for a minute that you have a hatpin."

"Are you trying to call my bluff?"

"Heaven forbid. It's just that we do have more up-to-date ways than hatpins to fend off an assailant. There's mace, pepper spray, various forms of martial—"

"There's another thing. I haven't been completely straightforward with you."

"I'm astonished and appalled."

"I did suggest to Mr. Carlton that maybe *The Beacon* would want to do a story about his collection."

"Conveniently forgetting that Jesup isn't even in the same

county as *The Beacon*. Were you hoping neither Phil nor I would notice that?"

The speed with which she switched gears answered my question. "Phil's such a good photographer, maybe he'd like to take pictures of the collection, anyway."

Actually, it wasn't such a bad idea. Phil is a photographer with talent beyond what's required for *The Beacon*. Somehow, with a camera he can manage to invest ordinary objects with importance and meaning. Beyond that, he might be interested in the walking sticks. With the additional possibility of clearing up the question of whether Buck Carlton had Althea's walking stick, I caved in, just as Aunt Lulu had known I would. "As long as you come clean with Mr. Carlton, Aunt Lulu. Phil and I will not go under false pretenses."

"Of course," she said.

My parting shot was, "What did Hen say when you told him about your date?"

"If I had mentioned it to him, which I haven't gotten around to doing yet, I'm sure he'd have been happy to know I have a social life outside the family."

I thought she was wrong about that, but I didn't argue.

My conversation with Phil, after I'd given him the general outline, went something like this:

"Why not? It's a free meal." He pushed back from his computer without any indication of reluctance. I had stopped by *The Beacon* office to talk to him. When I'm on patrol, I can justify practically any kind of quick stop since the idea is to keep the community aware of a police presence, and to do it in a random, unpredictable way.

"You don't feel just the tiniest bit manipulated?" I asked. If there's one thing that annoys me about Phil, it's how easy he is to get along with.

"Sure I do, but that goes with being in the newspaper business. People are always trying to manipulate me into printing something, or not printing something, or putting some kind of spin on something I print. I figure I'm doing as well as can be expected if I more or less even out being the manipulator and being the manipulatee. Don't you think this would be a good story for a paper like *The Beacon?*" He raised his voice and called to Inez Wilkes, one of his reporter-columnists, who was out of sight behind the work-station divider. "Inez, don't you think a story about a man with a collection of walking sticks would be interesting?"

"As long as I don't have to write it," Inez called back. "I'm way behind on the series I'm doing on the drought."

"He lives in Jesup, Phil," I hissed.

"So a story for *The Beacon* is out, but it doesn't mean I won't go along with you," Phil said. "Don't know when I've been on a double date."

"That's beside the point," I said, lowering my voice, now that I was aware that Inez might be listening, no matter how far behind she was on the drought series. "Didn't I tell you how smarmy he is? And doesn't it make you gag to think of double-dating with Aunt Lulu and this older man?"

"You're the one fixated on the double-date thing, Trudy, not me. I think you're being very narrow-minded. Anyway, we aren't going to go somewhere and park and make out. Are we?" He adopted an eager, hopeful, totally bogus expression.

"Sheesh!"

"If I take my car, then they can have the *backseat.*"

"Please stop, Phil. I hate to admit it, but your imagination is even more vivid than mine."

"Comes from being in the newspaper—"

"You've already used that angle in this conversation."

"Do I bore you?"

"Not usually."

"What time shall I pick you up? And do I bring a corsage?"

So, HERE WE WERE, the four of us, in Jesup, pretending to be harmless pilgrims with an interest in walking sticks and a free meal. Even though we had in mind to do some police business, we had come for mid-day dinner on my day off, so we wouldn't be rushed. I'd been relieved to note that Aunt Lulu, the style setter, had evidently taken no more pains than usual with her appearance. Even so, in her purplish plaid blouse that went so well with the pinkish tint of her hair, she easily outshone Phil and me in our earth-tone cotton garb.

The directions Buck Carlton had given Aunt Lulu led us to a white frame house not far from the center of town and only a few blocks from the Azalea Acres Nursing Home. A similar house on the left, practically hidden behind a lattice frame holding hanging baskets of plants, protected from the sun by a towering oak, was a florist. The one on the right had a sign out front for Jackson and Jenkins, Attorneys at Law. It didn't take much of a detective to conclude that Buck Carlton's neighborhood had changed around him. Once surely entirely residential, the mixed use now put him within walking distance of just about any service he might need, unless, despite his denial, his walking sticks really were because he was mobility-impaired.

The house looked well kept, and through the open-sided carport we could glimpse a shady well-tended backyard garden with a hedge of azalea bushes, long past bloom, mostly hidden from the street.

When I looked up from my survey and deductions and turned back to the house, I was startled to see Buck Carlton, wearing a ruffled apron, standing in the open doorway watching us and hefting a huge butcher knife.

"My, aren't you lovely today," he said, smiling at Aunt Lulu. The sunlight glinted off his bridgework and the knife.

"I could say the same of you," Aunt Lulu replied, giving him a bright smile, but coming to a stop, with her eyes on the knife. "I've always been partial to a man in an apron. Don't tell me you killed the fatted calf on our account."

"Hm? Oh. This." He raised the knife and scowled like a comic book villain.

"You remember Trudy," Aunt Lulu said, taking a step backwards. I began to wonder why I hadn't given more serious consideration to the idea of Buck Carlton as a killer. At the moment, even though he was obviously joking, his silky, ingratiating smile looked predatory, menacing. Maybe he *was* a sexual predator, after all.

"Mr. Carlton, this is my friend Phil Pittman," I said, to break the spell.

"Of *The Beacon*," Phil added, fearlessly extending his hand toward Buck Carlton's knife-wielding hand.

Buck Carlton switched the knife to his left hand, in a flourishing gesture that made Phil recoil, before he lowered it and took Phil's hand. "Sorry. Forgot I was holding this. It came with a set of knives Irene bought from a door-to-door salesman, back when people still tried to sell things door-to-door, before everybody got to be afraid to open a door to a stranger. I was using it to try to pry loose a stuck drawer when I saw y'all drive up."

"Oh," said Aunt Lulu.

"Forgive my manners, keeping you out here. Come on inside. Dinner's all ready for you." We climbed the steps and passed through the door Buck Carlton held open for us.

Inside, the house was neat, if not spick and span. I, ever the detective, decided this was a man who knew it was important not to let the house get too far out of hand, but really didn't care much about it. That pretty much describes my attitude, too, come to think of it, and Buck Carlton seemed to be doing a better job than I usually do of keeping ahead of the mess. I was having a hard time deciding what I thought of the man. My estimation of him went up when I saw he'd gone to some trouble with the table. A gardenia floated in a crystal dish, and the cloth napkins had been folded into standing bishop's hats.

"My, my," Aunt Lulu said as Buck held her chair for her while Phil did the same for me. Good manners do set a certain tone! "This is so nice."

"I saw the napkin thing in a Martha Stewart column somewhere," Buck Carlton said.

"I remember when Betty Crocker and Heloise were the goddesses of good homemaking," Aunt Lulu said; "and everything wanted to have the *Good Housekeeping* Seal of Approval. I guess that's all too old-fashioned for the likes of you."

Buck Carlton beamed.

"But you shouldn't have gone to all the bother for us," she added.

"It wasn't any bother, really. I did the napkins while I was watching television." He started toward the kitchen but paused in the doorway, apparently hungrier for someone to talk with than for whatever he and Martha Stewart had chosen for dinner. "Mostly I eat by myself, or I get something and take it over to the nursing home to eat with Irene, so I enjoyed having a reason to do something extra. I started taking over in the kitchen when Irene had her first spell. She'd been getting forgetful even before then, but that was the last straw. Don't give me much credit. I did it in self-defense. Didn't want the house to burn down around us because she forgot she had something on the stove. I flatter myself I do pretty well. You can give me credit for that. Irene says I have a flair for it. I'll be right back. Don't you go anywhere, now." With that flirtatious postscript, flung in Aunt Lulu's direction with what looked like a leer, he disappeared into the kitchen.

He returned moments later with a potholder in each hand gripping pre-made dinners, still in the microwavable trays. I'm not a snob, but this didn't impress me. And salads of iceberg lettuce topped with a glob of French dressing didn't reflect too much Martha Stewart, either, although he had gone to the trouble to arrange the salads on individual plates.

On the drive over, Aunt Lulu, getting cold feet w-a-y too late, had told us she'd stifled the impulse to offer to bring dessert. I started wishing she hadn't stifled it. It would have been nice to look forward to something like her Carolina Trifle, with pound cake, vanilla custard, and fresh fruit. Even if Buck Carlton came up with something he hadn't bought at Sam's Club, it wasn't likely it would hold up against Aunt Lulu's Carolina Trifle. Okay, we were supposed to be doing some police work, I told myself, and the meal wasn't all that important, but still.

"It sure did brighten up my day when you said you'd come," Buck said, once he'd settled down. "Anybody nice enough to come visit Irene like that, I knew you'd be somebody I'd like to get to know better. And I'm always happy to show off my walking-stick collection." He sliced into Sam's chicken Kiev, and melted butter oozed onto his plate. He hadn't offered us fried chicken or a turkey dinner with dressing and cranberry sauce, no doubt to support his high opinion of himself as a cook.

Nodding at the centerpiece, Aunt Lulu said, "I've always loved gardenias. I used to wear a gardenia perfume, I like the smell so much. It can be overpowering, though, and it's a little out of fashion these days, I'm afraid. Is this one of yours, or did you get it from the florist next door? It seems awfully late for gardenias."

"I've got one bush back in a corner that gets confused," Buck Carlton explained. "Every now and then it puts out a bloom or two. It must have been fate that produced this one for you. A woman who's interested in my collection and my garden! This is my lucky day." Phil and I might as well not have been there.

"Maybe so," Aunt Lulu said. She obviously had decided to flirt with the man—in the line of what she perceived to be duty, no doubt. We were going to have to have a talk. Or maybe I'd tattle on her and let Hen do the talking. I took a bite of chicken Kiev to hide my smile.

Through the rest of lunch we talked of varieties of azaleas, mulch, insect spray, and fertilizer.

The dessert was one our host had unquestionably made himself—a scoop of lime sherbet on top of canned fruit cocktail. Probably not as bad for you as Carolina Trifle, I consoled myself.

"Well, are y'all ready to see the collection?" Buck Carlton asked when we'd come to the end of the food and a discussion of thrips, also known as woodworm, an insect pest apparently well known to both Aunt Lulu and Buck Carlton.

"Oh, yes," Aunt Lulu said.

"I'm sorry we can't use a story about your collection in *The Beacon*," Phil said, "but I think Miz Huckabee explained that, and you know how small-town community newspapers are." Then he surprised me. He likes to do that. "But I talked to Milton Whitcomb over at *The Press-Sentinel*. Milton knows I take better pictures than he does, so he wanted me to go ahead and take some pictures, and he'll get in touch with you later about interviewing you for a story. Does that suit you?"

"I'm flattered at your interest," Buck said. "Until Lulu mentioned it, I never had thought about anybody writing a story about it, but of course it suits me."

"Let's get down to business, then," Phil said, hefting his camera bag as we followed Mr. Carlton into another room.

"My goodness!" Aunt Lulu's astonishment at the sight of all the walking sticks was surely genuine, if a little overdone. Irene Dasher hadn't been wrong to praise her brother's collection. There were dozens of walking sticks showing what I thought was an amazing range of materials and ingenuity for such a utilitarian object.

"Never had a family, so I can spend money on things like this instead of braces and college tuition," Buck Carlton said. "After a trip to the Little White House up at Warm Springs years ago, I got interested in that walking-stick collection of FDR's. Just a part of his collection is there. People all over the world used to send him walking sticks, and naturally they'd send the ones that were out of the ordinary. A lot of 'em, the ones that sent ones they made, were probably hoping for some publicity for their walking-stick business, but they say most people didn't know how bad off FDR really was, pictured him walking around making a dashing figure, I reckon, when he could hardly walk at all. He couldn't use them, but they do make a nice collection."

"Your collection is amazing enough," I said. "A presidential collection must really be something."

"We'll have to go up to Warm Springs and take a look one of these days," Phil said. He's always on the alert for interesting short trips that take us out of Ogeechee. I gave him a smile before returning my focus to the walking sticks.

It was obvious which ones were most prized. They were in what must have been a custom-made stand—four narrow tiers with rails to hold them in place while showing them off. I spotted the black one with the silver horse's head that Buck Carlton had had with him at the nursing home. There was an undulating wood one with a cobra head for a grip, and one that he showed us how to pull apart to reveal a sword.

An umbrella stand held half a dozen everyday models, including a brown wooden one, the kind you'd think of when somebody says "cane," the kind Althea Boatright had used.

Several sticks in Buck Carlton's collection were replicas of those in FDR's collection. I hadn't realized before what a wonderful ally a newspaperman can be. Even if he acknowledges he isn't after a story, Phil can't help asking questions. He distracted Mr. Carlton, leaving me to emit nonspecific approving sounds, and snoop. While the others looked at the fancy sticks, I busied myself with the plain sticks in the umbrella stand. If Buck Carlton had killed Althea and taken her cane by mistake, in exchange for his, this was probably where he would have put it. I made a point of running my fingers down the length of each stick as I returned it to its place. None was chewed up as Martha Tootle had said Althea's was.

"Is that the whole collection?" Phil asked, doing that thing photographers do with his camera, pointing, squinting through a lens, crouching, dodging here and there. "Or do you keep the heirlooms and jewel-encrusted ones in a vault somewhere?"

"Couldn't enjoy 'em if I kept 'em locked up," Buck Carlton said. "I like to have the whole collection at my fingertips so I can use whichever one I want to. My security is that nobody much would think a bunch of walking sticks would be worth stealing. And I don't tell anybody which ones are valuable."

Aunt Lulu and I glanced at each other when he said that. Naturally, we both looked them over again, trying to guess which were especially valuable.

"Why don't we get a couple of pictures of you holding up a fancy walking stick?" Phil said, fiddling with his glasses, now that he was through fiddling with the camera.

Without hesitation, Buck Carlton pulled out a dark stick with a lacquered finish and a design in red that seemed to be a dragon twining up to the handle, where the dragon held a marble in its teeth. "One of the people at the nursing home's in the Army Reserve. Had a stint in Bosnia a while back. Brought me this from there. Run this picture, it'll give him a charge."

"Good," Phil said. "Another local angle. Milton will like that." He clicked off several shots of Buck Carlton holding the Bosnian cane, to go with the close-ups of some of the individual canes, and some shots from farther back that showed the whole collection.

"How about some pictures with the ladies?" Buck Carlton asked when Phil stopped clicking his camera.

"Why not?" Phil asked, grinning at me. "Ladies? Care to join him?"

"Go ahead. Get a walking stick," Buck Carlton urged.

I repressed my knee-jerk reaction at being called a lady and chose the sword cane. Aunt Lulu's choice was green and gold and looked like cloisonné. The three of us posed, looking— as photographs later proved—very much like a not-very-well-rehearsed vaudeville act.

When Phil finally quit amusing himself by taking far more pictures than *The Sentinel* would ever use, Buck Carlton said, "Let me show you around the yard. It's not every day I have lovely ladies—and a gentleman—come visit, and I hate to have you hurry off."

He took an aluminum walking stick with a four-pronged base from the umbrella stand, explaining that it didn't sink into the ground like the others, and ushered us back through the kitchen and out the back door. We moved slowly down a gentle slope to the back of the long, narrow backyard, and I noticed our host feeling around for a firm place to plant his walking stick as we strolled, admiring and discussing the needs and proclivities of the various plantings. He might not want to admit it, but he did need that stick. And we had only his word for it that there were no more of them.

"I like to sit out here in the evenings," he said, when we'd come back to the house after working our way past pink impatiens, red nicotiana and bougainvillea, multicolored lantana, white petunias, and the confused gardenia bush with three lackluster blooms well past their prime. "It's not too hot right now, so if you aren't in a hurry, how about another glass of tea?"

"Tea would be nice," Aunt Lulu said.

He pointed his cane at a stack of white plastic lawn chairs, and Phil and I took the hint. We pulled four of them from the stack and set them at the edge of the carport, where we had a good view of the flowers.

"Y'all just sit, then. I'll be right back. There's a family of pesky half-wild kittens that come out of the underbrush if you sit still long enough. Can't get rid of 'em."

"Let me help you," I said, imagining him making four trips to carry the tea along with his walking stick.

Phil winked at me, pushing his luck. "You ladies sit and rest. I'll help with the tea."

"How're we doing?" Aunt Lulu whispered as soon as the men—excuse me, the gentlemen—were out of sight and we ladies were seated.

"I didn't see anything that could have been Althea's cane," I said. "And as far as we know, he wouldn't know there's any reason to hide it. The killer's not supposed to know he has the wrong one, right?"

"Right, but he might have figured it out."

"And if he did, then he's on to us, and he probably poisoned the dinner."

"I could have done better, but I don't think it was actually poisonous," she responded uncharitably.

ELEVEN

BUCK CARLTON'S YARD showed the care his house didn't, everything neat and well trimmed.

"It's easy to see where he spends his time," I whispered. "Even the floor of his carport is clean. I didn't think there was such a thing as a car that doesn't drip."

"He must use some product Martha Stewart recommended," Aunt Lulu whispered back.

"Or, obviously, he doesn't park there!" We were so impressed with our powers of observation, and our wit, that we giggled. Then to avoid getting caught looking like we were scheming, or being catty, which we were, we quit whispering and started trying to spot kittens. It's one of my favorite pastimes, and I get a fair amount of practice at it. Between us we glimpsed three—or was it four?—tiny faces peeking out of the petunias. They disappeared with hardly a flutter when the men returned with the tea.

I was amused and grateful to see that the tray Phil carried held some funeral-home fans. They may sound old-fashioned, but graveside services can't be air-conditioned, and modern technology has yet to come up with something that suits the situation better than cardboard with a handle. Aunt Lulu and I helped ourselves to tea and fans.

"It's late in the season now, but back in the spring my yard was the prettiest spot you've ever seen," Buck Carlton said as he took his seat, for all the world like a man with nothing worse on his conscience than feeding guests a store-bought dinner. "This year the dogwoods and wisteria outdid themselves. And I had one camellia that put out red and white flowers on the same bush. Not red-and-white ones, mind you. Red ones and white ones. Different flowers. I'm sorry I didn't have one of them for you."

Aunt Lulu waved his apology away with her fan. "The gardenia made up for it."

He beamed.

"Mr. Carlton…"she began.

"Buck, please."

"Well, then, Buck, I have a confession to make."

He looked crestfallen. "A confession to make? To me? What could it be? You aren't interested in me? You already have a gentleman friend?"

As Aunt Lulu was composing her answer to that, I made the mental note that "gentleman friend" somehow sounded even worse than "boyfriend."

"Oh, no. It isn't that," Aunt Lulu said, with admirable composure. "I like you very much, and I'm sure we'll be friends. We are all interested in you, but not just because you're such a nice man." I was impressed with the extra, ambiguous stress she put on the word "just." She's good.

"I…we did want to see your walking-stick collection."

Phil and I dutifully nodded agreement.

"I don't hold that against you," Buck Carlton assured us all. "That doesn't call for a confession."

"And we wanted to find out anything else you could tell us about the connection between Althea and Charles Sykes," Aunt Lulu continued. "Because of what you and Irene told us the other day, we could think of a reason, even if it was a pretty lame reason, for Charlie to want to harm Althea, but nothing you said explained why she'd have wanted to hurt him. Maybe his death was an accident, after all."

"I don't see how anybody would ever know the truth of it, with both of them gone," Buck said, "but it would be a pretty gol-darned big coincidence, pardon my French."

I decided it was time for me to remind everybody that I represented law and order. "Too much of a coincidence to ignore," I said. "There are two things you could help us with. Finding out why Althea Boatright might have killed Charles Sykes on purpose is one thing. The other is finding out who might have wanted to kill her."

"I've been thinking about that since you came to see Irene and me," our host said. "You said then you had some questions about how she died, and you were looking for a connection between her death and his, so I figured out you thought somebody had killed her. But I don't understand it." He shook his head, apparently mystified.

A kitten, black with white paws, quietly eased out of the bushes. It drank from the end of a coiled hose and slunk away again. It seemed to me the kitten kept a wary eye on Buck, and, sure enough, when he saw the kitten he brandished his walking stick in that direction. "Got to stop that drip," he said.

I wondered at a man who'd begrudge a kitten a drink of water.

Aunt Lulu said, "I think Mr. Sykes must have gone to Ogeechee to see her about something and made an appointment with her, or else she wouldn't have known where to find him, whether she ran over him on purpose, or not. And if he did that, they must have met beforehand or, after all that time, she never would have recognized him. I think they had met before, and he infuriated her or threatened her in some way."

"Enough for her to want to kill him?" Buck Carlton was waving his walking stick again. "How could somebody from that far back be a big enough threat to her for her to want to do that?" Good question.

The white-pawed kitten edged out of the bushes again. It was Aunt Lulu who sent it scampering this time, when she suddenly sat up in her chair. "Maybe he was threatening to make some kind of trouble for her," she said.

"That's an interesting idea," Buck said. "I could see if Irene knows anything about that. She keeps up on gossip pretty good, since people who visit her have to talk about something. Of course, with her hearing, she might not get it right, but she might know something. Wouldn't that be something, now?"

"Something. I don't know what, but something," Aunt Lulu agreed. "Would you ask her?"

"Anything for you, dear lady."

"As long as you're at it," I suggested, even though I wasn't his dear lady, "see if you can find out why Mr. Sykes might have gone to Ogeechee to meet Miz Boatright after all those years."

He nodded. "All right."

"It would help to know exactly when it was that he left Jesup in the first place," I suggested.

He nodded again. "Was run off right after high school. I remember that. You think he might have been carrying a grudge against Althea about that all this time?"

"Maybe."

"I could check around and see what kind of family Charlie still has. They might know something about whatever business he had with her. Maybe he was trying to blackmail her about that old scandal."

"Althea would have gone to any lengths to protect Leland," Aunt Lulu said.

"Leland's her husband?"

"No, Leland's her son. Bert Grinstead was her husband,

Leland's father, but he's been gone a good while now and she married Rowland Boatright."

"What's her son like?"

"A lot like Althea, actually. Not a trace of Bert Grinstead in him anywhere."

"Is that a fact." It wasn't a question the way Buck Carlton said it. He nodded thoughtfully.

"Well, that's what people say, but of course, he did go into the grocery business after his daddy." Aunt Lulu smiled at him, encouraging him. I smiled at her, encouraging her to encourage him. He might turn out to be a helpful source of information.

"As long as you're willing to be helpful," I said, knowing I was pushing my luck, "for the record, can you tell us where you were the day she died?"

"Me?"

"Just for the record. I am a police officer, you know."

All four prongs of his walking stick hit the ground with an angry thunk. "So all this about wanting to see my collection and talking about Charlie and Althea is really because you think I killed her?"

Aunt Lulu began making soothing noises, and I was about to get pushy, but Phil saved us. "You can't blame me for whatever it is the ladies are up to," he said.

I knew he was faking the earnest, good-old-boy camaraderie because he called us ladies again. "I'm here because I wanted to take pictures of your collection."

"So you're just an innocent bystander?" Buck Carlton asked.

Phil grinned at him. He has a nice, innocent, engaging grin.

Buck Carlton frowned back at him. "They aren't just ladies. They're police," he said.

"Just one of us," I said. "And you really could be a help, besides telling me where you were that day so I won't waste any time investigating an innocent person." I tried my version of Phil's engaging grin, adding the date and the day, not yet two weeks past.

He appeared to be thinking about it. The end of his walking stick rested on the ground and rotated slowly back and forth on one of the prongs. But before he could speak, a sudden agitation of the gardenia bush behind him drew all our attention. The black and white kitten with the nose that looked like it had been poked into somebody's floury business, belly on the grass, eyes on the stick, crept out of the petunias.

"Those rascals," Buck Carlton said, abandoning the conversation for the distraction. "They chase lizards up that bush. Wouldn't think there'd be room for 'em, but there they go."

We all laughed far too much as one of the kittens went too far out on a limb and swung crazily toward the ground.

A gray and white ball of fur jumped out of another branch, colliding with the black and white one. Both tumbled to the ground, looked startled, and bee-lined for the petunia bed, then renewed their assault on the bush.

Phil, pushing that engaging grin to the limit, did what he could to defuse the situation. "I think all this is a waste of time. I look at the obvious, and it seems obvious to me that if anybody did kill her, it had to be one of the Grinsteads."

Buck Carlton swung around to face him. "That would be this Leland, Althea's son, and his wife? Why do you say it had to be them?"

Phil spread his hands as if to say it was obvious. "The place was locked up so tight Trudy had to break in to get to Althea. Whoever killed her must have had a key."

Buck Carlton leaned heavily on his four-pronged walking stick, then he turned to me. "You think this boy would kill his own mother?"

"Maybe not on purpose," Aunt Lulu said.

Buck turned and glared at her, a measure of his agitation.

"If that's right, if it's open and shut, then what's all this business about Charlie?"

"Mostly, Buck, it's curiosity by now," Aunt Lulu told him. "At least for me, it is. Curiosity about an old friend and a whole side of her we never knew."

On that note, the party more or less fizzled on out. All three kittens, just beginning to ease out of the bushes again, darted back when Buck picked up his stick. We thanked our host for lunch and left.

We were halfway home before I realized that Buck Carlton still hadn't told us where he was the day Althea died. There isn't necessarily anything sinister about a person not wanting to be adopted by a family of itinerant cats, and I tried not to hold it against him that he didn't like cats, but even if he was a unique version of Martha Stewart, with a way with flowers and a knack for keeping his carport pad clean, he was also, until further notice, a murder suspect.

TWELVE

A SIGN IN THE post office says the mail will be put up by ten in the morning, so the place buzzes every day about that time. There's no telling who you'll bump into.

I bumped into Ellen Chandler, dressed in a beige T-shirt with blue round-the-world postmarks on it. Laminated cancelled stamps hung from her ears.

"Do you save that ensemble for your trip to the post office every day?" I asked, stepping aside to allow her plenty of room to bend down to her box.

She smiled. "You underestimate my girls, Trudy. I have three distinct post office outfits. The pink one has envelopes on it and the other one has a hand-painted scene of a mail truck."

"With truck earrings?" I guessed.

"I don't know where they get their ideas—or their materials," she said. "Look at that," she said, jerking her head toward the entrance and Melva Boatright, squeezed into turquoise slacks and a matching knit shirt that showed off every detail of a figure better loosely draped and kept obscure. I'd never seen her without perfect make-up and hairdo, but some tactful friend would be doing her a favor to introduce her to a full-length mirror.

"Mornin', Melva. You sure look nice," Ellen said, shaming me for my uncharitable thoughts. "It's hardly worth the trip down here, most days. I don't get much besides bills and junk mail. Here's one wants to sell me a trailer and another one that'll put siding on my house, and me with brick. It's hard to see how it pays for them to mail all this junk."

"That's the truth," Melva agreed. "The personal mail I get isn't one tenth of what I find in my box. Homer says the government subsidizes junk mail to help the economy, supposed to be good for businesses, but it beats me how it can pay them to pay people to run the post office just for the junk."

"Does Homer use bulk mail for his business? I don't know that I've ever gotten anything from him."

"Oh, probably not. His work is so specialized, it's referrals from contractors, mostly."

"That must keep him pretty busy," Ellen said.

"Busy enough most of the time. Not so much lately." Melva bent toward her post office box, key in hand.

By now, I had retrieved my own handful of junk mail and was wondering if the way Ellen was spinning the conversation meant she was playing detective for my benefit.

"Seems like somebody told me y'all are getting ready to build a new house," Ellen said.

Melva straightened and turned back to Ellen. "Don't I wish! Who told you that?"

"Oh, I don't know. I just heard it somewhere. Maybe it was just that you were wanting to build."

"Well, that's not news," Melva said. "Homer's been promising me a new house for years but putting me off with one excuse or another. He's too busy or we can't afford it or…something."

"My first husband, Crowell—you remember him?—he was like that. He didn't have the backbone to stand right up and say so when he didn't agree with me. He'd act like he thought it was a good idea but never did get his rear in gear when it got time to deliver the goods. You think Homer's just stringing you along?"

"I wouldn't want to say that." But the expression on Melva's face said it plainly enough. "I don't think he's ever given up on getting the old Boatright house back and living there. His daddy built it, you know. Put all kinds of special details into it that you wouldn't find in any other house."

"I never knew that," Ellen said.

I was shamelessly eavesdropping. Maybe this would lead somewhere.

"What kind of special details?" Ellen asked. "You mean built-ins? Bookcases? That kind of thing?"

"Oh, yes, that kind of thing. But Homer says, and I know he got this idea from his daddy, that if you have a safe or a big lock on a door, it's a tip-off that you have something valuable inside, so it's exactly where a thief would look and go to no end of trouble to break in. From what he and Susannah have said, their daddy put secret compartments all over the house."

Ellen smiled in what looked to me like a conspiratorial way. "Maybe if you suggest putting in some of those hiding places, Homer'll get around to building you the house you want. I learned with all my husbands if I could point out where their interests ran with mine, I could usually get what I wanted without much fuss."

Melva jiggled her key ring. "Most of the time I manage to get what I want one way or another, anyway. I'll say that for Homer."

"With Althea gone, maybe you and Homer could get the house back. Leland and Clarice may not be all that attached to it. Why don't you get Homer to make them an offer?"

I was impressed with Ellen's spur-of-the-moment manner of delivering this suggestion.

"Not Homer," Melva said, lips tightening in exasperation. "He'd think if he did that, showed an interest in the place, Leland would jack the price up just for spite. Under the circumstances and all."

"He could be right," Ellen said. "Even without the circumstances, I don't know how I'd react if somebody showed up out of the wild blue yonder and offered to buy my house."

Melva's key ring jingled more vigorously. "You have to admit old places like that have a lot of character, but I'd rather have a new place, myself, with up-to-date wiring and heat and air-conditioning you can count on. And some closet space. Not that Clarice hasn't done what she could to make it livable—what Althea would let her do, anyway—but that flowered-y carpet she put in the living room wasn't much of an improvement, if you ask me.

"I don't think Homer's all that sentimental; when you come right down to it, I think Homer would rather build a nice new house to live in, too. It might be different for Susannah, but I think all Homer wants is to be in the house long enough to go through it and check out all those little hidey-holes. Maybe there's something his daddy forgot to take out. Rowland went pretty quick, you remember. Might not have had time to take care of every little detail." Melva's eyes had taken on an unpleasant greedy glint.

Ellen nodded. "About as sudden as Althea went. We'd been playing bridge the day she died. Martha Tootle found her, you know. Poor Martha's not much good in an emergency. I can just picture her standing there on the porch in a dither looking around for help. She said she saw you drive by, but she couldn't get your attention."

I didn't remember Martha saying any such thing. Maybe this was Ellen's admirable way of fishing for an alibi. Melva looked surprised, but I didn't think it suggested guilt. She didn't even sound especially interested when she asked, "Really? I sure didn't see her."

"But you were driving by?" If Ellen was just fishing, she was doing a good job of it.

"Hmm? Oh, I don't know. Might have been. The house on a main street like it is, I go past it quite a bit. I think I'd remember if I'd seen Martha Tootle standing there waving. Did she say I waved back?"

I was sure Ellen was making this up as she went along, so she was free to answer however she chose. She chose, "No. She said you acted like you didn't see her."

"I'm glad of that. I wouldn't want her to think I'd ignored her on purpose, especially in an emergency like that."

Ellen and Melva moved aside for Fred Womack to get past to his mail box, and I edged out of the way, but not so far I couldn't keep an eye and ear on Ellen's interrogation. Melva had either figured out what Ellen was up to or was truly unconcerned. "Oh," Melva said. "That was a Tuesday, wasn't it, when Althea died? It couldn't have been me. On Tuesdays I usually go over to Vidalia with my sister to the big Super K store for groceries. Homer doesn't like to give Leland our business, not for so much as a loaf of bread, so we started going over there before Food Lion came, and we haven't changed our habits. Too bad Homer and Leland feel that way about each other, since I guess technically they're stepbrothers, but it isn't like they grew up together."

"So you heard about Althea when you got back from Vidalia?" Ellen asked.

"I guess so," Melva said without much interest. "Francine and I usually have lunch somewhere over there. I wonder who it could have been Martha mistook for me."

"I have no idea," Ellen said. I guessed that was true enough. "Did you go to Vidalia in your sister's car that day? Maybe it was Homer Martha saw driving your car. She might not have noticed more than just the car."

I admired Ellen's neat, smooth segue, but Melva gave a tight smile.

"I don't know how anybody'd mistake me for Homer, or vicey-versy, no matter what we were driving. Anyway, it couldn't have been Homer, either. He's been spending all day every day lately trying to finish up the work on the old McCall place that backs on the Durrence pond. Nice property except being so close to that pond makes the bugs worse. I think they'd have been smarter to knock the whole thing down and start over, but they like the old place, they said. I know they've spent enough to buy a new place, or build one, and I can't complain about that. Homer hasn't had all that much work lately. Not everybody can afford the kind of work he does."

Ellen was certainly being thorough. Having done what she could about checking Melva's alibi, she kept after Homer's. "Does Homer have a crew working with him over there, or does he work by himself?"

The jingle of Melva's keys took on an impatient sound. "All kinds of people, working on different things. Every time I've ever been by there, it's been like an ant hill. They do so much coming and going nobody knows for sure where anybody'll be from one minute to the next so they all carry those beepers so people can get in touch with them."

"Well, you know Martha," Ellen said. "No telling who she saw."

"Maybe it was my old car she saw," Melva said, stepping closer to the bank of boxes so that a young woman with three toddlers could pass. "Homer'd been acting like he couldn't afford to get me a new car like I wanted, not the nice one I wanted, anyway, but then he went and traded the old one in and got me my car. It's a Coupe de Ville, with all that new stuff on it, what Homer calls bells and whistles. But then he up and surprised me with it for my birthday last month. He had me worried about where the money was going to come from to pay a big business loan he had, too, but he had it all the time.

From what I've heard, that's how his daddy was, secretive about money. That's why it wouldn't surprise me if he got rid of some of that property Homer and Susannah stay so worried about and didn't feel like he needed to tell them, or even Althea, he'd done it. Yes, Homer's a lot like his daddy that way. He likes to keep me off balance, doesn't want me to know all his business. I don't like that trait in him, but I guess I don't have any right to complain as long as the bills get paid."

A man holding on to the hand of a crying toddler glared at the jam of women in his path, and we broke it up.

"Oh, goodness!" Ellen said. "Here I am keeping you, and I'll bet you have more to do than stand around in the post office gabbing."

Melva nodded.

I reviewed what Ellen had wormed out of Melva. Melva was—probably—having lunch with her sister in Vidalia at the time of the alleged murder and Homer was—probably— working on the McCall place with an ant hill of people all around. No way to be sure about any particular minute, though, with people coming and going all the time. In real life, most people find it impossible to swear where they are during crucial moments and have somebody else confirm it.

As Melva jingled past me toward the exit, I heard her muttering to herself with a peevish curl to her lips. "I thought everybody knew I had a new car."

I turned to Ellen. "Do you have a Sherlock Holmes ensemble? Something with a magnifying glass or a deerstalker?"

She didn't even look embarrassed when she shook her head in denial, and she didn't pretend not to know what I was talking about. "Closest I can come is a pretty green one with black fingerprints all over it."

Cancelled stamps swinging briskly from her ears, she marched to her car.

THIRTEEN

THINKING I'D DRIVE around a little and provide a bit of discreet police presence in the community after the post office encounter with Ellen Chandler and Melva Boatright, I didn't go straight back to the station house. Purely by chance, I found myself on the street where Martha Tootle lived, and I couldn't help noticing a gathering of cars and people in her yard.

The sight of Jerome Sharpe, standing in the midst of a handful of flurrying women, drew me nearer—not that I thought for a moment Jerome needed my assistance against a handful of flurrying women, you understand, but something about the scene suggested this was police business.

As I came closer, I recognized the women in the flurry: Martha Tootle, Aunt Lulu, and Ellen Chandler, who must have gotten there only a minute or two ahead of me. Something was clearly up.

"Oh, Ellen," Martha was saying as I came into earshot, "Somebody broke a window in my cute little car!"

Ellen Chandler's postage stamps waggled in indignation. "What a shame! I'm so sorry! I know how proud you are of this little car. Did they steal anything?"

"No. The CD player and all the CDs are still there, and so's the radio. So why would they break in? Just pure-D meanness? There wasn't anything else to take. You know how I hate a junky car. I was just telling Officer Sharpe, I don't… Oh." A strange look passed over Martha's face.

We waited for an explanation that didn't come. Instead, like a hostess at a tea party rising above a troublesome kitchen contretemps, Martha changed the subject. "Oh! Where are my manners?" As usual in times of stress, Martha's— Mahtha's— *r*'s all but disappeared and we got, "wheah ah mah mannahs," which is a little thick but not incomprehensible. "Does everybody know everybody? Lulu, this is Offisah Shahp. Offisah Shahp, this is Lulu Huckabee."

Jerome smiled and touched his forehead in an approximation of a salute. "Yes, ma'am, I know the name," he said.

"I've heard of you, too, and what an asset you are to the police force," Aunt Lulu said. She gave Jerome a wide smile and then turned back to her friend. "Now, Martha, what? What's the matter?"

"Nothing. I'm fine. I just remembered…"And then Martha remembered enough that she stopped talking again.

"What is it, ma'am? You remembered something that was in your car?" Jerome used his best freight-train, female-melting voice, a big, slow, calm, rumbling sound that would soothe any fears and keep any booger man away, the kind of voice anybody would want on guard, lulling you to sleep, but it didn't seem to soothe Martha.

"No, I, uh, I remembered I have a coffee cake in the oven. Is this going to take long?" For somebody whose pet automobile had been vandalized, she sounded oddly impatient.

"Don't be silly, Martha," Aunt Lulu said. "Taking care of this is more important than that. Somebody else can go see about the coffee cake."

Nobody budged in the direction of the kitchen. And risk missing something?

"That's all right," Jerome said. "Y'all go on and see about that cake. If you don't have anything else you want to tell me right now, I'm going to see if I can lift some fingerprints. You never know what'll turn up when you do that. And if it's a car-theft ring—"

"Ohhhhh!" Martha wailed.

"Or drug dealers—" This time Jerome, who is very quick on the uptake, waited for Martha's wail. She didn't disappoint him.

"Ohhh! Did you hear that, Lulu?"

"Whoever did it," Officer Sharpe continued placidly, "might turn up in our computers, and we'll catch 'im. Some-times we get lucky like that."

"I don't think—" Martha started, but once again cut herself off in mid-think. She shook her head.

"Okay, then, ma'am. I'll see what I can find. You don't want to watch me making a mess all over your car with this finger-print stuff. When you get the window fixed, they'll make another mess, so you might want to wait and clean it up all at once. I'll put a piece of cardboard over that window before I go." His smile was as calming as his voice. "Y'all just go on, and don't worry about it. Unless there's something else—?"

"No," Martha said a shade too firmly to be convincing. "No. There wasn't anything in the car. I'm sure of it. I can't think of anything else to tell you. Thank you."

"Well, all right, then," Jerome said. "I wouldn't worry about it if I was you. It was probably just some young'un without a thought in his head, but we'll keep an eye on your place for a while, just in case. And you call us again if you see any little old thing at all that worries you, and I'll come back. Will you do that, now?"

"If you think it was children, why would you take fin-gerprints?" Aunt Lulu asked. "Would you have children's fingerprints?"

"No, ma'am, probably not. Every once in a while people get interested in having their young'uns fingerprinted in case they get lost or kidnapped. Makes 'em feel safer. But they keep the fingerprints themselves. I didn't mean I think it's young'uns, but I like to cover all the possibilities. That's what adds up to good policin'. Besides," he added with a grin, "this'll give me some extra practice on lifting fingerprints, and Miz Tootle can tell everybody I took fingerprints, and maybe whoever it was will break down and confess. That happens once in a while, too. Y'all go on and see about that cake, now." With that, Jerome flipped his notepad closed, in a gesture of dismissal that even Martha couldn't ignore. "I know where to find you if I think of anything else I need," he added, in case there was any doubt.

"Certainly," Martha said. "Good. Thank you. You go ahead. We'll go now."

With a wink in my direction, Jerome turned toward his car for the fingerprint kit as Martha grabbed Aunt Lulu by the arm and started toward the house.

I interpreted Jerome's wink to mean—and I know this is giving a mere wink a lot of interpretation—that he'd had about enough of Martha Tootle for the time being and that he figured something else was going on and if I could downplay my police officerness and play up my family friendness, I might learn something useful. Since that pretty much went along with my thinking, I trailed the three women toward the house.

"What's the matter with you?" Aunt Lulu asked Martha.

"Shhh. The killer!" Martha whispered, casting a nervous glance back at Jerome, who looked up from the handle on the inside of the door nearest the hole where the car window used to be and smiled peacefully in our direction. My disguise seemed to be working, though, because Martha didn't seem nervous at my presence.

Aunt Lulu whispered back. "What are you talking about? Officer Sharpe will be arresting you for being out in public without a custodian if you don't watch out."

"Well, if you don't want to know!" Martha huffed.

She had misjudged her audience, or imposed on all of us too often. We all knew that no power on heaven or earth would prevent Martha from telling, when she was good and ready, and that begging would only slow things down. We kept quiet.

Martha stuck out a petulant lip and led the way to the kitchen, picking up speed when we got close enough to hear the persistent rasp of the oven timer. She rattled the oven door and rattled the cake pan onto a cooling rack. She waved her hands in the oven mitt and generally created an atmosphere of forcibly repressed speech.

Ellen gave in. "What did I miss?" she asked.

"Well," Martha said. "I think we're about to solve the murder!"

"Really?" Ellen asked. "I can hardly wait to hear what that has to do with your car."

"Sit down and I'll tell you," Martha said. We all sat. But Martha, now that she was sure she was the center of attention again, didn't want to get right to the point.

"That's the meanest-looking deputy I ever saw in my entire life," she said. "I declare, if I'd done anything wrong, I'd have confessed just looking at him. Might have confessed anyway. He must scare people to death."

I was tempted to explain that Jerome's specialty, after scaring people to death and squelching fights in juke joints, was humoring eccentric women, but I settled for, "He's a good officer."

Martha still wasn't ready to come to the point, not with the seductive topic of Jerome so handy. "I thought he was kind of weird."

"What did he do?" Ellen asked.

"It's not so much that he *did* anything. I don't know whether it was his earring or his hair that got me the most,"

Martha said. "Did you see his earring? Flashy gold stud. Good thing he was wearing a uniform or I'd've had a heart attack at the sight of him! I'm surprised Hen doesn't have a dress code or something."

"There's a dress code," I offered. "Officer Sharpe is in uniform. Men can wear jewelry, just like women can. Hen calls that earring 'equal opportunity' jewelry."

"What does that mean?" Ellen asked.

"It means that men and women can wear jewelry. To quote Hen as nearly as I can, it's within regulations as long as it isn't ostentatious enough to detract from the solemn official dignity of the uniform."

"That sounds like Hen," Aunt Lulu commented.

"As a practical matter," I continued, "Jerome Sharpe or any other officer, male or female, can wear that stud, but nobody—male or female, can wear a big hoop that somebody might grab in a bar fight. At the risk of sounding like Hen again, do you have any idea how much an earlobe can bleed?"

I was pleased to see Martha blench. She recovered quickly, but did abandon the earring topic.

"Well, yes, but there was the hair, too, so curly and wild looking."

"I know there's a rule about haircuts," Aunt Lulu contributed. "The hat has to fit right. His hair was short enough. Martha, you aren't suggesting that Hen should have rules against curly hair, are you?"

At this rate, we'd never get back to Martha's cryptic reference to "the killer."

"Well, you can't talk away that earring." Martha might not have heard Aunt Lulu. "One earring! One looks even worse on a man than two would: more lawless, more dangerous, or something, like a pirate, like it's somebody who doesn't know the rules or doesn't care about them. Or lost one and doesn't even care about that. In my day—"

A discreet rumble at the screen door caused Martha to gasp.

"Excuse me, ladies," rumbled the pirate himself. "Just wanted you to know I'm finished out here and I'll be going. You try not to worry, now."

"Thank you," Aunt Lulu said, since Martha seemed to be choking on something.

I was disappointed that Jerome left without hanging around to cadge a piece of coffee cake. I took it to mean he felt I should continue the investigation. Either that or he couldn't take any more of Martha.

"He listened to me, and then he asked me if I'd ever had this kind of trouble before, like it was diarrhea or something," Martha continued once Jerome had gone, "and I said no I hadn't, and he asked me if I had any idea who it might have been, and I said I thought the police were supposed to find out who did it, and he said that's right but sometimes people know if there's somebody who has it in for them, and since there wasn't anything taken and not much damage, he just wondered." Martha was pacing now, working herself up again.

"Well, anyway, I do have to say he was polite enough. He listened to me, and kept nodding his head real slow, like he was taking it all in, and he wrote everything down. Said he'd write up a report and I'd have to come in and sign it."

"Are you planning to change your story before he gets that report all typed up?" Aunt Lulu asked.

"Why would you ask me that? Why would I want to change my story?"

"Since I don't know what story you told him, I have no idea," Aunt Lulu said. "But I know you well enough to know you're up to something."

"You really do know somebody who has it in for you?" Ellen asked, earning a reproachful glance.

"Why would anybody have it in for me? I'm not a school teacher, and I don't have any kids around that might have irritated somebody without me knowing, and I'm not Black or Jewish or gay or anything like that. But I think—"

"There's a doctor over in Claxton who has a car like yours," Ellen volunteered. "Maybe whoever did it thought it was his car and they were after drugs."

"No, I think—" Martha's voice was getting louder with each interruption.

"When did it happen?" Aunt Lulu asked.

"You sound just like Officer Sharpe, and I'll give you the same answer I gave him. How would I know when it happened? It's not like I caught somebody doing it, thank heaven. No telling what they might have done to me if I'd come along to catch them in the act. All I know is I haven't driven it since day before yesterday, when I saw you at the grocery store, Trudy. I went out this morning to move it on into the garage out of the way for y'all this morning—they were coming over to talk about the case, Trudy." She offered this as though she thought it was an acceptable apology for not inviting me, instead of an egregious interference with the police, and then, apparently sensing her *faux pas,* she hurried on. "That's when I noticed the broken window. The way I had it pulled in there, sort of sideways and that big hydrangea on one side and Jim L.'s car on the other, whoever did it was pretty well hidden.

"Now, if y'all are ready to listen to me, I'll tell you what I think." As if she hadn't been doing just that.

Aunt Lulu and I managed to sit with a semblance of patience, but Ellen Chandler pulled a deck of cards out of her purse and began laying out a complicated game of solitaire on the coffee table.

Finally, realizing we weren't going to encourage her any further, Martha continued. "I think it was Homer Boatright."

"You think what was Homer Boatright?" Ellen asked, looking up from her game as though that's all she'd been thinking about.

"Who broke into my car."

"Homer?" Ellen looked doubtful. "Come on, now, Martha! I've heard the construction business has been slow lately, and goodness knows Melva is high maintenance, but I doubt Homer's been reduced to rummaging through cars."

"Not cars. Just my car. Remember at the grocery store the other day, Trudy, when I was showing you the walking stick and medicine of Althea's that Clarice gave me? Well, Homer saw it! And he was limping. I think he'd lost his walking stick."

"Homer doesn't use a walking stick, does he?" Ellen asked.

"Not usually," Martha agreed. "Lately he has been, but he didn't have it the other day, did he, Trudy?"

"No, I have to say he did not have a walking stick when we saw him, and he was limping, but if you are jumping from that to the idea that Homer Boatright would need a walking stick so desperately he'd break into your car for it instead of buying one, Officer Sharpe might easily come to the conclusion that, as Hen might put it, you ain't doing a good job of connecting all the dots. You might as well try to blame it on the FBI or little green men from outer space." Maybe Hen had known what he was doing after all, sending Jerome Sharpe to answer Martha's call.

Martha puffed up and shot me a resentful look. "I didn't say Homer was trying to steal *a* walking stick. What he wanted was *that* walking stick."

"You haven't been lying to Officer Sharpe, have you, Martha?" Ellen asked.

"Of course not."

"But I heard you tell Officer Sharpe nothing was missing," Aunt Lulu said. "On principle, Martha, I don't believe in lying to the police. It sets a bad example."

"I didn't lie to him. It was the truth. There wasn't anything for a breaker-in, Homer, to take. I took it to the police, along with the medicine of Althea's that I got from Clarice. Trudy told me to, and I did." Martha's look of aggrieved innocence would have done justice to a saint.

"But Homer went inside the store. He wouldn't know that's what I did with it. He'd think it was still in the car."

"What about Leland?" Ellen asked, barely beating me to it. This happened in front of Leland's store, after all.

"What *about* Leland?" Martha retorted.

"Don't get prickly, now." Aunt Lulu weighed in on the side of law and order. "Be fair. You jump right on Homer, but what about Clarice and Leland? You took the cane and the medicine from their house. Didn't you say Leland didn't seem to like it?"

"Well, yes." Martha fiddled with her scarf.

Aunt Lulu persisted. "So if you're casting about for suspects, don't you think they are at least as likely as Homer?"

Martha folded her hands and looked prim. "Suspects for my car or for Althea?" she asked.

"I thought you were assuming it was the same person," Ellen said. She turned to me. "I agree with Martha that it's a pretty big coincidence. Whoever broke into the car must have done it because they were after the cane."

"Or the medicine," Aunt Lulu offered. "Or the drugs in the doctor's car. There are still several possibilities."

"I've had my network busy, like I said I would," Ellen announced. "Y'all want to hear what I found out?"

I'd been about to protest their interference, their assumption that they would solve the mystery of Althea Boatright's death—an assumption bolstered by the fact that Martha Tootle had gone to the trouble to make a coffee cake for guests—but I didn't. Hen, or my grandmother, or somebody else who's pretty smart, used to tell me I'd never learn anything with my mouth open, so I shut my mouth, ever alert to the opportunity to learn something.

"Of course we do," Martha said.

"What do you want first?"

"Since we don't know what you've got, we can't answer that question," Aunt Lulu said. "Why don't you just start?"

"Well, Armond, my lawyer ex-son-in-law, called. We were more or less right about Althea leaving everything to Leland. There were a few bequests to charities and the church, but nothing worth killing for. I mean I don't think the Baptist Church is so desperate for a new kitchen they'd have sent one of their deacons over there to do her in, even if they knew they were in the will."

"Probably not," Martha said, "but that church kitchen could really use a new stove, one of those restaurant kinds, and—"

"That was a joke, Martha," Ellen pointed out.

"Oh."

"So if we think she had enough property to kill for, it looks like Leland is it."

"And if we don't think so?" Martha looked smug.

"Leland still looks like it. Charlene and Armond's boy Ronnie—the one who can't get it in his head that one of these days he's going to get in deep doo-doo for betting money he doesn't have and has made some acquaintances he'd be better off unacquainted with—Ronnie told Armond that Althea's boy had run up some big gambling debts and was having trouble paying them off."

"Leland?" Stark incredulity met this announcement, and the name was pronounced with various shades of amazement on the part of Martha and Aunt Lulu. I, of course, held my tongue.

"Leland gambling?" Aunt Lulu asked.

"That's what Armond said Ronnie said," Ellen said.

"Althea told me Leland wanted money for the store," Martha reminded them. "He would have known better than to expect Althea to help him pay gambling debts, so if he had gambling debts he would have told her he needed it for the store."

"He needs it for the store, too, if you ask me," Ellen said. "Charlene's second husband's daughter Renee is a checker over there, and she said Leland's been talking about wanting to expand some so they can compete with the supermarkets."

"Leland ought to know he's got a captive market here. Nobody's going to drive clean to another town just so they can shop in a supermarket."

Melva Boatright does, I thought.

"Well, there's the Food Lion," Martha said.

"I'm just telling you what Charlene said Renee said," Ellen continued.

"Sounds like you've been doing a lot of grapevining, Ellen," Aunt Lulu said.

"What's the point in having a family like mine if you can't get some good out of 'em once in a while?" Ellen answered.

"We might as well have coffee and some of that cake while it's warm," Martha said. "Don't anybody say anything while I'm in the kitchen."

Obediently, perhaps thoughtfully, we sat quietly, watching Ellen lay out an intricate solitaire and move one card at a time, until Martha returned with a tray of coffee cups.

"Thank you," Ellen said. She took a sip of coffee and put a red jack on a black queen and studied the layout before she spoke. "And Little Whit's wife, the pharmacist, said there wasn't anything wrong with those pills."

"What pills?" I asked, in as mild and unthreatening a way as I could manage.

Martha stopped cold on her way back to the kitchen and I could almost see the wheels turning as she tried to think of an acceptable answer.

"Would that be some of Althea's pills?" I asked helpfully. I remembered Martha reaching for her phone when she went back to her car that day in the parking lot at Grinstead's Market. She must have reached for the various pill containers as well, and skimmed off a few before turning them over to Hen.

Martha nodded, speechless, for once. Aunt Lulu broke the moment of silence that followed this rare occurrence.

"So," Aunt Lulu said, "it wasn't the medicine."

"I've said all along somebody pushed her down," Martha said. "And if whoever did it was going to do that, they wouldn't have done anything to her medicine."

These women had so much faith in their connections that they couldn't, wouldn't, even bring themselves to trust the police toxicologist report on the presence or absence of un-expected drugs in Althea's system.

"But... Oh, oh, there's Jim L.," Martha said suddenly. "I wonder what he's doing home."

But it wasn't Jim L. Tootle whose steps Martha had heard on the porch, it was Ogeechee's Chief of Police, Henry Huckabee himself, who added himself to our party.

"Good morning, ladies," Hen said after Martha, wonder-ing aloud why Jim L. would knock instead of just coming on in, had opened the door.

"I appreciate your coming, Hen," Martha said. "I didn't think that other officer was taking this very seriously."

"What? Your car break-in? Yes, ma'am, Officer Sharpe is taking it seriously. He's working on his report this very minute. He'll be talking to you again about that. Could you spare me a cup of that coffee? It smells a lot better than that stuff down at the station house."

"Certainly. You just sit on down, and I'll bring it to you. You put anything in it?"

"No, ma'am."

"And you'll have some coffee cake, too." Martha didn't wait for an answer.

"You didn't just drop by for a cup of coffee, did you?" Lulu asked.

"Tell the truth, this is in the line of duty," Hen said, looking sorrowful. "Officer Sharpe, who is not just another pretty face no matter what you ladies might think, reported to me that it looked like my mother and her friends seemed to be conniving at something. No offense, Officer Roundtree, but I thought you might need some backup here."

"No offense taken," I lied, but he knew I was lying, so it might not count as a real lie in the list of my sins.

Martha Tootle, the main conniver, sailed into the room with plates of coffee cake in time to hear what he'd said. She looked guiltily at Aunt Lulu. Aunt Lulu, more experienced, kept her gaze steadily on her son. Ellen Chandler smiled at me.

"Did he say what we are alleged to be conniving at?" Aunt Lulu asked. "At what we are alleged to be conniving?" she amended.

"No, ma'am, but he reported that he had the distinct impression that Miz Tootle had remembered something that had been taken from her car. Something she didn't want to mention to him. Now, Miz Tootle, if you're smuggling drugs or bootleg whiskey, I can see why you wouldn't want to tell him about it, and I tried to picture you in one of those professions, but couldn't quite bring it into focus. Then I recollected your stopping by the station house the other day to drop off some things, and I asked myself if those things might have figured in this crime, if somebody knew you had them and thought you still had them."

"What did you answer yourself?" I asked in petty revenge that revealed I had taken offense.

He didn't bat an eye. "I said to myself, 'Self, you ought to go have a talk with those ladies. Women. Because if there is a connection, they might have put themselves in danger with their meddling. Anybody willing to bash in a car window might be willing to…' Well, I don't want to scare you, but you can see my point. Now, is there anything any of you would like to tell me?" He took his time looking from one of the women to the other. They all shook their heads in a ladylike way.

Ellen studied a cuticle; Martha touched a napkin to her lips. Only Aunt Lulu, from years of practice, could stand up to Hen's gaze.

Silence.

"We appreciate your concern, son," Aunt Lulu said, finally.

"It's more than just filial and professional concern," Hen said, standing up so he could tower over the women and hope to intimidate them, since leaning on his knees and puffing up hadn't done it. "If it's police business, then it's police business."

"I have a suggestion," Ellen said.

"Yes, ma'am?" Hen was polite.

"If you think Martha's in danger, why not take her into protective custody?"

I was impressed by Hen's self-control. He didn't gape, goggle, or grin. Possibly, he thought Ellen was teasing Martha. Even if she was, I liked the suggestion so much I didn't want to risk anybody seeing any logical flaws in the plan. "You could take her in, Hen, and I'll follow you. Lights and sirens. Big show. And we'll let everybody know that she's cooperating fully with the police."

I shouldn't have been surprised that Martha loved the idea, too. "Handcuffs?"

Hen allowed himself a grin, then. "Why not? It's on the

silly side, but why not? The bigger the fuss, the more likely for everybody to talk about it. It'll be all over town in fifteen minutes that the police have whatever it is you had, and if there is somebody who's going around killing off mature ladies, he or she will know you don't have it. You'll be safe. Well, Miz Tootle, it sounds like you're agreeable. You ready to go right now?"

"Just let me leave a note for Jim L.," Martha said. "Do I need a change of clothes?"

Hen and I exchanged glances. He sighed. "No, ma'am. We won't keep you overnight. This isn't really protective custody, you understand, just a big show of you cooperating with the police."

Martha looked disappointed.

"Spending the night in jail isn't as much fun as it sounds like," Hen assured her.

"So all I get is a ride in a police car? Big deal."

"You also get to make as big a story out of it as you want to, and it might keep you safe," Hen countered. "Take it or leave it."

"Oh, all right."

He turned to the other women. "Now, with all the respect due your gender and your mature years, I have a suggestion."

No doubt expecting that his suggestion would be for them to butt out, they didn't look eager. He surprised all of us. "You are uniquely qualified to spread the word, since *The Beacon* won't be out for another few days, that Martha Tootle did have some possible evidence in a murder case, but that she has turned everything over to the police."

Aunt Lulu and Ellen nodded.

"We can do that," Ellen said. "Don't worry, Martha."

Martha bit her lip.

"I'll drive her," I offered.

FOURTEEN

MARTHA TOOTLE'S PROTECTIVE custody was fun as long as it lasted, but it was short-lived, and we soon settled back down to routine. A three-car pile-up west of town that involved a car fire and a brawl at a juke joint that involved a couple of hunting knives took my attention so thoroughly that you could have knocked me over with a corn tassel a few days later when I looked up from what I was doing and saw the dapper Buck Carlton standing right there in the station house.

"Well, good morning," I said, unable to keep the surprise out of my voice.

"Good morning, Officer Roundtree."

"What brings you to Ogeechee?" I asked.

"I'd appreciate it if I could talk with Chief Huckabee," he said. "I've been investigating the death of Althea Boatright, as y'all asked me to, and I think it's time to report what I've learned."

"Oh? You've found out something?"

"Yes, I have."

"You don't want to tell me?" I prompted.

"I'd rather talk to him, if you don't mind."

"Let me just go see if he's in the middle of something," I offered.

If Hen was in the middle of a donut, I might give him a chance to finish, but that was about the only thing I could imagine that would be too important to be interrupted for what would unquestionably be an entertaining interview. In fact, he was in the middle of a telephone conversation. He looked up when he saw me.

"One of Aunt Lulu's special friends wants to talk to you," I whispered. I'd been on the fence about Buck Carlton, not sure whether I liked him or not, but that "if you don't mind" had tipped the scales against him, even if he hadn't said it with a lot of attitude. It was "if you don't mind" in a quiet, paternalistic way that assumed he ought to talk to a man.

"Lord, not Martha Tootle again, I hope." Hen grimaced.

"No. A special friend." I tried to leer, which got his attention. "Mr. Buck Carlton of Jesup. He says he has important information about the Althea Boatright murder." Okay, he hadn't actually said "important information" and I was stretching a bit.

"Hold on, Trudy," Hen said, and turned back to the telephone. "Mama, I need to cut this short. Seems like I've got one of your little friends down here wanting to help me with the Althea Boatright case, and I think I'd better go listen to him."

My conclusion, that Hen was a little miffed over Aunt Lulu's interference in the case and was out to make her suffer a little, was strengthened by his next words. (Yes, I lingered outside his door.)

"No, he has not run afoul of the law. What kind of company do you keep, anyway? He's being a good citizen, come in to assist us and didn't even hold out for a ride in a police car." Hen's voice sank to a raspy pseudo-confidential whisper. "What has me worried is he told Trudy he wanted to talk to me man-to-man."

I wished I could hear Aunt Lulu's end of it, but maybe I didn't need to, to follow the gist.

"It's the man-to-man business that has me worried, Mama, especially since he mentioned he's a good friend of yours. Is he one of those old-school, by-the-book types? He ain't about to ask for your hand, is he?"

Pause.

"Who? Oh, excuse me. I figgered you'd know who I was talking about. You got so many admirers you can't keep track? Describe him? I ain't seen him yet. Trudy?"

So he'd known I was listening.

"What's he look like?"

He relayed my description, word for word: "A good-looking gentleman with a beautiful moustache. Sound like anybody you know?"

Pause.

"Lord have mercy on my eternal soul, the very man! She recognized him!" If I hadn't known Hen better, I'd have believed the amazement in his voice. Of course, Aunt Lulu wasn't fooled, either. "I always said I got my brains from your side of the family," he went on. "But, Mama, I've got to know how long you been carrying on with this man? You want me to give my blessing or go find a shotgun?"

Pause.

"No, ma'am, he can't hear me, but I'd better go see what he has to tell me… No… No… No."

I could hear Aunt Lulu's squawk clear out in the hall.

"I can take care of this, Mama. It's my job. You better keep after that kitchen tile. I don't think it ought to wait a bit longer. I've been meaning to talk to you about it. You can't just leave your scrub bucket right there in the middle of the floor. What would the neighbors think?… No… No… No."

He hung up. "Let's talk to him in the conference room," he said to me. "I'll be right there."

I showed Mr. Carlton to the conference room, offered him something to drink, and went to get us some coffee. By the time I returned to the conference room with a cup for Buck Carlton, Hen had joined him. In spite of what Hen had said on the phone, they didn't seem to be discussing a prenuptial agreement or a dowry, but the weather. We got down to business, but had barely established Mr. Carlton's credentials as an old friend of Althea's, when Aunt Lulu appeared at the door, having made pretty good time for someone who would have had to change out of her housecleaning clothes—things she wouldn't wear out of the house if it had been on fire, things that didn't even match her current hair, things that wouldn't be further degraded by caustic cleansers of the kind Aunt Lulu didn't want to inflict on Elfreda. Buck came to his feet and bowed over his walking stick, today a sturdy one that looked like twisted roots. Hen, a little slower, came to his feet, too. "Mama. What a surprise."

She merely smiled.

Hen ushered his mother to the chair he'd been occupying, the throne-like chair the mayor occupies at council meetings. He sat beside Buck on the front pew, which the city bought a few years back when a church renovation made them surplus and the congregation gave the mayor a good deal on what he thought might lend a properly reverent atmosphere to council meetings. Even if the pews didn't achieve that, they are nicer than the folding chairs the city used before. I hovered near the door, prepared to mutiny if Hen tried to send me away on some other chore, but unwilling to intrude just yet.

For all the world like a woman who thought she'd been invited to the party, Aunt Lulu smiled at Buck. Either she'd decided she liked him, or she was teasing Hen. "That was certainly quick work. I can hardly wait to hear what you found out."

"Speed and efficiency are my hallmarks, dear lady," Buck said, smiling back, "but I didn't expect the pleasure of your company."

Hen was unable to stifle a grimace.

Buck continued, "I'd hoped to put it all to rest and spare you the trouble."

"Nonsense. Althea was my friend, after all. Tell me what you found out," Aunt Lulu ordered.

"I found out why Althea ran over Charlie," Buck Carlton said with uncharacteristic simplicity. He didn't even smile suggestively at Aunt Lulu when he said it.

"That's what these two assigned you?" Hen asked. He'd been leaning back comfortably, arms folded, conveying mild skepticism and marginal interest. Now he leaned forward and fixed his iceberg-blue gaze on Buck Carlton. I took his reference to me to mean he knew I was there and intended to stay, so I took a side pew near the front where I could see everybody and not miss anything.

"My sister, Irene, and me, yes."

"Well, let us hear it, then."

Buck Carlton turned to Aunt Lulu. "Dear lady, I want you to know I didn't let on I was investigating a murder."

"Good." Hen and Aunt Lulu spoke together. I was beginning to wonder if Buck Carlton had so many romantic entanglements that, afraid of calling the wrong name in moments of high emotion, he called all his women friends by some nickname. Bad as "dear lady" was, it could have been worse. At least, it wasn't "sugarplum" or "snookums." Maybe he just didn't trust his aging memory with anybody's name. I'd have to pay more attention.

Buck Carlton studied the twisted wood of his cane while he cycled his thoughts back to the beginning, then looked up at Hen. "Your dear mother asked me to see what I could find out about Charlie and Althea. When I was talking this over with Irene, she reminded me Lewis Long and Charlie used to pal around together back in school, and it seemed like if Charlie had told anybody his business, it would have been Lewis. So I went and had a talk with him. I told Lewis that Irene and I had been reminiscing, which is true as far as it goes, and Charlie's name came up, and Althea's. That's all it took to get old Lewis going. Always was a talker and now he doesn't get out like he used to, he'll talk your arm off and your leg too if you'll sit still for it."

"I know people like that," Hen said.

Mr. Carlton continued, "He said at that reunion a few years back, the one Charlie came to, Charlie told him he had talked to Althea about something he referred to as unfinished business. None of us is as young as we used to be, except perhaps your lovely mother." Buck paused to smile at Lulu. "And Charlie said something about how he wanted to get his affairs in order and do right by his heirs. You have to remember, now, that reunion was three or four years back, so we can't expect Lewis to remember exactly, since he probably was half-cockeyed at the time on some of that blackberry wine Roberta Hines-that-was-Wooten brought to the peanut boilin'. She'd left it buried too long and it would have taken the varnish off a doorknob. Whoo-ee!"

"Charlie Sykes's unfinished business," Aunt Lulu said.

"The reason Miz Boatright ran over Mr. Sykes," Hen said.

"Yes," Buck continued. "Lewis said Charlie showed him a marriage license with his name on it, and Althea's. Lewis was all set to josh him about that, but Charlie was serious. Said he wanted to put things right with his child bride, just like in a fairy tale, although his bride didn't wait for him like they do in the stories." He tapped the floor sharply with his cane and swung the tip up to point in Hen's direction. "Now, what we have here is a drunk remembering what another drunk told him several years back, for whatever that's worth. Took me by surprise, I'll tell you. We all knew Charlie and Althea had been a hot item, but nobody knew things had gone that far, not even Irene."

Hen snorted.

"You don't have any call to act like that, Hen," Aunt Lulu said. "If Althea and that man she ran over were married, then it makes it look a lot less like an accident, doesn't it? I think that would make it what you police call a vehicular homicide."

"Mama, I keep telling you not to read the police manuals."

"Don't sass me, young man. Am I right?"

Hen sighed. "All right. Yes, you're right. And just in case you were thinkin' of sayin' anything about why we didn't haul your Althea Jordan Grinstead Boatright—maybe Althea Jordan Sykes Grinstead Boatright, if what Mr. Carlton is telling us is the truth—off to jail for committing vehicular homicide, I'll remind you that if we'd known she'd been married to this man—if that's the truth, and getting a license doesn't prove they actually got married—we would certainly have taken a close look at the circumstances of the accident. At the time, she never let on she knew him, though, so we had no reason to think there was anything more than met the eye, and what met the eye was a doddery old woman with bad eyesight, bad reflexes, and a bad dog running into a stranger."

"So now we know," Aunt Lulu said, "and Althea's not saying she knew him makes it suspicious, doesn't it?"

Buck Carlton tapped the floor with his cane again. "There's another thing."

Hen settled back in his pew and closed his eyes in a good imitation of an attentive listener. "Ready when you are," he prompted.

Buck Carlton turned to Aunt Lulu. "Do you know when Leland Grinstead was born?"

"No, not exactly," Lulu said.

"Hold on a minute, here," Hen said. He gave up trying to sit still and listen, and began pacing up and down in front of the pews like an evangelist at altar call. He turned on them, making me glad I'd chosen a seat off by myself. "I'm having one gold-plated heck of a time keeping up. What does Leland Grinstead's birthday have to do with the price of squash?"

Buck Carlton explained. "Isn't it possible that Charlie Sykes could be Leland Grinstead's father instead of whatever-his-name Grinstead? That could be how Charlie would have been able to cause trouble for Althea. Do the police have ways to find out that kind of thing? What about that DNA testing we hear about?"

Hen had a few questions of his own. "Was this your idea, Mama? Y'all sure covered a lot of ground over that lunch you had. And I have to tell you, I'm disappointed in what a low mind you have. Now you're impugning Leland Grinstead's birth?"

"No, not impugn, not if Althea and Charlie were married." She waved the notion away. "You have to admit that if Charlie Sykes had been married to Althea and was threatening to tell people, she might not have liked it."

"Maybe not, but being married more than once isn't a crime. Even good church-going people are doin' it these days. Why would she need to kill him?" Hen asked.

Aunt Lulu changed her ground. "Well, maybe she wasn't ashamed of it. Maybe that wasn't it. Maybe he'd made a lot of money out in Texas or somewhere and was going to leave his money to Althea and she knew it, and didn't want to wait for it."

"I didn't like her much," Hen said, in understatement, "but it sounds like you had a worse opinion of her than I did, if you think she'd have killed a man for either of those reasons."

"We never really know people, Hen," Aunt Lulu said.

Buck pointed his cane at Hen again. "What if Althea and Charlie got married but never did get divorced—say she thought he was dead or something, or didn't know how to get in touch with him to divorce him—and she didn't want him messing up her reputation here in Ogeechee by turning up and claiming she was a bigamist."

"Or what if Althea didn't want him to get any of her money?" Aunt Lulu said. "We've been acting like he was the one with money, but she had plenty. Maybe she killed him to make sure her money from Bert Grinstead and Rowland Boatright couldn't be in dispute. Could the Boatrights contest what Rowland left her if she was married to somebody else when she married Rowland?"

"Do the police have ways of checking on that?" Buck Carlton asked.

"I will pause here to point out to you that even if Charlie Sykes was her intentional victim, even if we did mess up on that and let her get away with murder, she's past being brought to justice under any statutes, ordinances, or regulations enforceable by the City of Ogeechee, the State of Georgia, the United States of America, the United Nations, or anybody else short of God Almighty."

"Well, yes," Aunt Lulu allowed.

"And even if we could explain why she would be guilty of such a heinous act, which we do not need to do, for the reasons I just laid out, I don't see how that bears on her own death. You think this Charlie Sykes came back from beyond the great divide to get even with her? After all this time?"

Aunt Lulu turned toward Buck Carlton. "I want you to know I did the best I could to raise him to be more respectful to his elders."

That brought Hen to a stop. He crossed his arms and bowed his head in defeat.

Buck Carlton nodded. "What I think is those Sykeses, Charlie's brother's family, found out about the marriage and killed Althea because they were afraid she'd get his money."

Hen took three deep breaths before responding to that. "That's an interesting theory, Mr. Carlton. Do you have any facts, any evidence at all, to base it on?"

"Well, I don't know for sure."

"I didn't think so," Hen said. "Now, that might make some sort of wild-eyed sense if Althea had died, or, all right, been killed, soon after Mr. Sykes came back to Georgia and got in touch with her, but that's not what happened. She didn't die until after he did."

"And if Althea had inherited money from Mr. Sykes, how would killing her now do them any good?" Aunt Lulu asked. "That's weak." She sounded apologetic, like she didn't want to hurt Mr. Carlton's feelings.

"Maybe it was revenge," Mr. Carlton said. "If you're out for revenge, it doesn't necessarily do you good, it just makes you feel better. Maybe it was revenge because she left them poor, or maybe just for killing their uncle or brother or whatever he was to them. I don't want to tell you your business, Chief Huckabee, but I'd investigate the Sykeses, if I was investigating and I was the police. Maybe the Sykeses thought if Althea thought she was entitled to Charlie's money, she could contest his will and take it away from them."

"If you're obsessed with motive, you have to concentrate on what motive Althea would have had for killing him. Everything hinges on that." Aunt Lulu seemed sure of herself. "I don't think it could have been money. She had plenty of that. But it's ridiculous to think it could have really been an accident, knowing what we know."

"Ridiculous," Hen repeated. He turned to Buck Carlton. "Now, Mr. Carlton, I don't know you very well, so I'm giving you the benefit of the doubt here. I do know my mama, and I'm sure she's not slow-witted. So I think you'll understand me when I say that from where I sit—and where I sit—where I usually sit," he amended, with a nod toward Aunt Lulu in the throne, "is the big chief's chair at the Ogeechee Police Department—it looks like if she was murdered it had to be an inside job, not one of your Sykeses; one of the Grinsteads since, by accounts of witnesses on the scene, the place was locked up tight as two ticks in carnal embrace.

"And since I don't think either one of the Boatrights is particularly slow-witted either, if one of them had knocked her down, whichever one of them it was would have had the sense to unlock the door and mess the place up a little bit. It would have been amateurish, which makes sense because they are amateurs, but it wouldn't have been stupid. The smart thing would have been to wait till it was too late to do Althea any good and then call up in hysterics and tell Dawn that their dear mother—or mother-in-law—had slipped and hit her head. But they didn't do that. And nobody else coulda been in there and got out. Therefore, in spite of one or two unexplained details, I have to conclude it was an accident. Is that clear?"

"It was murder," Aunt Lulu said.

"Maybe they aren't very smart," Buck suggested.

Hen's sigh came from somewhere near his toenails. "Mr. Carlton, I'm giving you the benefit of the doubt; you do the same for the Grinsteads. Mama, give it up. Go back to your housecleaning or bridge playing or whatever, but give this up."

Hen showed his exasperation by abandoning his elders and turning to somebody he could order around. Me. "Trudy, you better start taking notes on the things they want the police to check on. What was it? DNA testing? Leland Grinstead's birthday? Oh, yes, who was really Leland Grinstead's daddy? Matter of fact, I kind of like that one. That kind of question mighta done fatal damage to Althea's status down at the Baptist Church, so it could be a motive, if she had a son she'd been passing off as Bert's. Mighta come as a nasty surprise to Bert, not to mention Leland, and if I knew Althea, she'da been a lot more worried about Leland than Bert."

A quiet tap at the door announced the presence of Jerome

Sharpe. "Could I see you a minute, Chief?" he rumbled. "There's something here you might want to know about."

"Certainly." Hen sounded relieved to have an excuse to leave. "Now while I'm gone, I want the two of you to take a little time out and think about what I've been telling you. I hope you can find it in your hearts to mend your meddlin' ways."

"You must be proud of him," Buck said to Aunt Lulu as soon as her son was out of the room. "I wonder sometimes what I missed, not having a son."

"Thank you. You aren't seeing him at his best, but I think he is a fine man," Aunt Lulu said. I felt like gagging, but stifled it, wanting to stay and listen to them instead of getting to work on the bogus assignment Hen had just given me.

Aunt Lulu continued. "And he's usually good at his job. I don't know why he's being so narrow-minded and obstinate about this."

"I wouldn't worry about it," Buck said. "If we're right, he'll come around. And if he's right, we'll come around, won't we?"

They shared a smile of hypocritical agreement, then Buck Carlton asked, "Is that Grinstead's Market just across the street? Where Leland Grinstead works?"

"Yes, it is."

He seemed to ponder. "Would he be working today, you think?"

"He works just about every day. So does his boy, Jordan."

"Jordan. That would be Althea's grandson. That was Althea's maiden name, Jordan."

"Yes, I know. Shh! Hush!"

"Wha—?"

"Listen!" Aunt Lulu insisted in a whisper, finger to her lips, moving closer to the door. Buck Carlton looked astonished, perhaps at her unladylike manners, but he did hush.

From the corridor on the other side of the closed door, we

could hear Hen's voice and the deeper rumble of Jerome Sharpe, subdued, but not inaudible, especially if one were to amble closer to the door, which Aunt Lulu, and then Buck Carlton, did.

"There's no doubt about it, Chief," Jerome said.

"Son, one of the best things I ever did was recognize you've got brains as well as brawn. Now, tell me what you think it means."

"Well, sir, I got the fingerprints ID'd, but I haven't got around to making any sense out of it."

"It'll take some explainin'. You want to go haul him in and talk to him about it?"

"Not especially, nossir. Something tells me he'd rather talk to you about it. I take care of the women who make cookies. You're the chief. What they taught me at the academy, that means you take care of prominent citizens."

Hen laughed. "And the headaches that go with it. Yessir, you've got brains all right. But don't you think it'll be interesting to see what Mr. Prominent Citizen Leland Grinstead has to say to explain his fingerprints on that car?"

"Yessir," Jerome said. "I surely do."

FIFTEEN

THE DOOR OPENED suddenly into the conference room from the hall, nearly hitting the eavesdroppers who'd been indiscreet enough to stay near the door. I tried not to look smug.

Hen and Jerome weren't well into the room before Aunt Lulu, not in the least apologetic, spoke. "You've identified the fingerprints on Martha's car!"

Hen didn't answer until he and Jerome had seated themselves at the conference table, Hen reclaiming the throne. Comfortably invisible there in my pew, I had the unkind thought that Hen had made Jerome come with him for moral support. "Yes, ma'am," he finally answered. "Officer Sharpe has identified the fingerprints. Knew I'd get my money's worth out of him."

"And you're going to tell us all about it?" his mother asked, advancing on him.

"The police don't normally tell civilians all about their investigations, Mama. With the reading you do, you ought to know that sometimes that tips off the perpetrators. Your books probably call them the perps."

"They do not." Aunt Lulu bristled visibly. "Not the technical ones, anyway. Just some of the fiction. But don't change the subject."

"You can't blame me for trying," Hen said.

"Oh, yes, I can. I can blame you for trying to keep us out of an investigation we started when you didn't even think there was anything to investigate."

"Well, we do have a car break-in to investigate, and we're capable of taking it from here," Hen said. "Thank you both for your help." Both Aunt Lulu and Buck Carlton ignored the dismissal.

"A car break-in? I hadn't heard about that. Something to do with Althea's death?" Mr. Carlton asked.

Since Hen didn't repeat the lecture about civilians he'd just given Aunt Lulu, but looked at his mother, I realized he was interested in hearing how she'd explain it.

"Somebody broke into a car that had evidence of her murder in it, but they didn't get anything because it had already been turned over to the police."

"What kind of evidence?" Buck Carlton asked.

Aunt Lulu seemed about to tell him, but Hen harrumphed and she thought better of it. Facing Hen and Jerome, Aunt Lulu looked from one impassive face to the other, then turned to the frankly expectant face of Buck Carlton. She darted a smile in his direction and said sweetly to her son, "We couldn't help overhearing you in the hall. Would you like Mr. Carlton and me to interview Leland Grinstead for you?"

Hen curled his lip in disgust. Jerome stifled a grin. Buck did not stifle his grin. Hen breathed in deeply and exhaled hugely before he spoke.

"All right, Mama, I give up. I don't want you two and the rest of your motley band messin' around in this any more. I throw myself on your mercy, in the full understanding that any promises I extract from you would not be worth the breath it would take to speak them. So, lady and gentleman, I officially inform you that Officer Sharpe here has been sharp enough to discover one of those flukes that makes policin' such a constant wonder and amazement."

Aunt Lulu smiled at Buck, who smiled back.

"Go on," Aunt Lulu said.

"Thank you. Now, let's just hear the evidence and see what we can make of it. Officer Sharpe? Take your time and make clear to these two civilians what we have and what we do not have. I promise you they're gonna be hanging on your every word, but don't let it make you nervous. They are well-intentioned and, I believe, mostly harmless."

"Yessir," Officer Sharpe rumbled. He cleared his throat. "Mornin', Miz Huckabee, sir," he began. A glance from Hen brought him up straight in his chair. "I found a match for the fingerprints I took from Miz Tootle's car. It's a wonder I did, considering the prints wouldn't normally be in the AFIS—"

"They're civilians, son, in spite of how they act," Hen reminded him.

"Yessir. AFIS—Automated Fingerprint Identification System. It's how we identify fingerprints."

Hen, of course, amplified. "The system holds information from twenty million cards, and every one of those cards has ten fingerprints on it. Used to be it would take a room full of monkeys more time than anybody had to find a match, even if there was one, but now it's computerized it goes quicker'n scat. Used to be nothing but criminals in there. These days everybody from people who want to teach school to people who want to be foster parents get in. And who else, Officer Sharpe?"

"People who are applying for a liquor license, or renewing a liquor license, have to undergo a background check," Jerome Sharpe said.

"That's where our fluke comes in," Hen said. "Tell 'em, son."

"Yessir. Sir. Ma'am. Grinstead's Market wants to expand into wine and beer vending, and Mr. Leland Grinstead's fingerprints are temporarily on file up there in Hotlanta—excuse me, Atlanta—so when I sent the prints in from Miz Tootle's car, there was a match."

"I do declare," Aunt Lulu said, just as though she hadn't

already heard the conversation in the hall. She and Buck Carlton exchanged a look. "Leland Grinstead."

"Hold on, now," Hen said. "Under the system we have in this country, Mama, we do not automatically send a posse out to lynch Mr. Grinstead. We give him a chance to explain how his fingerprints got on that car."

"Well, it's obvious, isn't it?" Aunt Lulu asked.

"Not to the impartial eye of the law," Hen informed her. "Mr. Grinstead runs a grocery store. Just for instance, now, don't you think it's possible he helped Miz Tootle put some groceries in her car?"

"No, I do not think that is possible. Leland Grinstead? If she needed help, he'd send one of his clerks to do it."

"Maybe he leaned against the car in admiration while Miz Tootle or Mr. Tootle was braggin' on the car. They've been doing a lot of that, I hear."

"I see your point," Lulu said. "It's obvious to me his fingerprints on Martha's car have something to do with Althea's death, but we do need to give him a chance to try to explain."

Hen sputtered. "*We,* if I understand who you mean by that word, do not need to hear how he'd explain it. We, the police, will talk to him about it. And, no, I don't think it's obvious that the presence of his fingerprints on the car, even if he cracks under police interrogation and admits he broke into the car, means he had anything to do with Althea's death. Maybe you know something I don't?"

"Oh, I'm sure I do, son," she said.

"About this case?" He ended on an interrogatory note and looked hopeful.

Aunt Lulu smiled at him. "Maybe not about that. But this proves we were right, doesn't it? Leland knew she had the evidence. Hen, you and Officer Sharpe and your fluke have solved a crime you didn't even believe in." She turned to Buck Carlton. "See there? I told you he was good!"

"I appreciate your testimonial, Mama, but you're getting ahead of things. I am going to ask Officer Sharpe to amble over to the store and invite Mr. Grinstead to drop in over here for a chat. He oughta be back from lunch by now. We'll ask him to do some explaining about his fingerprints on the car. He may be able to do that. And, with your permission, even if he did break into the car, we'll think about it some more before we accuse him of murdering his mother. That's two different crimes."

"You don't have to be snippy," Lulu said.

Hen grinned at her. "I know I don't have to, Mama. Fact is, I do it because I enjoy it. Now, Officer Sharpe, if you don't mind—"

"Yessir." Officer Sharpe came smartly to his feet, nodded a polite goodbye, and left the room.

"I never really believed Martha about somebody murdering Althea, either, Henry," Aunt Lulu said into the silence that prevailed after Jerome Sharpe left.

"May I then ask why you kept after it?" Hen asked.

"Well, it was possible, wasn't it? And you wouldn't want a murder to go undetected, would you?"

"No ma'am, not personally or professionally. Now, I'd take it mighty kindly if you civilians would run along, go have lunch or something, and let your police force get on with investigating things."

"I know you have all sorts of things to tend to. You go right ahead. Don't worry about us. We'll be fine." But Aunt Lulu did not match these words with any kind of activity that suggested she was getting ready to go out to lunch or anywhere else.

"Keep an eye on 'em, Trudy," Hen ordered as he left the room. "Get rid of them," he muttered as he stalked past me.

Silence spread, grew, crept into the corners under the rearmost pew, and began lapping at my shoes. I got the distinct feeling from the way Buck Carlton glared at me that he'd have liked me to go tend to some other duties, along with Hen, leaving him a clear field for amorous advances on Aunt Lulu, so I said, "Nice of you to come all the way to Ogeechee to give us this information, instead of just calling."

He stroked his moustache. "I started to call, and then I realized that if I came here, I might have the good fortune to see this dear lady again. I didn't expect to see her here at the police station, though. That was just my good luck."

"It worked out very well, then," I said.

The silence began to spread again. "Today's senior day at the new Italian restaurant," I pointed out. "Y'all really ought to go have some lunch. No telling how long it will be before anything interesting happens around here."

My companions looked at each other. I'd have sworn the idea of spaghetti with meatballs and garlic bread appealed to Buck Carlton, but Aunt Lulu said, "It's still early for lunch, and if we leave now, Hen won't let us back in."

"If you don't leave, he might lock you both up for interfering with an investigation," I suggested feebly.

Aunt Lulu glanced at Buck, but for once he wasn't gazing at the dear lady but was gazing out the window.

Hen bustled back into the room. "Y'all still here? It's senior day at Lotsa Pasta."

"I tried that," I told him.

"You can leave the problem, the case, the investigation, whatever you want to call it, in the capable hands of the police, now, Mama," Hen said.

"Did I mention that one of Ellen's relatives found out about some gambling debts of Leland's?" she asked. "That could be a motive for wanting Althea's money."

"No, ma'am, you hadn't gotten around to mentioning that. Musta slipped your mind," Hen said with heavy irony.

"I didn't want to mention it if it was just gossip, but if you've got evidence against him, then this would help explain it."

"I know how you hate gossip," he said. She didn't respond so he tried another tack. "I don't know what your sources are, but you might want to check and make sure they were talking about Leland. I never heard of him gambling and, while my network might not be as good as yours, I do hear things from the street."

"Who could they possibly confuse with Leland?"

"Depends," Hen said.

"On what?" Lulu asked.

Buck had been pacing back and forth in front of the window facing Grinstead's Market. "Here they come," he announced.

Hen and Lulu joined him at the window and watched the placid Jerome Sharpe and the agitated Leland Grinstead walking across the parking lot toward the police station. Buck seemed intent on their every move, his body twitching in sympathy with Leland's gestures. When Leland waved a hand to make a point, Buck waved a hand, and seemed fascinated by the movement. When Leland balled up his fist and frowned in the direction of the police station, Buck reflected that balled-up fist and that frown. Jerome Sharpe's stolid, unemotional demeanor obviously didn't inspire him the way Leland Grinstead's agitation did.

When the two men passed out of sight around the side of the building, Buck drew himself up tall and spoke.

"I can't let you put that poor man through your police interrogation, Chief Huckabee. I might as well tell you now and save everybody a lot of trouble. I killed Althea."

SIXTEEN

"I'LL SIT HERE quietly and just listen while y'all get this straightened out," Aunt Lulu offered.

Hen didn't quite laugh out loud at the idea. "No, ma'am. With all the respect due your years and our relationship, I have to tell you that I do not believe you are capable of doing that. This is gonna take a while. We will need to sit down and take statements, and I don't see any way at all you can be of assistance. You will offer opinions and advice. You will be in the way. You—"

"But, I—"

"See there? Trudy?"

"Come on, Aunt Lulu."

"Buck?" Whether she was hoping for enlightenment or deliverance, Aunt Lulu's hopes were in vain.

"I'm sorry, Lulu," he said.

"But—" Aunt Lulu looked back over her shoulder at Buck Carlton as I took her by the arm and guided her toward the door. Then, "What are you telling me you're sorry about? If you killed Althea, apologizing to me won't do any good. You can't possibly—"

Hen interrupted. "The sooner you let us get to interrogating Mr. Carlton and Mr. Grinstead, the sooner we'll know what's possible and what isn't. Trudy, you come back just as soon as you see her drive away, but not a minute sooner."

"Yassuh, boss," I said, not daring to look at Jerome. "Come

on, Aunt Lulu. I don't want to miss this, either. The sooner I
see you drive away, the sooner I can get back."

"Oh, all right," Aunt Lulu said.

I released my hold, poised to grab her again if necessary.
"Thank you."

"But I want you to call me as soon as you can."

"Yes, ma'am."

BUT I DIDN'T CALL Aunt Lulu as soon as I could. Discretion
being the better part of valor, I reasoned that if I waited long
enough, Hen would talk to her before I did, and I'd be spared.
So when I was free, instead of calling her, I called Phil and
suggested he might want to take me away from it all—as far
as the movie complex in Vidalia.

As it turned out, when we got to the movie theater,
nothing they had to offer looked interesting enough to get
us out of the car. We sat in the parking lot, and I continued
to sketch the high spots of my day for Phil. From long
practice, we both know he won't abuse my confidences by
scooping the opposition and breaking the story prematurely.
For one thing, there's no opposition to scoop, and for
another, even if he was willing to antagonize me, and I like
to think he wouldn't be, he might think twice about getting
on the wrong side of Hen.

As is my habit, I hit what I considered the high spots of
the story, and left it to Phil to fill in any details that interested
him by practicing his interviewing technique. I leaned against
the door and put my feet in his lap for him to massage while
he quizzed me. "Did Mr. Carlton say why he killed her?"

"Mm, that feels good! He says he did it out of long-
standing frustration, which turned to hatred because she didn't
return his teenaged passion."

"Ah! Sex-Starved Senior Citizen Stalks…" He stopped

massaging my feet in order to use his hands to sketch the headline in the air in front of my eyes.

"Not funny," I said, kicking him gently to remind him of where his duty lay.

"Probably not," he agreed. "He didn't strike me as the kind of person who'd feel passion for any particular rose in the garden of his life deeply enough to hold on to it for all that time. So, probably not sex-starved. How about 'Jaunty Jesup Gentleman Jerks... Jinxes... Joins'...help me, Trudy."

I kicked him again, still gently. "How about Cane Killer Confesses?"

"Not bad," he said, getting back to work. "You could write headlines for me in your spare time."

"It's the teamwork that does it," I said. "You inspire me."

"Ah, Trudy, that's probably the sweetest thing you ever said to me." He pressed a thumb deep between my toes. "Have I ever talked to you about reflexology?"

"Uh, no," I said.

"Somebody desperate to sell a book about it sent a copy to our book editor, for review, so I'm probably Ogeechee's resident expert on the subject."

"*The Beacon* doesn't review books."

"Ah, but the poor author doesn't know that, does she? Anyway, that's no reason for me not to read the book." Now he was working on the area behind my heel, below my ankle, so I wasn't inclined to argue with him. "Reflexology, as I am trying to explain, is very serious business."

"I'm sure it is," I said agreeably.

"The different parts of your feet correspond to other areas of your body. Serious practitioners believe that working on the proper part of the foot can cure ills elsewhere."

"No kidding?"

"It's to do with the chakras and the auras," Phil said. "But I won't go into all that now and risk boring you."

"As long as you keep up what you're doing, you're welcome to bore away," I said. "In a manner of speaking."

"I'd love to, but that's about all I remember. Back to business. Your business. Do you believe Mr. Carlton would track down and kill somebody who did him wrong half a century ago? It sounds far-fetched to me. Did you arrest him?"

"It was all we could do not to. He seemed set on spending the night in the pokey and supping on bread and water, but we reached a compromise. We took his statement, which was pretty unimaginative and lacking in any kind of detail that would lend credibility to his story, and Hen exercised the full extent of his considerable discretion in how he dealt with the situation. He didn't absolutely have to arrest Mr. Carlton, so he didn't."

"You let him go on his own recognizance? Confessed Killer Cruises? Is that what you usually do?" He began pinching and wiggling my toes, like "this little piggy" without the audio.

"Phil, you're as bad as Aunt Lulu, the way you bandy around police jargon. To answer your question, no, I never heard of turning a confessed killer loose, and that is not what we usually do, but there is nothing usual about this case, including Mr. Carlton's confession. Hen claimed he was sparing some judge having to read a lecture about the danger to the community and the risk of flight in the accused and sparing Mr. Carlton having to come up with bail. He did send him home with a flea in his ear, as the old saying goes, and the stern warning not to leave the state while we investigate further."

"So you are investigating further?"

"We're pretty much at a standstill on investigating, unless it would be poking around to see why Althea would have murdered Charlie Sykes, for whatever investigation that's worth. There is no doubt about somebody—Leland Grinstead—breaking into Martha Tootle's car, but there's nothing to investigate there, since we finally got Leland to admit he did that."

"Did he say why he did it?"

"As you might expect, he started out by denying he'd ever been within a country mile of Martha Tootle's car. Acted like he didn't even know what her car looked like. We all had a good friendly little laugh over that, and when we finally convinced him that fingerprints don't lie—or at least that there wasn't much chance they were lying in this case—he changed his story to how he must have brushed against the car in the church parking lot. When we pointed out how that didn't account for the prints inside the car he clammed up."

"He took the fifth and lawyered up?" I could tell Phil was teasing me, but I rose to the bait anyway. After all, he was massaging my feet. The man deserved something for his trouble.

"There you go again, sounding like Aunt Lulu and her police procedurals!" But I said it in a friendly way. After all, he was making me the beneficiary of his expertise in reflexology.

"Well, what?"

"In the face of our irrefutable proof and Officer Sharpe's inscrutable manner, Leland came up with another story. His final version, his confession, which we didn't like any better than we liked Mr. Carlton's, is that yes, he did break into the VW, and he will be glad to pay for the repair, and he hopes she won't press charges. When pressured to explain why, he admitted he probably wasn't thinking very clearly, but he thought Clarice had thrown out some important papers of Althea's when she went on her cleaning binge, and he knew Martha had taken some things."

"Why didn't he just ask Martha for them?"

"Says he was embarrassed."

"So embarrassed he resorted to crime? Really?"

I wiggled my toes to express that my skepticism matched his, and to get him back on task. Phil resumed his massage.

"You don't think there's any chance Buck Carlton is telling the truth?"

"It seems unlikely. I really don't know what to think. I don't like him much, but I don't know why, and it's beside the point anyway. Maybe I don't like the idea of a romance between him and Aunt Lulu. Maybe there's nothing more to his confession than a warped notion of how to stay in touch with her."

"Hmm. Dandy Confesses in Cry for Attention."

My kick that time was somewhat less gentle. "Oops," I said. "Sorry. Knee-jerk reaction."

He merely grinned at me. "Really, Trudy, maybe you are on the right track. He could be acting interested in Lulu because of her connection with Althea. Maybe he thinks she can keep him informed about the case." He was working his way up my foot now, pressing deeply into the ball of my foot. "So is it all over?"

"Ah. No, not quite. A certain amount of investigation is called for, even with a confessed killer on your hands. In the unlikely event we should happen to have to go to court with this, we wouldn't want to be unprepared. And if we decide to ignore his confession of murder, we need to be on firm ground."

"So you're going to check his story?"

"As much as we can. He was extremely vague on how he got into the Grinstead house, for instance, and his last words as he left the station house were to admonish us not to look any further for a culprit. We'll investigate. I'm not sure how, but we will. He's an odd man. I saw him standing outside Grinstead's Market after we cut him loose, just standing there."

"See there! That goes along with my theory. He's obviously interested in the Grinsteads, like he's interested in Lulu, because of the connection with Althea."

"Maybe you're right, Phil. Another odd thing, though. When he first started talking to us, he seemed to be trying to convince us that some of Charlie Sykes's family killed her. And then all of a sudden he changed his tune and came up with this confession."

"Do you think it's suspicious that he didn't take any convincing that she'd been killed?" Phil offered, thoughtfully manipulating my ankle. "If he did kill her, he wouldn't have trouble believing that. He'd go right ahead trying to frame somebody else. And you said he suggested revenge as a motive. That could apply to him as well as the Sykeses. Maybe he did kill her."

I sighed, partly out of frustration and partly because the massage felt so good. "We'll have to check on him. For all we really know about him, he might be capable of anything from making stew out of stray dogs to supplement his Social Security all the way up to running a white slave trade out of the Azalea Acres Nursing home."

"Police Probe Possible Perversions? The mind boggles," Phil said. He continued to work on my feet, concentrating so deeply that I began to wonder if I ought to find out more about reflexology before I let him practice it on me. No telling what he might be up to!

"Just how scientific is this?" I asked. "And should you be practicing without a license?"

"There was a good deal of anecdotal support for the benefits of reflexology—oh, and acupressure, I almost forgot that—in the book."

"Anything about putting women under your spell?"

"If there is, I didn't get to that part," he said. "But I'll keep reading. The most interesting thing so far is the woman who said her minister of reflexology cured her chronic constipation."

That did it. "Not that I don't admire a man who reads," I

said, putting my feet on the floor, "but I think it's time to go home. On the way, I'll call Aunt Lulu from the car. That way, if I don't like the way the conversation is going, I'll just pretend the signal is breaking up."

Phil started on the road back to Ogeechee while I punched in numbers. "Trudy, Aunt Lulu. Have you talked to Hen?" I asked hopefully, when she answered.

"Oh, yes. He told me he didn't arrest Mr. Carlton, and that he's not sure what to do with Leland."

"I'll bet it took him longer to tell it."

"I'm getting a fuller report now."

"From whom?"

"I'm entertaining a guest."

Something about the way she said it told me she wasn't talking about an average, run-of-the-mill guest like Hen or Martha. "A special guest of some kind?"

"Well, yes. Mr. Carlton came by after he left the police station, and we've been having a nice visit." She raised her voice for this last part, and I couldn't resist the thought that she did it to make sure he could hear her telling me.

"Are you worried about being alone with a confessed murderer?"

"Don't be silly, Trudy. Of course not. I had so much pent-up energy after I got home that I made a pound cake, and I have some fresh strawberries to go with it, if you'd like to come by."

"Let me ask Phil." I covered the phone. "Aunt Lulu says she'll give us some pound cake and strawberries if we want to go by her house."

"I think the price might be too high," Phil whispered. "I have a better idea."

"Buck Carlton's there," I said.

"Tell her we're on the way."

It wasn't more than fifteen minutes later when we got

there, but it was a long fifteen minutes. What if some of those lurid headlines of Phil's weren't so far off the mark? What if Buck Carlton was a killer so clever he'd offered a laughable confession to misdirect us?

"Don't worry," Phil said, either reading my mind or trying to reassure himself. "Even if he did kill Althea, that doesn't mean he'd have any reason to kill Lulu."

We were too late. When we got to Aunt Lulu's house, nobody was there. The kitchen door—the only way I ever enter her house—was locked. Her carport stood empty. Logic doesn't operate well in situations like that. No amount of telling myself that it was laughable to think of Buck Carlton as a killer, and so stupid that he'd harm the police chief's mother when he knew a police officer was on the way, kept me from wondering what had happened. I was on the point of alerting—alarming—Hen, when Aunt Lulu's car turned into the driveway.

"Oh, Trudy, Phil! I was worried I'd miss you and you wouldn't know what to think. Come on in. Buck had to leave right after you called, Trudy. He said he'd been enjoying himself so much he wasn't watching the time, and he had to get back to Jesup. So I drove him back down to Grinstead's Market."

"I beg your pardon?"

"For some reason, he left his car there and walked here."

"Maybe he wanted to enjoy a stroll through lovely downtown Ogeechee," Phil suggested.

"Or maybe he didn't want his car parked outside so anybody would know he was here, in case he was up to no good," I suggested.

"Really, Trudy!" Aunt Lulu said.

I'm afraid I blushed. "I didn't mean anything immoral. I mean romantic."

Aunt Lulu and Phil both looked at me as if I'd lost my

mind. "I mean, well, I'm afraid I meant maybe he meant to harm you. He's a confessed killer, after all."

"Oh, is that all? Well, he said he wanted to come and apologize for embarrassing me."

"He thought his murder confession would embarrass you?" Phil asked. "Trudy, I'm glad we didn't find a movie we liked. This is much better."

"He couldn't have apologized by telephone?" I asked.

"He's an old-fashioned gentleman, Trudy."

"So what did you do, if you don't mind my asking, besides listen to his apology and eat pound cake and strawberries?"

There was a gleam in her eye as she answered. "Oh, I showed him around the yard, and he wanted to talk about Althea. That's mostly what we have in common, after all."

As we followed Aunt Lulu inside for some pound cake and strawberries, I wondered why I had ever thought of going to a movie. With all the developing drama, comedy, and suspense right there in Ogeechee, we could give lessons to Hollywood.

SEVENTEEN

THE BEST TIME of day to do outdoor work in the summer in south Georgia is before the heat sets in. Luckily for me, I'm a morning person, and even after a day like the one I'd just put in, it was only about 7:30 when I went out to pick up the *Savannah Morning News* and found Digger Davis's Dodge Ram in my driveway.

Digger himself came into view from the far corner of the yard, pushing a wheelbarrow overflowing with yard debris—twigs, small branches, and pinecones.

"Mornin'," he called. A certain agitation of his head indicated he'd like to speak to me, so I waited by the truck till he arrived and lowered the barrow.

"Good mornin', Digger. Looks like you're just about through here. Thanks."

"Oh, yes, I like to get out with the early birds, even if I'm not after worms. Some people think it's a shame to waste the best part of the day on work, but when I got something to do, I like to get after it." He paused before adding, with a mischievous gleam in his eye, "Thought you'd want to know, too, about that Grinstead house."

"What about it?"

"Well, I got to thinking, after we talked about the trap I had Deloy put out. With you wondering what we mighta caught, got to worrying about it myself, so I figured you'd want me to look into it again."

"Ah…"

"No, you don't have to thank me." He said this with an expression that told me he knew very well I wasn't intending to thank him, so I waited while he took his time flexing and stretching his arms as if to work out the kinks brought on by pushing the wheelbarrow.

"What do you mean, you looked into it?" I prompted.

"Now, I don't want to give you the wrong idea. I didn't do it myself. Delegated. Got Deloy to do it. Have to show him who's boss every little once in a while, even if he is the up-and-coming heir-apparent to my exterior horticultural maintenance empire, and that was a good way to do it, so I sent him for another look. He mighta been lying, but what he told me is he could see a kind of a dragged path along under there, like it was made by a big snake or something, or somebody scootching along the way they'd have to, since there's not enough room to stand up under there."

"That's interesting," I said.

"Not that Deloy knows much about it," Digger went on. "He hated going in there to set the trap so bad he didn't want to have to go back to get it out, and he rigged a rope to it, so he could just pull it back out."

"So he doesn't—you don't—really know what's under there, or what might have been under there?"

"No tellin'," Digger admitted. "For all I know, it mighta been the booger man comin' for Miz Althea Boatright. Only thing I wonder is why it look 'im so long. Maybe even the booger man didn't want her."

He bent to the wheelbarrow after this pronouncement and began emptying it of his load of trash. I remembered my conversation with Elfreda. She had said something about whatever it was coming up through the floorboards to get Althea. Maybe there was something to that. Not the booger man, of course, but something. Somebody. Not a pleasant thought, even if whoever it was had been after something in the house, and not Althea.

LATER IN THE DAY, when I was having lunch with Hen and Phil at Kathy's café, I made the mistake of telling them about Digger and Deloy and Elfreda's comment, trying to make a funny story out of it at Deloy Davis's expense.

"Lots of people don't like being in dark, confined spaces," Phil said.

"'Specially if there might be creepy-crawlies under there with 'em," Hen added.

I think he winked at Phil when he said it, which would account for why Phil then said, "Of course, that kind of thing wouldn't bother you, would it, Trudy?"

Too quickly, I said, "Of course not."

"Don't see how we can call our investigation complete till we've made sure nothing came up through the floorboards for Althea," Hen said. "Even with a confession in our hands from Mr. Buck-and-Jive Carlton, we wouldn't want to go into court with a weak case."

And that explains why we paid a visit to the Grinsteads that afternoon, all three of us. Hen and I were there in the name of the law, to take a look under the house. For *me* to take a look under the house.

The way Hen put it to Leland, it was a somewhat delayed official response to Althea's earlier complaint that there had been trespassers under there, belated but reasonable.

Phil's angle was that there might be a story in it for the paper and it would be impinging on freedom of the press to try to keep him away. Not that Hen minded Phil's being there, you understand. I know there are some men who would want to spare their beloved any kind of discomfort or stress, who would climb up on a white charger—or down in the crawl space under a house—in order to prove their devotion. Likewise, there are women who see themselves as fragile flowers and are willing to give up all pretense of self-sufficiency and independence in order to let their men spare them the annoyances of having to deal with life, whether it's changing a light bulb or, for instance, going in the crawl space under a house. Phil is not one of those men and I am not one of those women. Usually I appreciate Phil's giving me credit for knowing my own mind and my own capabilities and treating me like an adult. So I didn't hold it against him, not much, that he seemed to enjoy the prospect of my undertaking this dirty job nearly as much as Hen did.

I changed out of my uniform into grungy work clothes, slathered on every kind of insect repellant I could lay my hands on, from Deep Woods Off! to Skin-So-Soft, and picked up a heavy flashlight. The space under the house might have been precisely calculated to be not quite high enough for me to go on all-fours. I could see why Deloy, to whom I owed an apology he would never receive, hadn't been eager to explore it. Seeing no alternative, I slithered through the opening in the brick latticework near the steps by the kitchen door and went to see what was to be seen. All that was to be seen, at first, was marks in the sandy soil that indicated where Deloy had put the trap and snaked it back out after it had been sprung. Why did I say "snaked?" I meant "pulled."

I focused on the job at hand and flashed my light on the ground in front of me. I was relieved to see no evidence of children spending time under there—no arrangements or constructions, no piles of paraphernalia—nothing that suggested anybody had spent any time there.

There was, however, a clear path leading toward the middle of the house. It wasn't footprints, but looked, instead, as though something had been dragged, or dragged itself, along. A broad smooth track with evenly spaced indentations along the side. A big snake? What Delcie would have called an allicrockie? The booger man? I calmed down somewhat when I realized I was probably making much the same kind of tracks. A person, then?

Looking under my armpit back toward the bright light in the yard, where I could see Hen's boots, Phil's loafers, and Leland's lace-up wing tips, I weakly wished, however briefly, that I was more of a clingy, helpless woman and that Phil was more of a macho male. I could hear the murmur of their voices, and peevishly blamed them for talking about whether spittlebugs or casebearers were worse for pecans in the long run when I was in such peril in the short run. Then Hen's voice rose above the murmur.

"Beats me why God had to give us casebearers and spittlebugs. And spiders. If all the spider eggs hatched out and grew up, they'd plumb take over the world. Lucky there are things in the insect and arachnid kingdom that think they're tasty."

And Phil, "Spiders are helpful predators. No telling how many other little pests they get rid of, things worse than casebearers and spittlebugs, which don't bother people as far as I know. Did you ever look at an old spider web and try to identify all the carcasses?"

Leland, probably innocently, trumped them both. "I had a bite once, musta been some kind of a spider, right between my shoulder blades where I couldn't reach it. That thing swole up full of pus and turned black, Clarice said. She had to clean it out with peroxide every night for a week before it went away. Said it nearly made her sick to look at it."

It was that moment, naturally, that a lizard chose to run across my hand. I didn't quite stifle my "urk."

"You all right, Trudy?" Phil called.

"Somethin' get you?" Hen inquired.

"I'm fine," I called back. "Just fine," I muttered.

I slithered deeper under the house, away from the sunlight, away from the conversation, but I couldn't get away from the train of thought it had started. Every week, the county extension agent has a column in *The Beacon* dealing with matters of interest to the local farmers. I do my best to read everything in *The Beacon,* which is the only reason I had read the recent column about millipedes and centipedes, and learned they like damp places, like what you find underneath houses. I suppressed a shudder and moved on along the allicrockie path, planning as I slithered how I would blind the beast with my flashlight, then jam it into his jaws while I made my getaway—and if I didn't get away, or didn't get away all in once piece, those wise-cracking overgrown adolescent humorists standing safely out there in the sunlight would be sorry, yes they would!

I was so engrossed in my fantasies that I almost overran the end of the trail. Suddenly, there was no more allicrockie track. More important, there was no allicrockie. I drew a deep relaxing breath, said a brief prayer of thanksgiving, and shone the light on the ground around me. Yes, this is where the trail stopped. Why? What was significant about this spot?

I turned over to lie on my back and ease my elbows while I thought about it. Playing the light overhead, I saw a square outlined in the floorboards, cutting across the otherwise regular line of the wood. A trapdoor. If there had been an allicrockie lurking somewhere, he could have taken me then. I was so pleased with my discovery I was oblivious to anything except the thought that I'd have to thank Elfreda for saying something came up through the floorboards. I pushed. It gave.

I settled back to the ground, thoughtfully considering my very next move. I was debating whether to slither out into the sunlight and share my news with the men right then or to go on up through the floorboards to see what I could see when a burst of male laughter from the yard made my decision for me. Onward and upward it was.

I pushed on the square above my head. It rose free, not attached by hinges, and I rose with it, slowly and cautiously, lifting the trapdoor with my head, into a space that was even darker than the space under the house. Something slid from the platform that was the door on my head, landing with several clatters on the uncarpeted floor. When my heart stopped pounding and I regained my senses, I realized I was emerging into a closet, in a dark corner, away from the door, where the trapdoor would be practically invisible, especially if something like whatever it was that had just clattered was piled on top of it. I could see a thin line of light. I kept rising, carrying the square door with me, until I was standing. The top of the floor was a little below my waist level, high enough to keep me from bounding out of my hole without thinking about it, and that instant's hesitation allowed three distinct courses of action to occur to me.

I could sink back into the crawlspace, slither back out to the men in the yard, and tell them what I had discovered.

Or, I could climb into the room, which, in spite of the changes in decor and my unfamiliar perspective, I recognized as Althea's. From there I could make my way out of the house, circle around behind the men in the backyard and yell, "Boo!"

Or, I could go out the front of the house, make my way to a telephone, since I'd left my cell phone in my other pants, and call Hen or Phil on their cell phones with a story of being abducted by evil forces who'd been hanging out under the Grinstead house.

The second two options were undeniably more attractive than the first, but I was in the spot I was in because of a tendency to act without enough forethought, so I took time to think it over.

The trapdoor, probably a means of reaching the nearby plumbing pipes without having to come the way I had come, answered the question as to how somebody—but not Buck Carlton, surely—could have gotten into the locked house. The next question was, who would know about the trapdoor, and how could I find out? Leland? He hadn't grown up in the house, after all, and an adult might not have explored it like children would. Clarice? Even less likely. And it wouldn't matter if they knew about it, anyway, since they wouldn't have had to use it to get inside, unless they were playing a deep double bluff in which one of them killed Althea and was waiting for an accusation before revealing the trapdoor and the possibility of an outsider. Did Digger, Deloy, and Latilda know about it because of that business with the trap? Children, after all? I hoped not, but couldn't avoid considering the possibility that children who had meant nothing but minor trespass might have urged and dared each other into taking bigger risks and wound up scaring Althea Boatright to death. The Boatrights? Far more likely, since they would know all the ins and outs of the house.

Reluctantly backing away from the seductive appeal of options two and three, I replaced the shoes that had been in the box on top of the trapdoor, balanced the box on top of the door as best I could, and sank back into the crawlspace.

"It's sure taking her a long time," I heard Phil say as I approached the sunshine.

"Probably found treasure buried during the War Between the States, and's trying to hide it from us," Hen said.

Leland, the literal-minded property owner, said, "It would belong to me, wouldn't it? Even if it wasn't my family that buried it?"

"You'd have to get a lawyer to look into that," Hen opined, if you can call such a statement an opinion. "The laws about buried treasure can be hard to figure out. It might belong to the State."

"Or the Confederacy," Phil said.

"But…"

I couldn't stand it any longer. I scrambled out, graciously accepting Phil's offer of a hand to help me to my feet.

"No allicrockies or booger men," I said truthfully to the assembled cheerleaders. "And if you take a picture of me right now, it will be your last act on this earth," I said specifically to Phil. He grinned and lowered the camera. "No story," I added for good measure.

"I guess y'all can quit worryin', then," Hen said to Leland.

"I haven't been worrying about it. Just something Mama imagined, probably, but Clarice has been letting it worry her, so she'll be glad to hear it. Now maybe I can get her to go up to the lake this weekend."

"Let us know when you'll be gone, and we'll keep an eye on the place, just in case," I said.

"I call that service," Leland said. He couldn't keep the surprise out of his voice. "Y'all do that kind of thing?"

"Crime prevention is part of the job," Hen said. "It's not as glamorous as the car chases, the fights in juke joints, the drug busts, and the vice raids, but it's part of the job."

"Well, then, I'm serving notice we'll be gone overnight on Friday," Leland said.

Everybody seemed happy but me. I left them to their male bonding and went home. I'd wait till I was cleaner—and Leland Grinstead wasn't around—to share my revelation about the trapdoor with Hen. And Phil.

EIGHTEEN

WHEN I GOT TO the station house, far cleaner and happier than I had been, all eager to explain my idea, I found that Hen had gone off to lecture a high school group on the dangers of experimenting with drugs, whether prescription, over-the-counter, school science project, or made by loving hands at home. Seems like the pharmacy had been having a run on Coricidin HBP Cough and Cold medicine, familiarly known as Triple C. This aroused suspicion because July isn't the big cold and flu season in Ogeechee. Hen's hope was that he could convince at least one young'un that the drunkenness, sickness, and appalling suspension of good sense induced by the medicine was not a good thing.

Phil, apparently for lack of something better to do, had gone back to his own business. The community, after all, does count on *The Beacon,* if not for news, then to confirm the news that's already made the rounds.

I, for lack of something better to do, went back to my own business. I wrote up a report on my exploration of the Grinstead place, but my mind kept coming back to the two clear thoughts I'd had while standing with the top part of my body in Althea Boatright's closet: we needed to find out who knew it was possible to get into the locked Grinstead house through that trapdoor, and we couldn't be straightforward about it. Asking wouldn't work. Even in a churchgoing Bible-belt community like ours, a killer might lie.

My thoughts about what we needed were clear. What I didn't have was a plan. I left my report on Hen's desk and decided to patrol the part of town near *The Beacon* offices. And as long as I was there, I decided to see if Phil had any ideas. He turned away from his computer terminal with gratifying alacrity when I appeared and gave his attention to my problem while I twisted back and forth in the swivel chair he'd pulled up for me. After outlining my idea, I waited for Phil's ideas, which must have been written on the inside of his eyelids, judging from how he squinched them tight.

"How about this," Phil said, stretching out a foot to stop my swiveling. "You let the word get around that the CBI or the feds or somebody has a new DNA test that you're going to use in Miz Boatright's room. Say it'll show up who's been in there."

"Okay," I said. "Say I say that. Why do I say we haven't already run this test?"

"That's easy. The testing kit is so new and so expensive that a little ol' place like Ogeechee doesn't have easy access to it. You've had to wait your turn."

"Not bad," I admitted. "Everybody knows how red tape works. But I don't see how this scam does us any good."

"I was thinking anybody who shouldn't have been there might be worried enough to go back and try to destroy the evidence. You arrest whoever comes through the trapdoor."

"And how would he or she think he or she could destroy the evidence?"

That answer must have been written down on Phil's eyelids with the other one because he didn't have to think about it. He gave me a wicked smile as he said, "There are fumes in one of the ingredients in, uh, baby powder that interfere with the, uh, fuming process employed by the kit. So if there was baby powder sprinkled around, the kit wouldn't be able to read the DNA. Naturally, anybody with a guilty conscience," he continued, in case I wasn't keeping up, "would want to sneak in there and sprinkle baby powder around."

"I absolutely love it," I told him. "How do you feel about explaining it to Hen?"

"I'd welcome the challenge," he said.

"He should be back from the school by now," I said. "Springing this on him when he's fresh from a high school gig, it might not sound too bad."

Phil looked hurt, but I was sure he was faking it. Hen's reaction to the idea might be the most interesting thing to happen all day. We caught up with Hen a few minutes later at the station house.

"Trapdoor, huh?" Hen asked, letting me know he'd read my report.

"Yes," I said. "It opens up several possibilities, doesn't it? Tell him, Phil."

Hen listened to Phil and his laughter rumbled, grew, and exploded. "Any chance that CBI DNA test kit looks like a little vacuum cleaner?"

Phil, unperturbed, nodded. "Matter of fact, the one I saw looked just like one of those little hand-held models."

"You see it in a comic book?" Hen asked. "A long time ago?"

"I don't remember where I saw it," Phil said. "Or when."

"I bet you don't," Hen said.

"It doesn't matter. We don't have to order the test kit, remember?" I said. "I know it's flaky, no insult intended, Phil, but unless our top cop here has a better idea, I say we try it."

Hen thought it over, and he must not have been able to come up with a better idea, because he said, "Okey-dokey. It's flaky, all right, but I don't see what it can hurt. I turned Jerome loose on the walking stick and medicine Martha Tootle liberated from the Grinsteads, and he didn't come up with any useful prints. No prints but Althea's on the medicine; nothing but smears on the walking stick, which isn't surprising when you think about it. Mostly, it's the palm that contacts a walking stick. And the lab found nothing out of line with the medicine, either. We need a break and this nonsense might shake something loose." He grinned. "Okay. Our turn with this kit comes up next Monday. That gives our killer the weekend."

"Perfect," I said. "Leland told us he and Clarice are going up to the lake, and we said we'd watch the place. So all we have to do is make sure the word gets around that they're gone and we're planning to run that DNA test on Monday."

"Do you think anybody will really believe it?" Phil asked.

"Son," Hen answered, "the average run of people, if you put it to 'em right, would believe Lester Maddox was big on civil rights, that the Confederate flag came over on the Mayflower—"

"How will you spread the word?" Phil interrupted.

"We got to be a little subtle," Hen said. "We make a big announcement, it'll be obvious it's a trap. Besides that, we make a big announcement, it'll make a laughingstock out of the whole police force. We've got to have ourselves some deniability here. The way to do it is to leak it, and I know a leaky vessel or two that will serve our purpose."

"Who?" Phil asked.

"Well, seems to me like it's about time for my mama and her gang to do something useful instead of just thinking they're God's gift to law enforcement. Trudy, you take care of it. I've never been able to lie to my mama."

"I don't think I'll have to lie, exactly," I said.

"You better pay attention, son," Hen said to Phil. "Might help you know what you're dealin' with in your relationship."

I rose nobly above this provocation to go off on a tangent. "Let me make sure we all have the same thing in mind," I said.

"I pour this disinformation into a few leaky vessels like Lulu Huckabee, Ellen Chandler, and Martha Tootle."

"Check," Hen said.

"We do want the leaky vessels to believe it's a real test, don't we?" I asked.

"Ab-so-tively," Hen said.

"Then, isn't it even remotely possible that they would want to keep quiet about it, so as not to foul things up? If they're trying to be responsible, they might not leak anything."

"You have a point there," Phil said.

"These women? Nah. They'll leak," Hen said. "Don't tell 'em anything you don't want all over town."

"I do not mention a trapdoor."

"Definitely do not mention a trapdoor," Phil agreed.

"But definitely do mention baby powder," Hen said, grinning again.

"But what do I tell them that will convince them it's important but will still insure that they leak?"

"That's the weak part of the plan, all right," Hen said, already distancing himself from the whole idea. "You'll think of something. And if you don't, it won't matter. It's a flaky idea, anyway."

"Think you can do it, Trudy?" Phil asked.

"Sure," I said.

"Without compromising your upright moral character and sinking to outright lies?" Hen asked.

"Certainly," I said, reaching for a telephone. I asked Aunt Lulu if she thought her friends would like me to meet with them and give them a private, off-the-record update on the case, considering their special interest.

NINETEEN

WITH THE RESPONSIBILITY for the plan resting on my shoulders, Hen and Phil went back to other things while I tried to fix firmly in mind what I needed to accomplish in my meeting with the leaky vessels and how I could accomplish it. Aunt Lulu had told me she thought she could have Ellen and Martha at her house within an hour, and she was as good as her word.

Ellen Chandler showed up wearing a pale, peach-colored T-shirt with peaches embroidered on it, and small fuzzy peaches dangling from her ears, evidently nostalgia for the peach season which had already come and gone for the year. Her manicure, starting at the pinkies and working up to the thumbs, displayed a developmental chart of the peach, from blossom through ripe fruit, all the way up to a cone of what had to be peach ice cream. Aunt Lulu, relatively unimaginative, wore pink pants and a pink-and-white striped golf shirt. Martha Tootle was in unrelieved black—shoes, long-sleeved shirt, complete with dark sunglasses and an oversized black bag. I was in uniform.

Before I could begin my campaign of disinformation and misdirection, however, Martha Tootle wanted to report on a meeting she and Jim L. had had with the Grinsteads.

"They invited us over for dessert," she said.

"After what he did to your car?" Aunt Lulu asked.

"Because of what he did to my car," Martha said. "I'm pretty sure the idea was to be sweet as could be and talk us out of pressing charges."

"Did it work?" Ellen asked.

"Oh, we never were going to press charges, as long as he'd get it fixed, but I didn't see any reason to tell him that right off the bat."

"You milked it," Ellen said.

Martha seemed pleased, rather than offended, at her friend's guess. "Of course I did. You want to hear all about it, or not?"

"Of course we do," Aunt Lulu said. "Are you in a hurry, Trudy?"

"No, ma'am, not in too much of a hurry for this. I'm sure it will be relevant to our investigation."

If anybody suspected me of insincerity, they graciously overlooked it.

Just as she had undoubtedly milked it for the Grinsteads, Martha milked it for us, dramatizing not only her own role, but Jim L.'s, Leland's, and Clarice's, while the rest of us sat back and watched. I now recognized her costume as an actor's blank canvas upon which she would draw the appropriate character. It was no coincidence that her black bag contained props to help us keep straight when she was "doing" Clarice (a silk rose), Leland (a bow tie), or Jim L. (a baseball cap advertising Disney World).

"Right off, when Leland gave us a nervous smile and thanked us for coming, I said we had to come in that boat Jim L. drives instead of my zippy little bug." Martha held the bow tie at her neck, to make sure we connected it to Leland.

"Might as well get off on the right foot," I said.

"You might not be pressing charges, but you're making them pay," Ellen said.

"What did Leland say to that?" Aunt Lulu asked.

"Clarice jumped in and said they wanted to do what's right and to please come have a seat in the living room while she brought us a little something.

"Well, we let Leland lead us into the living room, but I didn't offer to help in the kitchen like I normally would, just to keep 'em on notice that it wasn't a social call. They re-did the living room. Did y'all know that?"

"Never have been over there that I can think of," Ellen said. "Wouldn't know if it was re-done. Is it pretty?"

"If you go for that overblown kind of thing. Wing-back Queen Anne chairs in a dark rose color that picks up the flowers in the rug. Old-fashioned class. Very Victorian."

Point of view is everything. I remembered Melva Boatright, saying the "flowered-y" carpet wasn't much of an improvement over whatever had been there before. Martha waggled the silk rose, which I now knew was supposed to suggest Clarice and her new flowered-y carpet.

"Clarice brought out this special coffee she gets in Savannah, in little china demitasse cups with roses on them. The demitasses told me she understood I was the one to sweeten up, because it just irritates a man to have to pick up such a teensy little thing. And a chocolate mousse cake, with strawberries dipped in chocolate on the side. Clarice knows I'm partial to chocolate, but I didn't say a word, just picked up my demitasse and nibbled at a strawberry.

"Well, we all took our time over the dessert, talking about who's been sick and who's getting married, people at church, like you do when you don't have much in particular to talk about. Let 'em squirm, is what I thought, but finally Clarice got up to go for the coffeepot and I saw her nudge Leland with her elbow when she went past him, so I knew we were getting down to business."

Martha picked up the bow tie. "Leland sort of cleared his throat and started in on how they'd been all upside down since Althea died. Said he'd lost some papers of Althea's and since he knew Clarice had been cleaning out and I'd taken some things, he thought—he hoped—maybe I had them instead of them being out in the dump somewhere.

"I just took another bite of that mousse cake and ate it real slow to show him I didn't care what he thought or hoped, and he said he didn't mean he thought I'd taken anything on purpose, just that they might have gotten mixed up with what I took.

"By then, Clarice was back and she said she'd told him and told him that all I took was the walking stick and the medicine, but there was no reasoning with him."

This was all pretty much the story Leland had offered us, so I wasn't interested in the content nearly as much as in Martha's dramatization and the smug, secretive look on her face.

The Disney World cap, and a deepening of Martha's voice, let us know it was Jim L. who said, "'You think your wife threw out important papers and my wife found 'em and didn't bring them back? You got a generally low opinion of women in general, or just these two?'

"I could have kissed his big ugly face right there," Martha said, as Martha. Then, with bow tie, "'Nothing personal, Martha. I know you'd have brought 'em back if you'd found 'em. It was more a case of me being beside myself with grief and worry. I'm a businessman. Wouldn't do me any good to have people think I can't keep up with important papers.'"

Then the baseball cap, "'I think this pickle is a sight more embarrassing than losing some papers, Leland.'"

Then the bow tie, "'It wasn't supposed to turn out like this.'"

And Martha as Martha, "So I said I guessed maybe it wasn't. It was supposed to turn out that everybody would blame it on juvenile delinquents and our insurance company would pay for it. And Leland said, again, that he was sorry and he admitted he hadn't been thinking straight, and he was practically kissing my feet he was so anxious to pay for the damage and set things right. I might have been ready to ease up on him, but Jim L. was mad about the insurance angle, I guess."

The baseball cap came back into play. "'You think you can do whatever you please and offer some half-baked excuse about stress or whatever and get off with an apology and writing a check? What makes you think having your mama die gives you permission to be a hoodlum? What about the aggravation?'"

Martha as Martha again, "Well, I took my cue from Jim L. and I asked Leland what he was going to do about my pain and suffering, when I saw what he had done to my cute little car. I felt absolutely violated, I told him."

"I wish I had been there," I said.

"He got a little snippy, then," Martha said, not seeming to appreciate my interruption. "Asked if we wanted him to go on a chain gang or wear a scarlet letter, or what. And Clarice said Hen had said it was up to us whether to press charges or not, and I gave Jim L. a nod to say we could relent, but I still wasn't quite through with Leland, now that we sort of had him at our mercy, so in a perfectly friendly way I asked him what kind of important papers Althea would have had in her bedroom that Clarice wouldn't have known about. I could tell he wanted to tell me to mind my own business, but he didn't. He thought it over, maybe thinking up an answer or maybe just deciding whether to tell me his business or not, but he finally said it was stock certificates, that Althea hadn't believed in keeping everything in the bank. And when I said I didn't believe Althea accumulated as much as she had by being stupid, Jim L. told me maybe it wasn't my business after all, and we went home pretty quick after that."

Martha folded her hands in her lap and ducked her head, so we assumed that meant the performance was over. I led the applause. Prematurely.

"But not before I told him I didn't for a minute believe there was some kind of random crime wave going on in Ogeechee, that there had to be a connection between the business with my car and Althea's murder. Yes, I called it murder, Trudy. Right out. And Leland gave Jim L. a look he didn't think I saw that said plain as day he thought I have a screw loose, and he said he didn't see how I got the idea there was a connection, since he was down at the station himself when Buck Carlton confessed. And Clarice—"

The silk rose had been out of action so long Martha had to fumble around to find it, but she finally found it and held it to her ear in a way that suggested a hula dancer. "Clarice said she heard Hen didn't even arrest him, even with a confession and all, and it was probably because she'd heard he was Lulu's boyfriend. I'm just saying what Clarice said, Lulu. Don't look at me like that."

"How would Clarice have heard about Mr. Carlton at all?" Aunt Lulu asked. "Much less that he was my friend?"

"Don't ask me," said our drama queen. "Anyway, I told her that besides being your friend, he was one of Althea's old boyfriends, and so was the man she ran over and killed, from when she was growing up in Jesup. Well, that got their attention."

"I'm sure it did," Ellen Chandler said.

Martha frowned at the interruption, "It was news to them, the connection between Althea and that man she ran over, and Clarice said maybe Buck Carlton killed her for revenge over that. Maybe he and the other man had been lovers, she'd heard about things like that, and I wanted to take up for you, Lulu, and not make it look like you had a homosexual boyfriend, so I told them that Althea must have been quite attractive when she was younger, to have all those men after her, and I fished around for Leland's birthday, too."

Aunt Lulu was beginning to puff up and looked like she

might explode, so I asked Martha how she managed to get from gay lovers to Leland's birthday. She took my question to mean how she had done it conversationally. I had meant mentally.

"I said that besides those other men, she'd attracted Bert Grinstead, and must have married him pretty quick after high school, unless he's younger than I thought he was. Well, Clarice jumped in before Leland could answer, saying Althea and Bert had had a whirlwind romance and Leland came along pretty quick after they were married."

Preparing for a lengthy speech as Clarice, Martha held up the rose. "'I remember somebody teasing your daddy about it at the party we had for their fortieth anniversary, Lee. He was already sick by then, and we hadn't been married long. I thought it was kind of sweet. Bert was quite a bit older than Althea, and you might not know he'd been married before, but that wife died before they had any children, so when he got this new young wife and she gave him Leland, he felt like he had a second chance at life. Bert worshipped Leland, he worshipped Althea for giving him Leland, and he put up with however she acted.'"

Martha abandoned the rose as she continued. "Then Leland said how Bert was a good daddy and he'd tried to be a good daddy to Jordan and bring him along the same way, but maybe even Bert would have had trouble with Jordan." Martha grinned. "I think Leland was so glad to be talking about something besides my car that he told us more family business than he meant to. He said he was a lot closer to Bert than to Althea even if Althea had always said he was more Jordan than Grinstead. Don't you think that might mean he isn't really a Grinstead?"

"Are you saying you think Charlie Sykes was his daddy?" Aunt Lulu asked.

"Or maybe Buck Carlton," Ellen suggested. "If he just found out he's Leland's daddy, maybe he got so mad with Althea he killed her."

"There's still the question of how he could have done it," I said. "But if he's really Leland's father, or thinks he is, it might explain why he'd confess if he thought we were about to arrest Leland for it."

"So he's just been using Lulu to find out about Althea, and about what the police know?" Martha asked.

"He hasn't been using me," Aunt Lulu protested. "I…"

"Trudy, didn't you say you had something to tell us?" Ellen said.

I began to pour my story into the leaky vessels.

TWENTY

MY ACT FOLLOWING Martha's would work for me in one way, I reasoned. After her dramatics, anything I said would appear, at least comparatively, straightforward and sincere. Choosing my words very carefully, per the plan I'd worked out with Hen and Phil, I explained the situation.

Carefully avoiding the lie direct, I told them I had heard we'd be getting the use of a DNA test kit that would help us find out who had been in Althea's room, and wasn't it funny that something as simple as baby powder would somehow mess up the results. We had a laugh at the limitations of modern technology, including side references to the huge power failure on the East Coast and the challenge of programming a VCR.

Coming back to my agenda, I went on to say that it wouldn't hurt if all our suspects knew about this test we'd be doing on Monday, because knowing we were about to get scientific evidence might make the guilty one nervous enough to make a mistake. "I'd like to be sure all our suspects know about this information," I concluded.

"You don't have anything to worry about," Martha said, her eyes lighting up at what was obviously a license to leak.

"Trust us, Trudy," Aunt Lulu said.

"You know how fast this will spread," Ellen said. "There's a church supper tonight, and I'll be surprised if the Boatrights aren't there. I'll take care of them."

We moved on to general conversation, into which I dropped the information that the Grinsteads were going up to the lake to spend Friday night and wasn't it nice that they felt like they could get away.

I WATCHED FOR Digger the next morning and strolled out to pick up my paper just as he was getting the wheelbarrow out of the back of the truck. I took it as a sign of divine approval of our plan that Deloy was with him and I wouldn't have to rely on Digger to convey the nuance of my disinformation.

"Just finishin' up, Trudy," Digger said. "Be outta here before you know it."

Deloy nodded agreeably.

"That's fine," I said to Digger. "I'll put a check on the kitchen table for you, in case I'm not here when you leave. Y'all have done a good job for me, and quicker than I expected, too. Be sure to use me as a reference when you go after new clients."

Digger beamed, and Deloy smiled in a restrained manner befitting the heir-apparent.

"And by the way," I added, including Deloy in my glance. "Thanks for telling me about your trap under the Grinstead house. Looks like you scared off whoever or whatever it was. The Grinsteads are going up to spend Friday night at the lake, and I know they wouldn't feel like they could go away if they were worried about the house being in danger. And speaking of that, I don't know if I told you, I've heard there's a new DNA test we're going to run first thing Monday that'll settle one way or another if somebody was in Althea's room and killed her."

"What kind of test?" Deloy asked. "How's it work?"

"I've never actually used it," I told them, and I described the test, as described by Phil.

"What won't they think of next?" Digger asked the universe.

"DNA, you say?" Deloy asked. "Don't you have to bleed or brush your teeth or something for them to get DNA?"

"I'm not sure," I said, "but I think this test is different from most of 'em. More sensitive. Funny thing, too, there's something in baby powder that messes up the results. Can you believe that?"

"What I believe is, it's gettin' so a man can't even breathe without some kind of police supervision of him," Deloy said. "Making his own DNA testify against him ought to be against his Fifth Amendment!"

"You be respectful, now! This woman here, who just happens to be in the police, is hiring you to clean up her yard, not give her your opinion on law enforcement. I apologize for the boy, Trudy. If you had young'uns of your own, you'd know you can't do a thing with 'em."

"No need to apologize," I said. In fact, I'd been amused at Deloy's bluster, clearly inspired by conversations with lawyers.

Digger turned to Deloy. "You been in the domestic horticulture business so long now you growin' roots, or you gone get to work?"

I mentally checked off Digger and Deloy. To insure thorough coverage of my end of the suspect pool, I went through a similar routine with Elfreda, trusting that she'd get the word to Latilda even if Deloy failed.

THROUGHOUT THE NEXT two days the leaky vessels reported in.

Ellen Chandler took advantage of the potluck supper at the Ogeechee United Methodist Church, where she managed to slide into line behind Susannah Boatright at the dessert table.

"I got off on the wrong foot right off the bat," Ellen reported, "by saying I thought Genelle Towner put too many pecans in her pie. Well, Susannah set me straight about that.

In case you want to know, it was her pie I was talking about, not Genelle's, and she uses the recipe on the Karo bottle, just like everybody else does."

"I hadn't been worrying about it," I said.

"Me, neither," Ellen said, "but now we both know. I asked her if she'd heard about them finding a prenuptial agreement in Althea's stuff."

"I'd sure be surprised if she had."

Ellen giggled. "Me, too, since I'd just made it up. Not to criticize your plan, but I don't think any of the Boatrights would be particularly worried about their DNA being in the house since they used to live there, so I embroidered on the story."

My heart sank. The trouble with a leaky vessel is that you can't be sure where it will spring a leak.

Ellen continued, "Since you said the idea was to make the killer nervous, I told her maybe with getting ready to go to the lake Friday night, Leland hadn't gotten around to letting the Boatrights know about it, but I'd heard they kept turning things up, things mentioned in Rowland's will, and I'd heard they were piling everything up in Althea's room till they could go through it. Then I acted like I hadn't meant to say all that and said maybe Leland and Clarice were waiting for a lawyer's advice."

"I think you've been spending too much time with Martha Tootle," I said.

"I did think I was pretty darned good, thank you. Then I asked her if she thought there'd be a chance Leland and Clarice might be willing to consider giving up that house since Leland might not want to keep on living in a house where his mother was murdered."

"Nice touch," I said.

"Thank you," Ellen said. "Susannah sort of shuddered when I said that, and I don't think it had anything to do with that artificial whipped cream Linette Glisson uses on her strawberry shortcake. So that's when I went ahead and told her about the DNA test on Monday and the baby powder."

"Sounds like you covered the ground pretty well. Susannah will surely tell Homer and Melva, and if any of them has anything to worry about—"

"She won't have to tell them," Ellen said. "I caught a movement out of the corner of my eye, about then, so I raised my voice just a notch and said, 'Of course, you might not want to live there either, in that case. But then, probably Homer and Melva would get it, wouldn't they? Oh, hello, Melva. Homer. I didn't see y'all. Have you tried that strawberry shortcake. Yum!' When I went to get myself some coffee, I could see Susannah talking up a blue streak to Homer and Melva."

"Well done," I said.

Ellen and I were sure we could, uh, leak into the suspect pool, so Martha Tootle and Aunt Lulu were freelance leakers, just supposed to drop the information about the DNA test and the baby powder wherever the opportunity came up.

Aunt Lulu sounded frankly testy when she told me about her conversation with Buck Carlton.

"He's still pouting because Hen didn't throw him in the pokey," she reported, and then in Carltonesque tones she added, "'The police cannot be relied upon to act appropriately, dear lady. I confessed as wholeheartedly as I could to the accidental murder of Althea, and they did grill me, but then they more or less brushed me off like an unsuccessful job applicant. As much as said, "Don't call us, we'll call you."'

"I told him I thought maybe they have to do some investigating and see what kind of a case they can bring, and he asked me what kind of a case they'd need since he'd confessed. People always think I know more about police work than I do," Aunt Lulu said modestly.

"How did you answer that question?" I asked her.

"I called on years of reading mysteries," she said. "I told him the police need some evidence that will hold up in court. They might think he did it and confessed to get them to bring a weak case. If they brought a weak case and he didn't get convicted, even if he did it, he'd be safe, because of double jeopardy. I reminded him of that old movie with Barbara Stanwyck and Fred MacMurray. Or was that *Double Indemnity?*"

"I have no idea, Aunt Lulu. That was before my time."

"He didn't know either," she said. "All Buck Carlton is sure about is that it hurt his feelings that nobody seemed to take him seriously, so I suggested that y'all believed him, but the jails are already overcrowded, and you didn't think he posed a great risk of flight to avoid prosecution."

"Very thoughtful of his feelings," I told her.

"I was a little annoyed with him by then," Aunt Lulu said, "so I suggested that if he really wants y'all to take notice, he could try to flee the jurisdiction. Well, he whined some more and said he thought you'd be so glad to have it solved you'd just take his word for it, so I told him that just proved the Ogeechee Police Department was good at its job because even to me it looked like his confession was pretty weak."

"I'll bet that really hurt his feelings, Aunt Lulu."

"I think it did," Aunt Lulu said. "So I told him he didn't have to worry about it because of this DNA test, which would prove his story one way or the other. He didn't seem to like that very much."

"Did you mention the baby powder?"

"Yes, Trudy. And he told me I ought not tell people about that because without the DNA you wouldn't have a case against anybody. The nerve of him, telling me what I should and should not talk about!"

I stifled a laugh.

The leaky vessels and I had done our job. Now it remained to be seen if we had shaken anything loose.

TWENTY-ONE

On Friday afternoon, Hen decreed that officers on patrol keep an eye on the Grinstead place, not as a security measure, as usually understood, but so that after Leland and Clarice were gone I could go on stakeout and watch to see if anybody showed up to make an assault on the trapdoor.

Jerome was the one who called it in. "They just drove by, heading out of town."

"Where are you?"

"Over here havin' a chat with Miz Coleman."

"She been seeing those camo men again?"

"Not for a while. We think maybe once they came down from off the motel and started wandering around in the woods, they kind of got lost. I keep checking with her, though."

"I understand completely," I said. "Well, come on and get me, and bring a cookie with you."

"Be right there," he said.

It was just about dark-thirty, as Hen might have put it, when Jerome dropped me off at the end of the lane that peters out about fifty yards beyond the Grinstead house. A footpath leads half a mile or more through tangled undergrowth around Durrence Pond before it comes out near the old Collins highway, but cars can go no farther.

Rather than announce myself by going through the lane or the yard, I cut through the underbrush and worked my way up to the garden shed that sits about twenty yards from the back door. Once inside, I hoisted myself up onto a sturdy workbench and verified that the windows, grimy though they were, would give me a good view in all directions. I opened a couple of them just a crack so I'd be able to hear and breathe better. Sitting still and passive, watching and waiting for something that may not happen is hard for me to do, so I had braced myself for a tedious, possibly unprofitable, evening.

That isn't even close to what I got.

I had just found a position I could tolerate for more than a few minutes—one that hit a balance between being so uncomfortable I'd have to fidget and being so comfortable I'd doze off—when I heard a car go past toward the dead end of the lane. I couldn't see it, but I could hear the car come to a stop. Doors slammed, then the clattery rattle of aluminum lawn chairs was punctuated by the voices of Aunt Lulu, Martha Tootle, and Ellen Chandler. I wondered what they thought they were doing, but I should have foreseen it. They'd have figured out that the house might be a target on Friday night. Martha's house is on the highway. She'd have been able to sit at her kitchen window and watch for the Grinsteads to head out of town. I used every ounce of self-control I could muster not to break my cover by going out there and giving them a talking to. I'd wait and see what happened.

Actually, except that they shouldn't have been there at all, they weren't doing such a bad job. They'd provided for their comfort, and even believing, as they must have, that the Grinsteads were out of town and nobody who was up to no good would appear before much later, they kept their voices down and relied on sign language as they found their own stakeout positions. Good instincts—and good organizational skills. They weren't but a few minutes behind the police, after all.

Martha, her unerring sense of costume fully in play, was wearing the appropriate outfit for sneaking around in the

dark—the same outfit stagehands, mimes, and actors use—
black slacks and a black turtleneck. She disappeared into the
shadows beyond the birdbath on the side of the yard away
from the lane.

Feeling goddess-like in my ability to see all from the
darkness inside the shed, I watched Ellen unfold her chair
behind a barbecue grill that sat on the concrete slab outside the
door to the shed. In her camouflage-patterned T-shirt and
jigsaw puzzle earrings, she blended beautifully into the
shadows from the shed and the tall trees lining the lane, even
better than Martha, in all black. I, of course, all-seeing though
I was, was not all-powerful. I realized I was effectively trapped.

The rustling from the corner of the shed just out of my
eyeshot had to be Aunt Lulu positioning herself deep in the
branches of the enormous hydrangea at the corner of the shed.

I was still quietly admiring the relative efficiency of the
leaky vessels when a shadowy figure, eerily elongated by the
glow of the streetlight behind it and carrying a monstrous
club-like weapon, detached itself from the trunk of the large
oak in the park-like yard across the lane and approached the
shed. From the sound of it, Martha dropped her chair and si-
multaneously made an unsuccessful attempt to stifle a shriek,
doing a fair imitation of the last moments of a small mammal
being swept up by a bird of prey.

"What's the matter, Martha?" Aunt Lulu asked in a loud
whisper. Her hydrangeas had kept the approaching menace
from her sight.

"Guilty conscience?" The shadowy figure spoke.

"Buck Carlton! Good heavens! What are you doing here?"
Aunt Lulu said. "Did you have to sneak up on us like that?
You took ten years off my life!"

"Ah, but you're beautiful when you're angry in the moonlight," he responded.

Various noises told me Aunt Lulu was fighting her way out of the hydrangea, still on the attack. "If you've been lurking under that tree, why didn't you help us with the lawn chairs?"

"I just got here," Buck said. He sounded hurt.

"But why? Why are you here?"

"I wanted to visit with Mr. Grinstead, Althea's son," he said. "I had no idea there was a party. I didn't mean to sneak up, and I wasn't lurking."

"It isn't a party. Leland isn't here," Aunt Lulu said.

"If he isn't here…" Buck's voice trailed off.

"Is this man a friend of yours, Lulu?" Martha asked. I couldn't tell from her tone whether she was still annoyed at being frightened, whether she was deliberately rescuing Aunt Lulu from Buck Carlton's embarrassing question, or whether she simply wanted to be introduced to a good-looking man.

Either way, Aunt Lulu seized on it. "Martha, this is Buck Carlton, from Jesup. Buck, the woman you nearly scared to death is Martha Tootle."

"Charmed," Buck said.

"Likewise, I'm sure," Martha said.

"Ellen's here somewhere," Aunt Lulu said. "You met her when we came to talk to your sister."

"Y'all better be quiet," Ellen called from the barbecue grill. "This isn't supposed to be a tea party."

"What is it supposed to be, exactly, if the Grinsteads aren't at home?" Buck asked.

There was a moment of silence, nobody, apparently, wanting to answer this one. Then Ellen's voice floated out. "We were hoping we'd catch somebody trying to break in."

"Oh," he said.

"Didn't I mention when we talked that the Grinsteads were going away for the weekend?" Aunt Lulu said.

"Oh, my, you might have. This old memory of mine just

isn't what it used to be." A pause. "Well, as long as I'm here, I can wait with you for somebody to break in." He made a sketchy bow over his walking stick. "I'm prepared for action." He hefted his weapon. "My bully stick, very much like the one of Teddy Roosevelt's on display at Franklin's museum."

"Heaven forbid it comes to that," I muttered. If we had violence with this cast of characters on the scene, there was no telling what the result would be.

"Oh, all right," Aunt Lulu said.

"Then take your positions," Ellen said. "No telling when it'll start coming down."

Buck bowed agreement, his shadow doing fantastic contortions on the ground in front of him.

"What's coming down?" Martha asked.

"That's a figure of speech," Ellen explained. "It's police slang. It means when things start happening."

"Well why didn't you just say so?"

When nobody answered that question, Martha asked another. "Do you think we'll be surveilling all night?"

"The word is 'surveillance,' Martha," Aunt Lulu answered a bit impatiently. "We have it under surveillance."

"But it's from a French verb, *surveiller,* meaning to overlook or watch out—*sur* means over, *veiller* means watch—so it ought to have a verb form in English and if it did, it would be *surveille.* You aren't the only one who can read, you know." I was as surprised by Martha's sharpness as by her erudition. Clearly whatever school she had attended offered French as well as drama.

"Under the circumstances, I agree we should be quiet," Buck suggested, his whisper interrupting Aunt Lulu's rebuttal to Martha's rebuttal.

"Right." Aunt Lulu and Martha spoke together. They melted back into the darkness of their cover. Buck returned to the bench in the shadows of the neighbor's oak. We had the back of the house covered from every angle. Activity subsided. We surveilled. And the cloudy moon, the gibbous moon, the highwayman's moon, shed its wan light on erratic rustlings and muffled snorts no more obtrusive than what might have been produced by, say, stray dogs, squirrels, armadillos, even deer.

Some time later—in my lair, it was too dark to see my watch—I became aware of the approach of something largish through the underbrush to my left, the non-lane side of the shed, the Aunt Lulu and Martha Tootle side. The noise, which seemed loud in the quiet of the night, grew closer. It made more noise than I'd have expected of a deer, and somehow it sounded large, larger than a deer. I'd never heard of woman-eating animals in these thickets, and if there'd been a recent prison escape, surely Hen would have mentioned it. Besides, I was safe inside my shed. I wondered if the women outside had heard the noise and if they were as much at ease as I was.

Aunt Lulu's nerve broke when whatever was making the noise stumbled into the bush under which she was huddled.

She had already started screaming when I heard, "Blasted all-fired stump!" The voice was male, familiar.

I was considering breaking cover when flashlight beams from both directions wavered and came to rest on the figure of Homer Boatright, who was now cursing more vividly and trying to shield his eyes from the light. I decided to bide my time.

"Don't shoot! It's Homer!" Aunt Lulu bluffed.

The wavering beams came closer in a narrowing circle, like primitive hunters encircling and confusing their prey. Even Ellen had come out from behind the barbecue grill to help.

"What in the all-fired name of holy blazes is going on here?" Homer Boatright yelled. "What is this? Help! Help!"

"Oh be quiet," Aunt Lulu said. "We have you dead to rights!"

"Lulu Huckabee? What are you talking about?" Homer asked. At least he had stopped yelling.

"What are you doing here this time of night?" Martha asked.

"What is this, some kind of ladies' aid vigilante posse?" Homer asked in return. "And what business is it of yours if I come to visit somebody?"

"Do you always come through the woods in the middle of the night when you go visiting?" Martha asked.

"The Grinsteads aren't home, and you know it," Ellen said.

"I'm taking names," Homer blustered. "I've got Lulu Huckabee, Martha Tootle, and Ellen Chandler." By now he'd moved into my line of sight, and I noticed that he, too, was dressed as if for intentional skulking. Like Ellen, he'd opted for camo. Unlike Ellen, he wasn't wearing earrings.

"Anybody else out there?" Homer craned his neck and dodged around as though trying to see around the blinding glare of the flashlights. His trick ankle didn't seem to be bothering him.

Not wanting to have the police associated with what was turning into a debacle, I still kept quiet. So, I noticed, did Buck Carlton, but my estimation of him rose a bit when a glance at the bench from which he'd been surveilling showed it empty. He and his bully stick were out of sight, but comparatively quiet sounds from behind my shed suggested he was circling to come up behind the others.

"We're watching over the Grinstead house in case somebody tries to break in." Aunt Lulu said it in a reasonable but accusing tone. "You aren't on visiting terms with them, from what I know. Did you come to break in?"

Homer let out a whoosh of air and tried again. "I like to take exercise at night when it's cooler and when people don't keep stopping you and asking if you're in trouble. When I got to the lane and saw your cars parked there, I decided to investigate. That's a funny place for cars, especially since I'd heard that Leland and Clarice were out of town."

"You're changing your story pretty fast," Martha said. "A minute ago you said you came to visit them."

"You knew they were out of town, and you came by to keep an eye on things?" Martha asked.

"I don't like your tone, Martha," Homer said.

"Stop right there!" Buck's voice was as startling as the fact that a bright light had just come on nearer the house, right over the back door.

A woman wearing jeans, sneakers, and a dark T-shirt, stood beside the steps. She stared wildly from the light to the group near the shed and then back, calling to mind movies of prison escapees who didn't quite make it over the wall before the searchlights caught them for the guards and their machine guns. Her face was stricken; her hands brushed at the dirt on her jeans. If she'd hoped to get away unnoticed she'd made a big mistake.

"Is this who we were waiting for?" Buck asked, turning to Aunt Lulu.

"Susannah!" Homer said.

"Homer?"

"Where did she come from?" Martha asked.

Ellen answered, "She came from the house and didn't realize that light over the porch was motion sensitive. We have one like it by our garage. I guess the rest of us are too far away to set it off. Where were you hiding, Susannah?"

"Meet Susannah Boatright, Homer's sister," Aunt Lulu said to Buck.

"Can we make a citizen's arrest, or do I get to hit her with my bully stick?" Buck asked. From my vantage point, the moonlight glinting on Buck's dentures gave them an evil sheen.

Homer moved between Buck and Susannah.

Aunt Lulu spoke, "Susannah, I'm sure I speak for all of us when I say we'd be interested in knowing where you've been, and why."

Susannah glanced at her brother, then busied herself with a thorough dusting-off of her jeans.

"I swear she didn't come out of the house," Martha said.

"Susannah?" Aunt Lulu prompted.

Susannah might have attempted an explanation, but she was spared when everyone's attention was diverted by the throat-clearing rumble of a mufflerless car turning into the lane. More traffic on a dead-end lane in the middle of the night? A rust-eaten Plymouth, ghostly in the moonlight, came to a stop on the grass between the back steps and the shed. Annoyed at the intrusion into my sightlines, I moved to another window.

Homer approached the car, followed by the rest of the group. I went back to my original window, where I could now hear and see better than ever.

"Help you?" he said.

"Trying to act like he really was looking for somebody to help," Martha whispered to Aunt Lulu. "Ha!"

"Uh. No." The voice wavered. Even the steadiest of tourists, having made a wrong turn onto a dead-end lane, being challenged by an angry man, and seeing various insubstantial shapes floating out of the woods and waving flashlights in her general direction might have wavered. This woman was plainly frightened. Surrounded, escape cut off, even the dispirited engine sputtered and died.

"Who is it?" Ellen asked, peering into the window on the passenger side.

The driver tried to crank the motor. When it didn't respond, she leaned on the horn.

"Latilda?" Aunt Lulu was peering into the car. With an air

of surprise, she told the others, "This is Latilda Wilcox. Elfreda's granddaughter." To Latilda, "Latilda, it's Lulu Huckabee. Be quiet. We aren't going to hurt you, but I think you'd better tell us what you're doing here."

"Uh." The horn stopped blaring. Latilda looked from one to another of the faces gathered around the car. She seemed to gain some confidence from the fact that they were human beings and that she recognized some of them. She spoke to Aunt Lulu, but her nervous gaze flitted from one to another of the others. "I, uh, left something here."

"Wouldn't it be easier to find in the daylight?" Ellen inquired.

With obvious relief, Latilda focused on the one face and the one question. "Yessum, usually, but in the daylight I've always got Deloy hanging around and I didn't want him to know I'd lost it." She turned to Aunt Lulu. "His daddy gave him a job under the house, but he made me do it, and I wouldn't do it without a good flashlight. Then when I turned around and started back, I didn't need the flashlight, and I put it down and forgot to get it. I wanted to get it before he found out and got on me about it."

Her voice grew firmer and I detected a hint of bravado, suggesting she'd had to talk herself out of tight situations before this. "I could just get it and go on, let y'all get on with whatever kind of party you're having out here in the dark." She tried for a friendly note. "What y'all doin' in the dark like this? Trying to fool the bugs? Deloy could probably get you a deal on a bug-zapper."

"It's a long story," Martha said.

Headlights swept the yard once again as another car turned in to the lane. The spotlight on the car's roof pinned the group, and the voice that instructed them rumbled like an earthquake, revealing the vehicle as a police cruiser and the speaker as Jerome Sharpe. "Don't anybody make any sudden moves. I don't want to hurt anybody, not 'less I have to, so just everybody keep calm." The addition of Jerome's spotlight to the still-glowing flashlights and the back porch sensor light gave the luster of a bright mid-summer's day to the scene, much like an over-illuminated stage set. I hoped Martha appreciated it.

Jerome came to a stop with his cruiser blocking the lane so that neither Latilda's Plymouth nor Aunt Lulu's Cadillac could escape without driving through somebody's yard.

"Evenin', folks. We had a call about a disturbance over here." He nodded to each one as he catalogued faces.

"Good evening, Officer Sharpe. It's good to see how efficient you are," Buck said when Jerome's gaze came to rest on him.

"Yessir, thank you. We aim to please. Hanging around in people's yard after dark, 'specially these people's yard, isn't what we had in mind when we let you loose, Mr. Carlton. It seems to me like you're out of your territory. Shouldn't a man in your position, you know what I mean, be behaving himself, maybe spending a quiet evenin' at home in Jesup with his television set, and not running around at all hours with a bunch of wild women?"

Buck examined his walking stick. "I just came to visit," he said.

"Uh huh." Jerome didn't sound surprised. "So, does that mean you the one's gonna try to explain all this?"

"Oh, no," Buck said.

Martha spoke up, offering as though it were an explanation, "We heard the Grinsteads were out of town."

"Um hmm." Jerome was patient.

"We, some of us I mean, were afraid somebody was going to try to break in. With them gone." Martha adopted an aggrieved tone. "You aren't accusing us of trying to break in—"

"No, ma'am, not yet—"

"—because if you are, we can all alibi each other."

"What she means is vouch for each other," Aunt Lulu amended.

"Vouch," Martha affirmed, with a nod at Aunt Lulu that showed she appreciated the difference. "Vouch. Not alibi. We were survei—watching out. Not breaking in." She shot a look at Aunt Lulu.

"And what gave you the idea somebody, anybody, was going to try to break in?" Jerome persisted.

"Arrest every one of them," Homer said. "They're the ones planning to break in, that's why they thought of it. They had the place surrounded, posted lookouts and everything else, so they could do what they wanted. No telling what they were up to, no matter what they say."

"And what were you doing here?" Officer Sharpe inquired. He seemed to have meant the question for Homer, but it was Latilda who answered.

"I was just turning around here, when they piled out of the woods all over me. Scared me nearly to death," she said virtuously, unconcerned that this was at odds with what she'd told the vigilantes earlier.

"That's not—"

"Ask him why—"

"What's going on out here?"

This last remark, delivered from the back porch in the irascible and unmistakable voice of Leland Grinstead, brought the rising hubbub to a halt.

"What are you doing here?" Martha asked.

"I live here. Remember?" He squinted in the light. "Martha Tootle? That you? You and your friends come to break into my car? I thought we had that business settled. Who-all's out there, anyway?"

"There's nothing to worry about, sir," Jerome said. "I've got things under control."

"I'd sure like to know what's going on," Leland said.

"We thought you were out of town," Martha unwisely explained.

Leland frowned at her.

"Clarice is out of town, not that it's any of your business. I started a migraine and decided not to go. And I want you to know all this uproar isn't doing me any good."

"We know Susannah was in the house, Leland," Martha said. "Did you invite her over, with Clarice gone?"

"What?" Leland asked. "What is that supposed to mean? Susannah who?"

They all turned to Susannah. With the extra time she'd had to work up an explanation, Susannah came up with, "I wasn't in the house. I was just hiding and watching, like everybody else."

"What were you watching for?" Buck asked.

"Whatever the rest of you were watching for," she said with an aggressive lift of her chin. "I was walking past and saw people here, and it worried me since I'd heard Leland and Clarice were going out of town. Anyway, I don't see why I have to explain myself. I have as much right as any of the rest of you to be here."

"I don't know how much right you think that is, any of you," Leland fumed. "The Bill of Rights doesn't give any one of you the right to create a disturbance in my backyard in the middle of the night." He turned to Jerome. "Are you going to arrest them?"

"My mama gets those headaches, and I know how bad they can be, Mr. Grinstead," Jerome said. "I've got things under control out here. Why don't you go on back to bed, and we can talk about this tomorrow. I'll have a talk with these folks, and I expect things will quieten down. If you decide to press charges, we can do that tomorrow."

"You stay away from my car," Leland said to Martha before he turned to go back inside.

"Hold on a minute," Jerome said. Leland stopped in his tracks and watched with the others as Jerome stooped and picked up something from the ground. He held it up in the light so that it was plain even from my vantage point that he was holding a small plastic bag with white powder in it.

"Anybody here know what this is?" Jerome asked. No one made a sound. "Let me put it this way," he said. "Anybody here not know what this is?"

He took his time, looking from one face to another.

"I don't know for sure," Aunt Lulu said, "but from what I've read, I'd say it looks like it might be drugs."

"Yes, ma'am, that's what it looks like," Jerome said. Everybody stepped back from Jerome, the bag, and the spot of ground where it had been lying. Even Latilda, still in her car, seemed to shrink away.

"Nobody's claiming this?" Jerome asked. "No? Then I'm going to have to take you all in for questioning."

There'd be no way to tie that bag to any one of them. I'd been watching the whole time, and with all the milling around, I couldn't have said when it appeared or who had dropped it— or who hadn't dropped it. Bluster or not, Jerome had everybody's attention as he undid the wire fastener on the bag. Development in the drug culture being what it is—even without the recent grisly deaths of a couple of felons who'd ripped off some ingredients for methamphetamine production and unwisely inhaled, cooking their innards almost instantly—police officers do not dip their pinkies into unknown substances and then taste them, no matter what you see on television. Jerome sniffed delicately, then quickly resealed the bag. His face was inscrutable.

"What is it?" Buck Carlton asked.

Jerome didn't answer. Instead, he drew himself up and presented his fiercest aspect.

"Folks, this is serious," he said. "The right thing for me to do is to haul you all in to the station house on suspicion, until we can search everybody."

Uproar is far too mild a word for what followed. My quick scan of faces showed expressions including what I'd have called mock horror (Martha Tootle), exasperation (Aunt Lulu and Leland Grinstead), amusement (Homer Boatright and Ellen Chandler), skepticism (Buck Carlton), uncertainty (Susannah Boatright), and fear (Latilda Wilcox). There was no witness to the expression on my face. Fascinated delight? Rapt attention? Intense concentration?

Aunt Lulu, admittedly in the most secure position, asked, "Are you serious?"

"That's correct procedure," Jerome answered. "Wouldn't want word to get back to my boss that I didn't know how to do my job."

Martha squealed. "Jim L. would never get over it."

"My grandchildren would love it if I spent the night in the clink. They'd never let me hear the end of it," Ellen said.

The others held their peace. Jerome, giving them plenty of time to reflect on their many and varied transgressions, took his time looking from face to face. While he did that, I reflected with amusement on the pros and cons of Jerome trying to haul this crew in. The pros were obvious—the whole town would enjoy talking about it, and the embarrassment might, just might, persuade Aunt Lulu and her friends to butt out of the police business. The only con I could think of was that I'd probably have to help.

To my surprise and the evident surprise of the rest of the party, after a lengthy silence, Jerome said, "I've got your names and know where to find you. You all promise to turn up at the station house tomorrow to make statements, and I won't haul you in now and make your children and grandchildren come and bail you out. You don't show up tomorrow, I come after you with sirens and shotguns. Everybody got that? The offer is good for exactly three minutes. Anybody still here after that can go with me now."

"Me, too?" Leland Grinstead asked.

"Yessir," Jerome said.

Leland disappeared into the house. While Jerome moved his car to let Latilda out, Aunt Lulu and her minions folded their chairs. They were in her car ready to go as soon as the lane was clear. I didn't see Buck Carlton leave, but he must have. When the varoom of Latilda's Plymouth faded and the dust from Aunt Lulu's Cadillac settled, only Jerome remained. He assumed his most imposing stature outside my window and rumbled, "Ollie, ollie, ox-in free."

"You didn't drop that bag yourself, did you?" I asked once I was outside and brushing cobwebs off my uniform.

"Uh uh."

"Then I can't believe you let them all go, without any kind of a search."

"For what?" he asked. "More baby powder?"

TWENTY-TWO

I COULD HARDLY WAIT to get to work the next day and see the fruits of Jerome's brilliant handling of the situation at the Grinstead house. He had given us the opportunity to question all the murder suspects while ostensibly investigating a drug bust. Beautiful!

The whole enterprise looked extremely questionable in the rearview mirror, even without the unforeseen involvement of Aunt Lulu and her friends. I wouldn't have been surprised if Hen wanted to distance himself and the OPD from the whole mess, or blame me for the whole thing.

Just about the only sliver of a silver lining I could see in the cloud of confusion was that practically everybody on our suspect list had showed up at the Grinstead place. On the other hand, not one of them had gone to the head of the list, based on revealed familiarity with the trapdoor.

Susannah Boatright came closest. She had materialized from near the house, maybe she'd even been under the house, strong evidence that she knew about the trapdoor and had used it—or been prepared to use it—but there was no evidence that she'd actually used it.

Her brother Homer would certainly not have come into the yard to investigate if he'd thought there was trouble, as he claimed, so he was surely on another errand of some kind, but we had no proof he was planning to go inside. Could they have been in cahoots? I'd have to give that possibility some thought.

Latilda's story had the ring of truth to it. It was easy for me to believe she might go to some trouble to keep from antagonizing Deloy. Even if she had been the one who set the trap under the house to catch Althea's booger, it didn't prove she knew about, or used, the trapdoor.

When I got to the station house, ready to start rehashing the events and braced to defend myself, if necessary, from the scorn of my exalted cousin and professional superior, I was surprised and pleased to find a delay. Leland Grinstead was already there, closed up with Hen in Hen's office.

Both men nodded to acknowledge the fact that I'd intruded myself into the already crowded space. Hen greeted me with, "'Morning, Trudy. We were just tryin' to decide who to charge with what over that uproar last night."

I nodded.

"But first," Hen continued, "Leland is going to give us a better explanation of why he broke into Martha Tootle's car the other day."

"I am?" Leland asked.

"Before we get on to your complaint about last night," Hen said.

"I already…"Leland began, looking defensive.

Hen waved him to a stop. "I know. You said you thought Martha might have had some important papers in it, papers belonging to you. You said you were embarrassed. I looked it up on your statement. Embarrassed. I can see that, all right. I personally think you'd have better luck with temporary insanity, but that's up to you. The thing is, we need more detail. What papers? In case you're the only person in town who doesn't know it, we've come around to the idea that your mother was killed by somebody she surprised going through her room. Burglarizing it. Now, to a country policeman like myself it seems like if that's what happened, you'd be interested in helping ús find out who that person was. There might not be any connection between the two things—your mother's death and your temporary insanity—and I might be off on the wrong scent here, like a hound dog I once knew who'd had his smeller messed up with chlorine, but it'll take some convincing to make me believe these two strange events aren't connected."

"I don't see…"Leland started again, with the same result.

"I'm not accusing you of killing your mama, accidentally or otherwise, Leland, not right now, anyway, but I think it might help us find out who did if you tell us whatever you can. At the very least, if you explain things, it'll help by keeping us from wasting manpower—personpower," he added for my benefit, "going down some dead end and having to back up before we can get our bearings and start off again on the right road." Sometimes Hen's folksy little metaphors get a little out of hand, but usually, as in this case, they are reasonably apt.

Leland fidgeted and opened and shut his mouth, giving the impression he was eager to be helpful but wanted to be sure Hen wouldn't interrupt him again. Finally, he managed to say, "Somebody going through her room?"

"That's one possibility."

"But she wouldn't have…" Leland stopped himself that time.

"She?" I asked. "Your mother?"

"I meant Clarice. She wouldn't have hurt Mama, even if Mama did find her in her room."

"Why would Clarice have been in there?"

He looked uncomfortable. Embarrassed. "Clarice felt like she had to do the cleaning in Mama's room. Naturally, that meant sometimes things got moved around a little bit. That upset Mama. She didn't like it, but it didn't stop Clarice."

"You're saying your wife made a habit of going through your mother's things?" Hen asked.

"Maybe I need a lawyer," Leland said.

"You about to incriminate yourself?"

"No, not unless you keep twisting what I say!" Leland was sure of that much, if nothing else.

"What else you got to say?" Hen prompted.

"It makes us look bad."

"You and Clarice?" I asked. Even to my own ears, I was sounding somewhat obsessive over pronouns this morning, but it is important not to take antecedents for granted.

"You can get over looking bad," Hen said. "Unless it's murder."

"There was this thing about that man she ran over, that Charlie Sykes."

I perked up. I'd almost forgotten about that.

"You know Clarice and Susannah Boatright are cousins," Leland went on.

"Uh huh," Hen encouraged.

"Well, they've managed to stay on pretty good terms, in spite of the wrangling between Mama and the Boatrights."

"Good enough terms that Clarice gave Susannah a brooch your mother didn't want her to have," I said, remembering the wrangle at the Hatfield House.

"She shouldn't have done that, and I told her so," Leland said. "Clarice and Mama didn't get along very well even before that, and once Mama found out Clarice had been going through things in her room, well, it got where I stayed at the store as much as I could."

"And what's this got to do with your breaking into Martha's car?" I asked.

"Clarice told me she saw a letter in Mama's room from that Charlie Sykes, along with a photocopy of an old marriage license with Mama's name on it. She didn't get a real good look because she heard Mama coming. Anyway, it didn't turn up in Mama's safety deposit box or anywhere else after she died, and I got to wondering about it. If Mama had been married to him, it was news to me, but why would she have kept it a secret? I got to worrying if it would affect her inheriting from Daddy, and from Rowland. And then I got to wondering what had happened to it."

It sounded like some of our (this pronoun referring to the OPD as well as the leaky vessels) wild-eyed speculations were close to Leland's wild-eyed speculations.

"Did you worry about whether it would affect our opinion of the accident that killed him?" Hen asked.

"Well, that too, a little bit, but not much, with her already gone. But I wanted to get a look at that license, and we couldn't find it. I knew Martha had taken some things when Clarice was cleaning out after Mama died, and her car was the last place I could think to look. That really is the truth, the whole truth, and nothing but the truth. So help me, God."

Taken as a whole, his story explained a few things, like why Althea had been so sure somebody had been going through her things. And why I'd been having the feeling that Martha Tootle wasn't being completely forthright when we were discussing what she'd had in her car. I made a mental note to talk to Martha.

"Do you think Clarice would have mentioned that marriage license to Susannah?" Hen asked.

"I don't know. You could ask her."

"We'll do that," Hen said. "Meanwhile, why don't you save us all some trouble and forget about pressing charges over what happened last night. There wasn't any harm done, was there?"

"I haven't had time to look around too much, but somebody broke a big branch off my hydrangea."

"They're like weeds. You'll never miss it by the end of the summer," Hen said.

"I'll think about it."

Leland went off to think about it.

"Sounds like I missed a good party last night," Hen said. "If I'd known how interesting it was going to be, I'd've arranged not to have to be on the other side of town distracted by an idjit who broke into Maddie Odom's house and got trapped in the utility room. Maddie said she'd been meaning to fix that doorknob, but now she's not sure she wants to."

"Oh, yeah, the happening place was definitely the Grinstead yard," I said. "And FYI, Aunt Lulu's the one who was under the hydrangea," I said. "Leland probably doesn't know that."

Hen fetched a big sigh. "You got any idea what those leaky vessels of yours thought they were doing?"

"*My* leaky vessels? It isn't my mother we're talking about!"

"You're the one thought she could prime 'em and turn 'em loose, if I remember right."

"And if *I* remember right, you're the one that came up with the leaky vessel theory in the first place."

"Don't be so touchy, Trudy."

"Me, touchy? Then don't ask me trick questions. You don't expect me to believe you didn't already ask Aunt Lulu what they thought they were doing, do you?"

"You know, Trudy, no matter what some people say, you're a pretty good police officer."

"What did she say?"

"She said they were working on the theory that the killer always returns to the scene of the crime."

"Did you tell her the best forensic handbooks have pretty much abandoned that idea, and they ought to look for more up-to-date material?"

"More or less, yes, I did. Doesn't mean she was listening, though. And when I asked what in tarnation they thought they were going to do about it if the killer did turn up, she said they'd thought about it, and Martha had her cell phone, and Ellen had a fire extinguisher, in case he—Mama said 'he,' so I'm not being sexist—tried to burn down the place to destroy the evidence, and she herself had brought a gadget that whoops like a car alarm if you set it off."

"Good grief. I thought things were wild enough as it was. Look at what we missed!"

"Lost opportunity is a sad thing to contemplate," Hen said, leaning forward and slapping his palms down on the desk in a gesture that indicated frustration as well as determination. "Okay. I got Leland's version of what went on last night, and Mama's. What's yours?"

I gave him the summary I'd worked out, generously adding that the women shouldn't even be faulted for failing to note that Leland wasn't in the Grinstead car when it left town, since the OPD had also failed in that regard.

"Leland says he had a migraine and that's why he was at home," Hen said. "Mama says Martha says she thinks he stayed home for a rendezvous with Susannah. What do you think about that?"

"It's interesting to think about Leland and Susannah Boatright carrying on, especially since Clarice and Susannah are friends as well as cousins, but I have trouble believing it. I don't think Martha believes it, either. She just wanted to say something snide last night. If Susannah had a rendezvous with Leland, she wouldn't have had to get in by way of the trapdoor. She sidestepped the question last night, but I'm sure I saw her come out from under the house."

"So you think she knew about the trapdoor?"

"Of course she did, just like Homer did. They grew up in that house, remember. And maybe they had planned to meet there and go through the papers Ellen said Leland was piling up in Althea's room. Did Aunt Lulu tell you what Buck Carlton was doing there?"

Hen laughed. "Not exactly. When I asked her about him, her answer was my favorite part of the debriefing, as she called it. She said she didn't invite him to help them watch the place, and it spooks her the way he keeps materializing and de-materializing, and can I arrest him for stalking."

"Stalking, maybe, but crawling under the house to get to a trapdoor doesn't seem like his style," I said.

"No, it doesn't, but I agree with Mama that there's something spooky about him. Why did he confess to a murder he didn't commit? And why keep hanging around Ogeechee? I'd be the last man on earth to deny my mama's womanly charms, but I think there's more to it than that."

"Maybe," I said.

"So, where does all this get us?" Hen asked.

"Not necessarily any further down the road, I'm sorry to say. Unless the one suspect who didn't turn up last night turns out to be the guilty one."

"Who's that?"

"Melva Boatright."

"Melva? You been readin' those books of Mama's, the ones where you know the killer is the least likely suspect?"

"No, but—"

"Try as I might, I can't see her crawling under that house to get to the trapdoor, any more than I can see Buck Carlton doing it. Anyway, if I remember right, the big clue you used to convince me there was something to this story was that goldanged walking stick."

"Well, yes," I conceded, "there do seem to be a goldanged lot of people using walking sticks, once we started looking for them."

"But not Melva."

"No. Not Melva. Maybe there's some connection we're missing here. Just for example, if Clarice saw a marriage license for Charlie Sykes and Althea Jordan, she might have mentioned it to Susannah Boatright, who could have mentioned it to Melva. She's her sister-in-law, after all, and they have the same financial interest in Althea. And then maybe Melva wanted to get a look at it for herself. Some people would tell you Melva's the greedy one in the family—"

"Greedier than Homer and Susannah?" Hen interjected.

"Could be."

"If you're saying it was Melva, how do you explain the switched walking sticks and how she could have gotten in and out of the locked house?"

I had no idea how to explain the walking sticks, and her knowledge of the trapdoor, or lack of it, was irrelevant, since I agreed with Hen that she would never have entered the house that way. So I said, "Maybe we've been wrong about Althea surprising somebody. Maybe Althea let her in."

"And let her back out and then went and concussed herself to death? So it's an accident after all, and the walking stick doesn't mean anything? But without the walking stick, there's no reason to think anybody besides Althea was there in the first place. Make up your mind, Trudy."

He was right, of course. I could handle that, but the smirk that accompanied his analysis irritated me.

"Give me a break here! I'm just thinking out loud. What about this? She—if it was Melva—might have still been in the house when we got there. We didn't search the whole house. We were concerned with taking care of Althea and had no reason to treat the whole house like a crime scene. Melva could have been hiding somewhere till she got a chance to get out."

"But Leland came while y'all were there, didn't he? She—if it was Melva—would have had to dodge him."

"It could be done. We can figure those things out once we're sure she's the one we're after. It's always easier to find proof if you know what you're looking for and where to look," I told him, just as though I hadn't learned it from him in the first place. "For now, let's say it was Melva. Maybe she got what she wanted from Althea's room and was too smart to be spooked by that stupid DNA-baby powder story of Phil's. And here's something else about Melva, Hen. I remember her mentioning the new carpet Clarice put in. The new carpet. Get it? With all the bad feeling over Rowland Boatright's will, the Boatrights and the Grinsteads haven't exactly been cozy lately. When would Melva have had a chance to see that new carpet? Maybe she was hiding in the living room."

"It's a point," Hen conceded. "But before you get too excited, you better find out when Clarice put the carpet in. Maybe it was before they had their falling out. Let's ask Clarice about that when we ask her if she told Susannah about the marriage license."

He called Clarice himself and turned back to me with a satisfied smile. "She has not socialized with the Boatrights since the carpet was installed. She's doesn't think she mentioned the marriage license to Susannah, but she might have, since they are still on relatively friendly terms."

"So you want to go talk to Melva?" I didn't really think it was Melva, either, but it was all I could think of at the time.

"Sure," Hen said, calling my bluff. "Maybe we can settle everything with her and won't have to haul in the whole bunch. You want to come?"

"You bet I do. Especially if we can go by way of Martha Tootle's. I think she has some explaining to do."

TWENTY-THREE

OUR TALK WITH Martha didn't take long. For once, possibly because she was guilt-ridden and we represented atonement, she did not indulge in dramatics. Her story was straightforward and convincing.

"Yes, I did take something besides the walking stick and the medicine. I took a box, but it wasn't stealing, if that's what Clarice is trying to claim. It was a pretty box like stationery comes in, and it was out there in the trash pile in the yard where Clarice threw it. I'd gotten sentimental over Althea, looking at the pitiful stuff Clarice was throwing out, and I decided to take the box for a keepsake, maybe keep handkerchiefs in it."

"What was in it? Stationery?" I asked.

"Nothing was in it."

"Can we take a look at it?"

We could, we did, and we found nothing except a collection of Martha Tootle's dainty linen hankies.

"Maybe somebody else took something from that box," I suggested, once Hen and I were back in the car and on the way to the Boatrights'.

"Or maybe there never was anything interesting in that particular box. Does make you think Leland thinks there's something missing, though," Hen said.

"Sure does," I agreed. "In spite of what he says, maybe Leland's missing something more valuable than an old marriage license."

"More negotiable, you mean," Hen said, turning in at the Boatright driveway.

The Boatright house was nothing to be ashamed of, in spite of Melva's well-known aspirations to something better, but it was nothing special, either. It wasn't as old as my house, for instance, and lacked the character of an older home, even one that has been remorselessly updated. On the other hand, it wasn't the kind of new, showy house you might have expected from a builder who could have used his contacts to do the work to make it into an advertisement for his business.

Melva's new Cadillac sat inside the open garage, so we weren't surprised when she answered the door. She was wearing a ruffled apron over her slacks and shirt.

"Homer told me about last night," she said. "He'll be home for something to eat in a little while, but he's not here right now. He said he was supposed to make a statement, but I thought he said he was going down to the police station. I didn't know you were coming here."

"Could we come in and talk to you, ma'am?" Hen asked. He can be polite when he wants to.

"I don't know anything about it except what Homer told me when he got home. I was watching television when he went for his walk."

"There are some things you could help us with while we wait for him," Hen said.

"Come on back to the kitchen, then, and we can talk there. I've got to keep an eye on the stove."

The inside of the house, like the outside, was surprisingly outdated and uninteresting for someone in Homer's business. Hen and I sat at a heavy maple table at one end of the kitchen and watched as Melva lifted lids from various pots that emitted the mouthwatering smell of cooking vegetables, turned down the heat under the pots, removed her apron, and came to sit with us.

"You like a glass of tea while you wait?" She made a move as if to get back up, as soon as she'd settled.

Hen answered for both of us. "This isn't exactly social, Miz Boatright. We have a few questions we need answers to."

"Questions for me?"

"Yes, ma'am."

"For instance," I said, "does Homer really like to go out walking at night?"

She shrugged, suggesting she didn't much care and didn't know why I'd be interested, then got up and took another look at the pots. "I'm going to have some tea. You sure you don't want some?"

"Yes, please," I said, before Hen could refuse for me again.

He sighed. "Yes, please," he answered.

Melva took her time getting ice from a tray—not even an icemaker? I thought everybody but me had an icemaker!—and pouring tea from a quart jar she had to go fetch from the back steps. She must have had a watchful eye on the clock, because with all her piddling around she'd just set the glasses down in front of us when we could hear Homer's car pulling up.

He came in blustering, which, added to his bright shirt and compact frame, made me think of a fighting cock—a bantam. "You got nothing better to do than come to arrest me because I'm slow getting over to give a statement? I'll get over there after I take care of a few things, but you want to know who dropped those drugs, you talk to that black girl first and leave the rest of us alone."

"Nossir," Hen said. "That would be racial *profilin'*, or maybe economic profilin', and we try to be real careful about it. We're plannin' to talk to everybody."

Unless we find out what we need to know while we're right here, I thought.

"We just try to keep after whatever needs to be done and

do it right," Hen said, being patient. "Matter of fact, we had some questions for Miz Boatright."

"I already told them I didn't know anything about it, Homer," Melva said, fixing another glass of tea, much quicker than she'd fixed the first three, and handing it to Homer.

"You must be pretty hard up for something to do." Homer kept his eyes on Hen while he drained the glass and handed it back to Melva for a refill.

"Nossir," Hen said, sipping his own tea. "We always have plenty to do in a hotbed of crime like Ogeechee. It doesn't all rise to the same level of urgency, not like the possibility of drugs at a scene we're already investigating because of a murder."

"Oh, Homer!" Melva put her hand over her heart.

"Calm down, Melva," Homer said, then turned to Hen. "You bring a search warrant or something, looking for more drugs?"

"Nossir. Matter of fact, we just came to talk, hoping we can clear up a few things. Somebody was with Althea Boatright when she died, and we believe whoever that was hastened her departure from this vale of tears. So far, nobody has come forward to admit to being that person. You understand me here? Somebody who shouldn't have been there was there."

"And what's that got to do with drugs?" Homer asked.

"No telling till we've investigated," Hen said, surprising me. "Maybe somebody was looking for drugs."

"Oh, my goodness!" Melva said. "You think Althea or Leland and Clarice were dealing drugs?"

"No, ma'am, I am not saying that. I'm saying we're investigating. If there's a connection between the drugs and her death, we'll find it. You see, even if whoever killed her did not go over there with murderous intent, went just to pick up a few things, for instance, the upshot was murder. In police language, Althea was killed in the course of a felony, so even if it wasn't premeditated, even if it mighta been half-way accidental, it's what we call a felony murder."

"Oh, my goodness!" Melva put her hand over her heart again.

"Don't look at me," Homer said. "The way I understand it, it happened when I was at work."

"That's what I heard," Hen said. "Matter of fact, that's where Miz Boatright comes in."

Melva went pale. "Me? Homer—"

"What you trying to pull?" Homer asked. "You trying to blame this on Melva? She wasn't even there last night."

"Althea Boatright wasn't killed last night," I said, earning a glare from Homer and a stricken look from Melva.

"I don't care when that woman died, you don't have any evidence to say Melva did it," Homer said.

"That's where you're wrong. We aren't going to tell you everything we know, but I don't mind telling you that part of what we have against your wife is her familiarity with the house."

Melva looked to Homer again. He didn't fail her.

"Come off it, Huckabee! Of course she's familiar with the house. It used to belong to us, to the Boatrights."

"Y'all been doin' a lot of visitin' over there lately?" Hen sipped his tea.

"No we have not, not since Daddy died and left it to Althea so she could turn it into the Grinstead house," Homer said. "What's who we visit got to do with anything?"

"Over to you, Trudy," Hen said.

"Then, Miz Boatright, how is it that you could describe the new carpet in the living room—carpet that the Grinsteads put in less than a year ago?"

"What carpet?" Melva might still have been coming out of her trance.

"What you called the flowered-y carpet in the living room."

Even with her own words coming back at her, Melva looked confused. Then, but slowly, a light dawned.

"Oh, that. Well, I didn't see it myself. Homer told me about it. Oh!"

Ah. Of course. Homer, scrawny Homer, would have known about the trapdoor and been able to get to it. Homer, who'd been using a walking stick for a while because of a leg injury—an injury inflicted by Digger Davis's varmint trap? Homer, who told Melva they couldn't afford a new car, and then came up with the money—money he'd gotten by stealing things from the Boatright-Grinstead house? Maybe it was bearer bonds and stocks that Leland Grinstead had been trying to find in Martha's car, instead of an old marriage license.

It might even have been Homer, in his camo outfit, that Mrs. Coleman had seen in the woods by the pond. It made much more sense for it to be Homer!

Hen was even quicker than I was. He turned toward Homer and said, "You have the right to remain silent."

TWENTY-FOUR

"HOMER? REALLY? Who'd have thought!" That was Martha Tootle.

I could tell Hen was having a hard time being as stern as he had intended to be when he set out to scold the leaky vessels that were gathered in Aunt Lulu's living room, along with Phil and me.

For one thing, they were all so pleased with themselves, so absolutely chock full of self-righteousness, that nothing short of a prison term would have damaged their self-esteem, and I wasn't at all sure he'd have been able to get them herded into a cell, even with the impressive Jerome Sharpe as backup. For another thing, it had to be conceded that they had identified a murder and, however clumsily, helped catch the murderer.

For a third thing, Aunt Lulu had just handed him a big bowl of her banana pudding, and he was far more interested in digging into that than lecturing them on their bad behavior.

Besides, it was obvious to me that if you could get past the complacent satisfaction that gleamed from each of their faces, they were making an effort to be conciliatory.

Hence, Martha Tootle's disgusting display of admiration for Hen's outstanding policin'. He wasn't using a spoon to do it, but he was eating up the admiration every bit as hungrily as he was eating the banana pudding. Not that he's ever averse to hearing himself talk, but under the spell of their adulation, he had graciously promised to take questions about what we were now calling the Althea Boatright case.

"No doubt about it. It was Homer," Hen said. "Althea's walking stick was right there in the umbrella stand by his front door. It woulda been easy to get rid of it, but he didn't have any idea he had the wrong one until Trudy pointed it out. As you know, Martha was willing to swear it was Althea's because of the gnawed places around the bottom."

Martha beamed, no longer fearing a jail term for stealing an empty stationery box.

"But couldn't somebody else have put the walking stick in Homer's house?" Ellen asked. "Susannah, maybe? Maybe she's framing him."

"It's a convincing frame, if that's what it is," Hen said. "As Trudy knows, once you know where to look and what you're looking for, you can usually find it. Officer Sharpe found Homer's prints on surfaces all over the house, and, yes, inside that hidey-hole. When we confronted Homer with that, he blustered some, and tried to make like he was just going after what was supposed to be his under his daddy's will. We'll never prove it, and I reckon we don't have to, but I think he'd been going in every once in a while, as the opportunity arose, and carrying out whatever he could carry at one time. Coin collection. Stock certificates. Jewelry. We've only got his word for it that he was helping himself to just the things he was supposed to have. That's a messy situation, because from what I understand, Althea was denying that she had some of that stuff—and maybe it really was supposed to be Homer's or Susannah's. That mess'll be in the courts for a while. Anyway, whether he was taking what was his, or not, Homer was breaking and entering to do it, and he did it one time too many."

"So Althea was right about somebody being in the house," Ellen said.

"Um hmm," Hen said. His mama had taught him not to talk with his mouth full, and he'd filled it as soon as he finished his last lengthy speech.

"Homer says he never would have hurt Althea or anybody else, but she came at him with her walking stick, and he just tried to protect himself and accidentally knocked her down," I offered. Hen nodded. "I can picture it. If he thought she was gone for the day, it would have been enough to rattle him when she showed up wielding a walking stick."

"Tell us again how you found the hidey-hole," Aunt Lulu said. Amazingly, she seems to be almost as fond of Hen's voice as he is.

"Susannah," Hen answered. "She was so upset at the idea that Homer had been making trips over there to help himself, and not coughing up her share, that she met us at the Grinsteads' and showed us where it was. There's a door concealed in the grooves of the paneling that goes around the bottom of the walls, and if you know just where to push, the door pops open."

"My granddaughter has doors like that on her kitchen cabinets," Ellen said. "Thought I never would figure out how to open them, with no handles or anything."

"That's why the chair was pulled out in Althea's room like that when we found her," Martha said. "He had to move it to get to the hidey-hole. We just thought Althea had knocked against it or something, didn't we, Trudy?"

I nodded graciously around my own spoonful of banana pudding.

"Did Homer have gambling debts, too, besides having a business slump and Melva to support?" Martha asked. "Ellen's stool pigeon said Althea's boy had gambling debts."

"No," Ellen said. "That turned out to be Jordan. If Leland knew about his son's gambling debts, on top of everything else he's had to worry about lately, it's no wonder breaking into a car made sense to him."

"I haven't seen Mr. Carlton around lately," Phil said, turning to Aunt Lulu. "What happened to him?"

While Aunt Lulu was still composing an answer, Hen spoke.

"He was hanging around a lot there for a while, but it wasn't just Mama he was interested in. All that digging into his past gave him the idea that his fling with Althea back in the dark ages might have borne fruit in the shape of Leland Grinstead. He never married, but at his age he likes the idea of having a son and a grandson, even one like Jordan Grinstead. When Buck came right out and asked Leland when he was born, he retracted his confession, which we appreciated since it would have cluttered up our case against Homer."

"We hadn't believed in his confession in the first place," I contributed. "He'd confessed because he thought he was protecting his son."

With just enough sharpness in her tone to make clear that she wasn't as entertained as the rest of the group was by talk of Buck Carlton, Aunt Lulu said, "Buck Carlton looked like a shady character because he was guilty, but not of murder. He was guilty of trying to hide the shameful secret that he no longer has a driver's license or a car. He managed to talk a friend into bringing him to Ogeechee so he could try to keep up with the investigation, but that friend got tired of it." She managed a smile. "A lady friend. I think she was trying to foist him off on me. It does hurt my feelings a little bit that a skirt-chaser like Buck Carlton was more interested in my car than he was in me."

"Obviously, the man has no taste," her son said, patting his mouth with his napkin.

"But he confessed to murder to try to protect his love child? How romantic!" Martha said.

"How ridiculous," Ellen said. "Sticking his neck out like that when he didn't even know if Leland was his son!"

"I think they ought to test their DNA," Martha said. "Althea could have lied about Leland's birthday."

"I think it's their business," Hen said.

"But maybe Charlie Sykes is really Leland's father," Martha persisted. "Weren't he and Althea married? Isn't that why she killed him?"

Hen leaned back and took a deep breath, to settle the banana pudding and address Martha's question. "That marriage license still hasn't turned up, so either it was a figment of somebody's imagination, somebody found it and destroyed it, or Clarice really did trash it when she was cleaning out Althea's room. We'll probably never know if Althea ran him down on purpose. Mighta been nothing more than her dog took a dislike to him. I always did say the dog was driving at the time. What strikes me about that is not why she killed him, if she did, but why she died so soon after."

"Coincidence?" Phil suggested.

Hen rewarded him with a snort. "Don't know how we'd ever prove it, but Homer might have known about Charlie Sykes—maybe when Charlie was trying to track Althea down, he found Homer first. So Homer could have known about whatever Charlie had on Althea. Maybe looking for that is what started him off poking around in the hidey-holes in the first place."

"Maybe?"

"Homer's not being too chatty on the subject right now," Hen said.

Eventually, the questions dwindled and Aunt Lulu's banana pudding ran out. As we left, Hen and Phil and I, Hen turned to Phil and delivered a blow he's been saving till we were away from the ladylike ears.

"Got a bone to pick with you, son," he said to Phil.

"What's that?"

"You started embroidering on the police news in *The Beacon.*"

"Why would I do that?" Phil asked cautiously. He knows Hen well enough to know this was a set-up of some kind.

"I don't know why you'd do it. Maybe it was inadvertent. Our official police report says Delmore Thigpen got drunk and shot all the windows in his house."

"Isn't that what *The Beacon* says?"

"Not quite."

"There was a typo, Phil," I said, having, as usual, loyally read every word.

"Can't catch all the typos, no matter how hard you work at it," Phil said, frowning. He had to know we knew a typographical error isn't all that rare and isn't anything to take seriously.

"You shoulda caught this one," Hen said, obviously struggling to control himself. "When you put an 'i' in 'shot' instead of an 'o' you get an entirely different picture."

He lost control then, barely managing to make himself understood when he added, "Son, that is one serious case of diarrhea."

"Oh, shoot," said Phil. But he grinned. "It'll be a long time before I hear the end of that."

Hen's grin matched Phil's. "And it'll be even longer before Delmore quits bragging about it."

* * * * *

About The Author

Linda Berry's Trudy Roundtree mysteries grow out of the same soil as her family roots. She was born in the small Georgia town that is the model for Ogeechee, and a cousin who's been a policeman in south Georgia for a number of years is the inspiration for Henry Huckabee. Her first publications were stories for children. She has also published short fiction for adults, poetry, a newspaper entertainment column, curriculum, and plays. She lives in Aurora, Colorado, with her husband, Jerry, and is a member of Colorado Dramatists, the Denver Woman's Press Club, Rocky Mountain Fiction Writers, and Sisters in Crime.